CORA BRENT

Other Titles

GENTRY BOYS BOX SET BOOKS 1-4
GENTRY BOYS (Books 1-4)

GENTRY BOYS SERIES
DRAW
RISK
GAME
FALL
HOLD
CROSS (A Novella)
WALK
EDGE
SNOW (A Christmas Story)

GENTRY GENERATIONS
(A Gentry family spinoff series)
STRIKE
TURN

WORKED UP
FIRED
NAILED

STAND ALONES
Unruly
HICKEY

Breathless Point (Coming soon)

DON'T MISS A THING!!!

Sign up for my newsletter and get early news on releases, cover reveals and special giveaways…

I always love hearing from readers so contact me at:
corabrentwrites@yahoo.com.

Check out what's happening on Facebook:
www.facebook.com/CoraBrentAuthor

Join my exclusive reader Facebook group:
www.facebook.com/CoraBrentsBookCorner

Add future releases to your TBR list:
www.goodreads.com/CoraBrent

Get your hands on the latest hot new releases

This book is a work of fiction. Any resemblance to persons living or dead is purely coincidental. Any similarity to events or situations is also coincidental.

ISBN: 978-0-9990021-0-0.

Cover Design: Sofie Hartley, Hart & Bailey Design Co.
Cover Photo: Sara Eirew

In This Life

Kathleen

Words that describe Nash Ryan:

Loner.

Unpredictable.

Wickedly hot.

Unforgiving.

Probably not the kind of man anyone should trust with an infant.

Definitely not the kind of man any woman should trust with her heart.

When Nash returned to town to take care of his baby brother I thought I knew exactly who he was.

It wouldn't be the first time I was wrong.

I also thought I was done giving my heart away until he proved differently.

But we don't have a chance because it's all ready to unravel.

And the secrets I've kept will be our undoing.

Nash

This isn't the first time I've known tragedy.

Maybe that's why I've always chosen to be alone.

But my life of solitude ends now because a terrible twist of fate has made me

the guardian of my four month old brother.

Suddenly I've got a kid to raise and a family business to save.

There's no time for anything else.

That's why Kathleen Doyle and I made this arrangement.

Once a skinny nerd girl who used to follow me around, she's now a single mom with flaming hair, a killer body and too many responsibilities.

We told each other it was just sex.

We told each other there were no strings attached, no expectations.

We lied.

And the consequences will cost us.

But I'm not surrendering this new family without a battle.

Because in this life we might only get one chance to have it all.

Chapter One

Nash

THE PHONE BEGAN BUZZING IN MY BACK POCKET AT THE exact second I pushed the key into the lock. I ignored it and opened the door to my apartment.

The drive home from Portland had been long and my adrenaline was finally wearing off. By now dried blood had stiffened over the broken skin along my right knuckles. The cuts stung when my excitable German Shepard licked at the wound with a sympathetic whine. Meanwhile, my phone issued one more plea for attention and then was silent.

"Easy, girl," I said, fending the dog off and heading for the kitchen sink.

I winced and flexed my hand under the stream of cold water. There was some antiseptic in the cabinet on my left. I twisted the top of the bottle off with my teeth and poured it over my split knuckles, hissing a curse when it throbbed like a bastard. The swelling would probably remain for several days and be a pain in the ass when the cuts scabbed over.

And yet I regretted nothing.

A few shallow scrapes were an acceptable price to pay for teaching some abusive dickhead a lesson. As I remembered the guy's pained groan as my fist connected with his jaw I smiled.

Nope, I didn't regret a thing about tonight.

I was still in the process of dealing with my injured hand when I heard my phone ping with a voicemail alert. My gaze landed on the digital microwave clock. It was half past two. There'd be no reason for a call at this hour. I lived alone, had no girlfriend, and barely said two words to any of my neighbors. The only reason I'd driven all the way out to Portland tonight was because an old buddy from college had a six hour layover in the city and I reasoned even an antisocial prick like me could stand to set foot in a bar once a season.

After I drove my friend back to the airport I circled back to the bar where we'd been hanging out. I had a reason, one that most people wouldn't approve of. I wanted to see if the son of a bitch who'd made his date cry was still around. And he was. He was a soft-bellied sloppy bastard who kept sucking back shots even though he wasn't the type to hold his liquor well. When he staggered outside a little while later I followed. He paused to take a piss in a gloomy corner of the parking lot and didn't even have time to drop his dick before I crashed into him. He likely chalked it up to an everyday mugging until the very end when I got close enough to smell his sour breath and the rank stink of his fear and hissed, "Don't you ever fucking hurt a woman again."

He would know what the words meant. He would remember the way he twisted the girl's arm behind her back and whispered something in her ear while her face twisted with pain before she managed to shake out of his grip. At least she had enough sense to run out on him and the fucker must have thought that was the end of it, never guessing what kind of man was watching from the other side of the bar.

After I slammed the spineless douchebag against the wall one last time for good measure I disappeared, unconcerned about cops. There were no eyewitnesses in sight. Plus I'd parked two blocks away and pushed a baseball cap down too low for any street cameras to catch my face.

I hadn't planned this, hadn't come out tonight with the intention of catching some asshole in the act of exercising his testosterone on a female just because he could. I never did plan these things.

But when I found them I reacted. I had to. Because I knew the terrible truth. All too often in this life justice didn't happen in time to save those who needed it the most. That was the thought keeping me awake at night, that if I didn't step in then no one else would.

Roxie pushed her food dish and whined again so I gave her some water and a handful of biscuits. She chewed happily while I opened up the sliding glass patio door and stared out at the beach. I could hear the north Pacific waves crashing against the rocks in the darkness. Earlier the weather had been calm but now the wind was fierce, the May air colder than usual. Everything about this environment suited me; the cold, the lack of sunshine, the storms that rolled in off the chilly ocean and battered the shoreline. I'd been living in this apartment for two years and I had everything I needed. My work could be handled from home and my rent was reasonable. That might sound like a lackluster life to some people but in all honesty I wasn't lonely at all. I didn't miss people, not really.

Hell, I could always talk to my dog if I got desperate.

Tonight my buddy had shaken his head over his Crown and Coke and begged to know if I was having any fun at all these days. I knew what he meant and blew off the question because I didn't like explaining myself and because he wasn't really that great a friend anyway.

If I wanted to find something pretty to keep me company I knew where to find it. There was a busy college town less than twenty miles away. Yet I didn't do that, didn't haunt the bar scene in search of willing college girls because I was no longer the casual hookup douchebag I'd once been. I didn't have anything permanent to offer anyone. My solitude had become too ingrained. Nothing and no one would change my mind about this self-imposed exile anytime soon.

As if objecting to my thoughts about solitude and exile the phone in my back pocket rang again. I closed the sliding glass door and withdrew the buzzing object. The number on the screen was an unfamiliar one. An Arizona number.

"Hello?" I said as the first instinctive feelings of unease bubbled in my gut.

"Nash?" choked out a voice. There was sobbing. "Nash, it's Jane."

Jane. Technically Aunt Jane. My father's younger sister drifted through life in a placid artistic haze while wrapped in the wardrobe of Stevie Nicks. We kept in touch via email but I couldn't remember the last time I'd talked to her. It might have been the last time I was back there in Hawk Valley. Four years ago. No, five years.

And now for some reason Jane had hunted down my phone number to call me in the middle of the night. And she was crying.

"What happened?" I asked and a sense of dread arose as I remembered something I tended to forget these days, that there were people in the world I cared about.

Through sobs and halting words she told me all of it.

I listened but I didn't comprehend, not immediately.

I should have anticipated that the most terrible things happen when you're least likely to see them coming. Fate was one cruel motherfucker and I should have remained ready for another blow. I wasn't ready for that agony the first time the bastard called 'fate' had decimated my life.

I wasn't ready now either.

I wasn't fucking ready at all.

Chapter Two

Kathleen

THE THREAT WAS ALWAYS THERE IN DRY SEASONS. SOME clueless camper might flick a cigarette into the thick brush or ignore the campfire warnings to roast some hot dogs because there's always some jerk that believes rules don't apply to him. And just like that ten thousand acres of green ponderosa pine would go up in smoke. The mountains were dotted with picturesque towns and cabins all over the place so there was a lot at stake when the alarm went out. Fire crews would spring into instant action to evacuate the threatened areas and they'd work tirelessly until the danger was contained.

Sometimes it wasn't enough.

Sometimes the combination of wind and flames would thwart the best efforts men could possibly give.

"Kat?"

The voice at the kitchen door was shrill. Three sharp raps on the wood followed.

"Kat, it's me!"

My stiffened joints complained when I disengaged from the hard wooden chair I'd sunk into when the sky was still dark. I tried to cross the room before my mother banged on the door again and woke everyone up. She was not renowned for her patience.

"Please, hush," I hissed when I cracked the door.

My mother blinked at me in the mid morning sunlight. "You

look awful," she informed me. Her list of assets had never included tact.

"Sorry, I didn't prioritize my beauty routine this morning." I opened the door wider so she could pass the threshold. She brought the acrid smell of smoke with her but that couldn't be helped. When there was a fire in the nearby mountains the haze and the stink inevitably drifted over Hawk Valley.

My mother made a beeline for the coffee pot, sighed when she found it empty and began noisily filling the carafe from the tap. "There are news trucks and fire teams everywhere," she said in a tone that implied their presence was ruining her day. "I couldn't even get my coffee this morning. The line was ten deep at Ed's."

"What a bummer," I mumbled, thinking of all the people who would love to count a ten minute wait for coffee as their biggest problem this morning.

"Yes it was," she said, not catching my sarcasm.

The coffee machine hissed as it warmed up. I rubbed my eyes, starting to feel the physical effects of last night's horrors. Mentally I couldn't do it yet, couldn't quite absorb the emotional torments to come. There was no end on the horizon. There would be crying and funerals and in time the sheer despair would subside but there would be no end. Just a sad new reality. And an orphaned child.

"Kathleen, are you all right?" My mother sounded concerned now. She really wasn't heartless. It's just that sometimes her sensitivity gauge got stuck.

I swiped at a rolling tear on my cheek. "I can't believe this is all real," I said.

She nodded and for the first time a look of grief passed over her face. Heather had been her niece after all. She'd been my cousin.

"I know," she said. "I never thought I'd see the day when I'd be a little bit grateful that cancer took my sister at a young age. But I have to say I'm glad she didn't live to see the death of her only child."

I reached over to grab a ceramic mug from the cabinet above

the sink. My fingers bypassed the whimsical pastel cup collection and closed around a souvenir mug that displayed a row of lush green pine trees beneath the words Hawk Valley Happiness in red script. There were dozens just like it sold in the Garner Avenue store my cousin Heather owned and operated with her husband, Chris. She'd designed these herself.

After I poured a cup of coffee for my mother I filled one for myself. We both drank our coffees black, one of the very few things we had in common. We sipped from our cups in sad silence as I thought about how different the world had looked twelve hours ago.

The winds had been very strong last night, stirred up by some meteorological collision that probably would have made sense to me back in my academic days. My only concern was that the noise would keep Emma and the baby awake. Luckily my three and a half year old daughter hadn't inherited my fitful sleeping habits but the baby was another story. He was only four months old and this was his first night away from his parents. He fussed as the wind battered the exterior walls and whistled through the tiny cracks it found. I rocked him for a solid hour before he settled down but I didn't mind at all. It was nice to feel the warm weight of an infant again. Now that Emma was past the throes of toddlerhood she often refused to be cuddled.

When Heather had asked me if I'd watch baby Colin for the night so she and Chris could enjoy a romantic anniversary at their cabin up in the mountains I didn't hesitate to accept. She'd almost changed her mind and brought him along but Chris laughed, called her a hovering mama bear and the two of them left for their anniversary trip alone.

Colin was finally asleep when I settled him in the portable crib in Emma's room and that's when I heard the first of the sirens. They could have been from anything. A car accident. A downed power line. I didn't dwell on them. Just as I was about to leave the room Colin released a sharp cry and I lingered in the doorway for a moment to see if he was waking up but he simply shifted and fell asleep once more.

Hours later I was awakened by a hysterical call from Chris's sister, Jane. She was the longtime girlfriend of the local fire chief so she'd heard the news first. The fire had moved quickly and mercilessly, swallowing entire acres in mere moments before a sudden burst of rain hushed its fury, not extinguishing it completely but giving the crews a chance to battle back. The first responders on the scene had the grim task of checking the half dozen cabins that had been engulfed. Only one was occupied. There would still need to be a formal identification of the bodies but everyone knew that cabin had belonged to the Ryan family for generations. And Jane confirmed to the authorities that her brother and his wife had driven up there yesterday evening.

Now I couldn't stop thinking about that lone shrill cry from Colin. I wondered if that was the moment his parents found themselves surrounded by fire. And I wondered if one of the tragic mysteries of the universe had occurred, if his infant mind somehow knew what had happened miles away up in the mountains.

"Mommy?" Emma padded into the kitchen like a sleepy angel in her pale blue nightgown.

"Hey, sweetheart," I said, holding out my hand to her.

She remained where she was, staring at me solemnly. She was old enough to have permanent memories of last night, of being awakened by the sound of sobbing adults.

"You're crying," she said.

"Come here, my pretty girl," my mother said and crouched down with her arms open. Emma glanced at me once and went to her grandmother.

Emma allowed herself to be lifted into my mother's lap. She yawned and said, "Colin's making noises."

"He's awake?" I asked.

She nodded. "He's making noises."

I had thought I would hear him if he cried. I set down my coffee cup. "I'll go see."

There were fitful gurgling sounds coming from Colin's crib but the second he saw me he erupted into a full blown wail. I lifted him while saying soothing words and willing my heart not to break into a million pieces over the thought of how much this sweet baby had lost.

"Somebody has a stinky diaper," I said with forced cheer and I tickled him after I laid him down on the changing mat. He smiled at me.

When I returned to the kitchen I found my mother feeding Emma a plate of chocolate chip cookies but I figured this morning I could refrain from arguing about the virtues of a healthy breakfast.

I took a bottle from the fridge, one that had been prepared by Heather, and settled into a chair with the baby. He eagerly latched onto the bottle and gazed up at me with wide blue eyes that reminded me of someone else. Heather had brown eyes. The blue eyes came from Chris's side of the family and it looked like Colin was going to keep them.

"How long are you going to be able to do this?" my mother asked.

"Do what?"

"Take care of that baby. You're already stretched thin between your job and school and taking care of your daughter."

I gritted my teeth. "Are you offering to help?"

She avoided the question. "Chris's parents are dead as is Heather's mother. Her father is alive but trust me, he certainly isn't going to pitch in. And don't get me started on Chris's hot mess of a sister. Jane can't even take care of herself."

Emma was watching us with wide eyes as she chewed her cookies so I didn't snap back that this was not the time to be slandering people who were devastated.

"I'm just thinking of you," my mother sniffed when I didn't respond.

"Then help me out by handing me my phone," I said. "It's right there on the counter."

At some point while I napped in the kitchen chair Jane had texted. I raised my eyebrows over the message although the news should have come as no surprise. Of course he'd be coming here. Chris had been his father and although I knew they weren't on the best terms I imagined the news still must have been a terrible shock.

"Nash is on his way," I said.

"Who?" my mother asked.

I sighed. "Nash Ryan. Chris's son. You remember him, right?"

She scrunched up her face. "Yes, vaguely."

"He's driving straight here from Oregon. Jane thinks he'll be here by late tonight."

She shrugged. "I wouldn't count on him for help either if that's what you're thinking."

Actually I was thinking about Colin. I was thinking about how he had a brother he'd never met and how that brother was now his closest living relative.

Colin waved a small fist in the air as he finished his bottle and I propped him up on my shoulder for a burp.

I had no idea what to expect from the return of Nash Ryan. There'd been a time when his name provoked all kinds of volatile feelings inside of me. For some confusing adolescent years I'd thought I was in love with him, before I understood that love doesn't mean trailing a guy's every move while consumed with obsessive lust. It was nothing, just a pathetic infatuation I'd barely thought of in ages. I just hoped for the sake of the little boy in my arms that Nash would take an interest in him. Colin would need all the love he could get.

More than anything, I hoped Nash had turned into a better man than the rumors implied.

Chapter Three

Nash

Twilight was settling again by the time I crossed the border into Arizona. Roxie lifted her head and stared out the window as we careened through the barren moonscape of the Mohave desert.

"I think we're due for a break," I said and pulled over into the sand about a mile down the road.

My dog was very well trained but I kept her on the leash as she went about her business. The full moon was starting to rise over the horizon and the colors of the sky combined with the vastness of the desert made the scene look like something out of a Star Wars movie. When I was a kid I'd been out this way once, with my dad. We were going to Lake Havasu. I could remember being fascinated by the open treeless spaces, full of sand and desolation, so different from the greenery of Hawk Valley, even different from the cactus-dotted stucco urban sprawl of Phoenix. It seemed impossible we were still in the same state. This is what people think of when they think of Arizona, this desolate desert. But it wasn't all like this.

Roxie lapped up the water I gave her when we returned to the truck. I swallowed a bottle of water myself and gazed up at the stars that were just starting to appear. My dad had been very into astronomy. He'd taken some classes at the local college but abandoned his studies after I came along and he knew he'd be working forever at the small family store in Hawk Valley, where an astronomy degree was about as useful as nipples on a man. But he'd never lost his love of the sky, often driving up to the big observatory in Flagstaff.

"That's the thing about the stars, Nash. Whether you can see them or not, they're always up there. Not many constants like that in this world."

I flattened the empty water bottle and tossed it in the glove compartment so Roxie wouldn't chew it up. After Jane's phone call I'd launched into furious action, hastily packing up so I could get on the road. It kept me from thinking. The last thing I wanted to do was think too hard. Driving made sense because I didn't have anywhere to leave the dog and anyway there were no direct flights to the tiny regional airport forty miles outside Hawk Valley. If I flew I'd have to get to Portland, wait around for a flight to Phoenix and then rent a car for the two hour drive to town. Or I could bite the bullet and drive straight through, avoiding all that hassle.

As for lodging arrangements, I'd figure that out when I got there. There was no telling how many days I'd be staying. I'd be there at least until the funerals, and until I knew the baby was taken care of.

Once I was on the road I found out there was no escaping my thoughts no matter how hard I tried. The empty miles gave me too much time to think. And too many fucking memories to think about.

The last time I'd talked to my father was four months ago, the day my brother Colin was born. We didn't speak for long and we hadn't spoken since. He regularly texted pictures; pictures of the baby, pictures of Heather and the baby, pictures of the three of them together as a perfect happy little family. Maybe he figured all those pictures would motivate me to take a trip out there and meet my baby brother. I thought about it. But Chris Ryan and I had always been oil and water. I believed I was doing their family a favor by staying away for now.

I knew how things would go if I took a trip to Hawk Valley. My dad and I would inevitably launch right into some petty argument or continue old competitive patterns. Heather would be uneasy about her role in the discord between us, though my father and I had been at odds long before she came along. And the baby was too young to know who the hell I was anyway.

So instead of visiting and stirring up problems I sent the kid a five hundred dollar savings bond plus a sappy card about happiness and blessings and shit.

Anyway, I was sure I had nothing to offer a brother at this point. We were twenty-five years apart for crying out loud. All over the place I saw men my age who were becoming parents themselves. My own father had a kid in kindergarten when he was my age. He and my mother were practically kids when they met at a party down in Phoenix and my dad began driving down there every weekend to see her. They sure as hell didn't plan for me. They couldn't even legally order a drink when I was born. They also didn't stick together for very long. I didn't remember Chris Ryan as an affectionate father. He could be harsh, unyielding. Sometimes he said things I found it tough to forgive him for. It was true that he'd mellowed out in recent years but by then the distance between us was too wide. I knew he saw Colin as his second chance, the chance to start all over and raise a child the right way. I didn't want to interfere with that.

Yet somewhere in the back of my mind I thought the day would come when we'd get another chance. Someday maybe he and I could sit on the creaking front porch of his old house with a couple of beers and have a conversation like fathers and sons did in all places and times.

Someday.

It was all too bitter a fucking pill to swallow at this point. I couldn't quite choke it down yet.

Darkness had long since settled when I finally reached the city limits of Hawk Valley. The place looked pretty much the same as it had the last time I'd seen it. Hawk Valley was a town stuck in time, maintaining a dusty kind of quaint charm while trying to keep its small businesses above water. The real estate boom and bust cycles of Phoenix didn't stretch this far north and vacation home buyers tended to bypass the place and choose mountain cabins instead. There was a small college on the outskirts of town but on the whole Hawk Valley was more of a pass through place that relied on the fringes of the tourist industry spending their loose change in the souvenir shops on Garner Avenue or grabbing a quick lunch at the local cafes. The people who lived there just got by and held onto what they had.

A shared custody arrangement meant I spent summers and vacations here as a kid. Then the summer I turned fourteen I became a permanent resident. It wasn't by choice. It was because the worst possible nightmare had come true. But that was the last thing I wanted to think about. The current situation was fucking terrible enough to handle without dwelling on the past.

The news was all over the local radio. Raging brush fire in the Hawk Mountains. Two lives lost. Blaze a hundred percent contained at this point. There was no information yet on how the flames had ignited but with high winds and dry conditions it wouldn't have taken much. The fact that the skies saw fit to open up just as the fire roared out of control was a lucky break for the emergency crews. It just didn't happen soon enough for my father and his wife.

Jane was too distraught last night to hand out many details. While I was paused at a traffic light on Garner Avenue I tried to call her to let her know I was here. I was worried about her. My aunt was a fragile kind of soul. She probably wasn't dealing with the death of her big brother very well.

"Hello?"

"Jane. It's Nash. I just got to town."

"Nash. Oh god, this is all so awful and I can't say how sorry I am. Jane's asleep in my room. She asked me to answer if you called."

I was confused. "Who are you?"

"Oh, sorry. This is Kat Doyle."

The matter-of-fact way the woman said her name made me

think it should mean something to me. I searched my memory but after twenty hours on the road all the connections were shot.

"I'm heading over to my father's house," I said, although I didn't know what I expected to find there. My voice cracked at the word 'father'. When I said it out loud I couldn't escape the truth that I didn't have one anymore. Chris Ryan, the man who taught me how to catch a ball and hammer a nail was dead. Sure, he had his flaws. So did everyone.

"Why don't you just come to my place?" Kat Doyle said. "I know there's so much to deal with but it doesn't have to all get done tonight. Jane badly needed to get some rest but she'll want to talk to you. And Colin's here. I'm sure you want to check on him."

I digested this information and asked Kat Doyle for her address. I couldn't even begin to list all the things that needed to be sorted out. Jane wouldn't be in any position to handle the funeral arrangements. There was no one on our side of the family who would take the reins and I knew Heather didn't have much immediate family either. But all that could wait for a few more hours. The woman who answered my aunt's phone was correct. I wanted to make sure my brother was all right.

Kat Doyle lived in a duplex among the old houses where some mining company had built housing for its employees some eighty years ago. The mines that were ten miles outside town had been closed since the Regan administration and at first glance most of these leftover houses looked like prime projects for one of those moronic home renovation shows.

The woman who answered the door had long reddish hair that curled halfway to her waist, a vaguely familiar face and a body that not even her shapeless t-shirt and flannel pajama pants could hide. Of course I felt like an asshole for even noticing her body in these circumstances but some things are just hard wired.

"Nash," she said and her green eyes were full of warmth and sympathy.

"Kat?" I guessed.

She nodded. "You might remember that I used to live three houses down from you. I was a few years younger though."

Something clicked. I recalled a skinny girl with a cap of boyishly cut red hair who always wore classic rock band shirts that were way too large for her. Kathleen Doyle was well known not for her looks or wardrobe choices but because she was a local legend, a damn genius who won every academic award ever invented by the Hawk Valley Unified School District and generally put everyone else to shame. She also used to follow me around all over the place even though I never acknowledged her.

"Kathleen," I said. "I remember you now."

A pleased smile tilted her lips and then faded just as quickly. Her eyes filled with sudden tears. "Heather was my cousin," she said. "I'm so sorry, Nash. We're all still in shock."

Standing outside Kathleen's door I could smell the smoke in the air. It was everywhere. Never again would I be able to light a campfire without wanting to fucking vomit.

Roxie stuck her head out of the window of the pickup truck and barked once, just to remind me she was still there.

"Settle down," I called and she whined once but sat down on the seat.

"You brought your dog?" Kathleen asked. She looked puzzled.

"Yeah. I was driving anyway and didn't know when I'd be going back to Oregon."

She appeared to mull that over and gave me a long look of appraisal that I couldn't quite interpret.

"Come inside," she said and backed up so I could clear the doorway. "Oh wait, what about your dog?"

I snapped my fingers in the direction of the truck. "Roxie, stay." I turned back to Kathleen. "Don't worry about her. She's well trained and the window's open. She'll be fine."

Kathleen Doyle's kitchen looked like a time capsule from 1983.

However, except for a few dishes in the sink everything was neat and clean.

"Coffee?" she offered.

"No thanks. I'm not a fan of caffeine."

She poured a cup anyway, probably for herself. "I'm too big a fan," she said. "I don't know how I'd get through a day otherwise." She set the coffee pot down. "Do you want me to wake Jane up? She's asleep in my room. She took a powerful sedative to calm down and Kevin—her boyfriend, Kevin Reston—didn't want her to be alone while he went to take care of fire department matters."

Kathleen paused to take a sip of her coffee. She leaned against the kitchen counter in her bare feet and pajamas and watched me. Again, I got the feeling her sharp green eyes were conducting a rapid assessment.

I leaned against the nearest wall and stared back at her. Now that I was here in Hawk Valley the reality was starting to sink in. My father and his wife were dead. My baby brother was an orphan. I hadn't cried yet but this girl was looking at me in a sad way that said she understood how much I wanted to. The fire had been a ferocious act of nature so there was no blame to assign but I wanted to scream and break something with my hands anyway. And even though I hadn't shed a tear yet I could easily sink to the floor and weep until the sun came up again. But I wasn't going to do any of that in Kathleen Doyle's kitchen.

"You sure you can't use some coffee?" she asked. "Or maybe a snack? I could whip up something if you're hungry."

"I'm fine," I said.

But in fact exhaustion was catching up with me. I hadn't slept last night and then spent twenty tiresome hours on the road thinking about regret and anger and loss and the time my pet mouse died when I was five and my father created a cigar box coffin for it before digging a hole and attending a very sincere funeral in the backyard.

"Do you want to see him?" Kathleen asked.

"See him?"

The idea was horrifying. All day I'd been willing my mind away from imaginary echoes of last screams and visions of charred bodies. It made sense that the remains would have been recovered by now and brought to town. The sight of blood had never bothered me, not even when it was my own. But I knew I'd break if I looked at what was left of my father.

"He's asleep in his crib," Kathleen said. "But you can take a peek in there."

I breathed with relief. "You mean Colin."

"Yes." She tilted her head. "Of course I mean Colin."

Kathleen set her cup down and motioned for me to follow her. The kitchen adjoined the living room, and then a short hallway branched off into two bedrooms. Kat led me to the smaller one and I blinked, trying to adjust my tired eyes to the dim light. There was a small bed occupied by a child. I had no idea what age the kid was but I could tell it was a girl. Kathleen touched the child's sleeping face and then moved on to the little crib in the corner.

He slept on his back, his balled fists over his head. We hadn't turned on a light but something about our presence seemed to disturb him because he scrunched up his face and let out a high pitched whimper that sounded like a small animal in pain. Then his face relaxed and he breathed evenly in peaceful slumber.

I didn't know jack shit about babies.

Yet as I stood in a dark room beside Kathleen Doyle while we stared down at the tiny creature that was my brother it occurred to me that he was the most amazing thing I'd ever seen. Something fierce and foreign twisted in my chest as I watched him and I found myself wishing I'd visited right after he was born. My dad thought I would. He'd asked, even offered to pay for the plane ticket though he knew I didn't need the money. I just needed to let old grudges go. And now that I was finally here, it was too late.

"You can pick him up," Kathleen whispered.

I reached out to touch the baby's cheek and then pulled back before I got there.

"Let him sleep," I said.

Kathleen tucked the thin cotton blanket around Colin's body and I took one last look before following her out of the room. She closed the bedroom door softly and took a seat on the living room sofa. Since there was no place else to sit I plopped down beside her.

"He's a good baby," she said and I noticed her eyes were teary again. "They just adored him, Heather and Chris. Heather was so happy to finally be a mom. They'd been trying to have a baby since they got married, you know."

I coughed once and shifted. "No, I didn't know." My dad and I didn't talk about such things, when we talked at all. There were reasons. Some of them had to do with Heather. The rest of them had to do with him and me.

Kathleen sighed and leaned her head back on the couch. "Jane got a call today from Brach's Funeral Home up on Hart Street. They're willing to take care of the arrangements for next to nothing. She's supposed to go there to meet them tomorrow."

"I'll deal with it," I said. A headache was blossoming, a bad one. I pinched the space between my eyebrows.

"You need some aspirin?"

"Yes please."

Kathleen retrieved a pair of pills and some water. I ignored the water and swallowed the pills dry.

She sat down again and pointed to my bandaged hand. "What happened?"

I'd forgotten all about the man in the alley. It seemed like that incident had occurred three years ago instead of last night.

"Scraped my knuckles on the concrete changing a flat tire," I said. I was a shitty liar. It just didn't come easily to me.

She didn't believe me. I could tell. There was something about the way her eyes changed that indicated she knew I was full of shit.

But she was polite enough to change the subject.

"How long has it been, Nash?" she asked. "How long since you've been back? About five years?"

"Something like that," I said, wondering how much she knew about the last fight my father and I had ever had. It was five years ago and our conversations since then had been carefully benign. But I remembered that night very well. Terrible things had been said.

"Go on. Marry her. It doesn't fucking matter to me. We're done."

Fights like that can cleanse or they can ruin. Usually the latter.

I wondered how much the woman sitting beside me on the couch knew. She was Heather's cousin after all and if Heather had trusted Kathleen with her baby then she might have also trusted Kathleen with her secrets. When our eyes met, something I saw in hers told me she knew a whole lot.

"Nash, I thought I heard your voice."

I looked up to find Jane had joined us. She was bleary eyed and puffy faced and it looked like she was holding onto Kathleen's paneled living room wall for support. I rose from the couch and embraced her thin body as she began to weep.

It was late and nobody was in a state to discuss anything serious, least of all Jane. Kathleen extended an offer for me and my eighty-pound dog to stay in her little apartment but I declined. However, I was glad to take her up on the offer to keep Colin here for the time being. I had decided to find a pet friendly hotel somewhere along the interstate but Kathleen produced key to my dad's house and suggested that I stay there. It was obvious Kathleen had taken temporary charge of things but I was in no position to argue.

"They just completed the renovation," she said. "And there are plenty of bedrooms."

"I know," I told her. I used to live in the damn house after all. For years it was an old Victorian eyesore that my grandfather never got around to restoring before he croaked on a golf course down in Scottsdale. Then it was my father's constant project, always full of building materials and half finished rooms. It sounded like he'd finally gotten the job done.

Jane wasn't really alert enough to drive but she insisted on going home so I offered to take her.

"What a beautiful dog," she said upon being introduced to Roxie, who was happy for the attention from a new person as she panted on the seat between us.

Jane lived with her boyfriend in a charming cottage three blocks away from the center of town. She seemed a little out of it as she kept petting Roxie but that was understandable. The last twenty four hours had been hell for her. Jane was a young teenager when I was born and even though she was in her late thirties now she'd somehow kept the fragile vulnerability of a young girl. I hoped the death of her beloved only brother wouldn't be the catalyst that sent her over the edge. As far as I knew, she'd been all right these last few years.

Jane's boyfriend came outside to greet me when I dropped her off. Kevin Reston was still wearing the uniform of the Hawk Valley Fire Department and his long face was drawn with exhaustion but he shook my hand and awkwardly offered his condolences before escorting my aunt inside.

I watched until their door closed and then did the only thing that was left for me to do. I went home.

The house was dark. When I stepped up to the front porch I accidentally kicked over an object. It was soft and I soon realized there were more just like it. Flowers. They'd been placed all over the front porch. I could also make out a very large poster board that had been propped up beside the door. The clumsy hand drawn letters said, "Chris and Heather. We love you always."

The outpouring was touching, and not unexpected. Hawk Valley prided itself on its small town vibe and my family was well known here. The tragic deaths of two pillars of the community would have left everyone reeling.

Roxie sniffed at the flowers as I fumbled with the front door key given to me by Kathleen. The hinges creaked as I pushed the door open. Immediately I was transported back to my childhood as I breathed in the scent of old wood and a vague mustiness that never completely dissipated. It was the smell of years and life and generations. But right now I just thought of it as the smell of sorrow.

I switched on the light near the door and the first thing I noticed was that the place looked far different than it had five years ago. The bones were all still the same but now adorned with antique furniture and tasteful accents. The paint scheme was far brighter, the lighting had been enhanced and everywhere I looked pictures hung on formerly bare walls.

I paused at eye level with a poster sized photo of the three of them; my dad, Heather and the baby. It must have been taken right after Colin was born. I'd been sent some photos of him wearing the same blue sailor outfit but those pictures were only of him. I'd never seen this one of the three of them before.

Roxie crept around with her nose to the ground, sniffing every corner. Her tail was down, as if she guessed this was a sad moment. After a few minutes she settled down on a braided throw rug while I couldn't quite tear myself away from the picture of a happy family that had been shattered. The smiling couple with their baby boy had no idea what fate had in store.

There was more grey coursing through my father's hair than I remembered. There were deeper lines around his eyes. And Heather was beautiful, her honey colored hair piled on her head in a loose bun. My dad's arm was slung protectively around her shoulder as she cradled the son who would have no memories of them. To Colin, Heather and Chris Ryan would only be people in pictures and stories.

I couldn't get used to the idea. Nothing about this was fucking fair. After my mother was killed I'd done nothing but cry in the days that followed. This time I hadn't yet shed a tear.

But then, as I sank slowly down to the floor in my father's empty house, I finally broke down and sobbed until my chest ached.

Chapter Four

Kathleen

THE FORECAST DIDN'T CALL FOR RAIN TODAY BUT THE SKIES opened up and the crowd began drifting away from the ceremony. There were a lot of unfamiliar faces, people from out of town. Maybe they were morbid curiosity seekers. The fire and its tragic conclusion had been all over the news.

"The husband and wife team owned a souvenir shop in the picturesque town of Hawk Valley. They leave behind an infant son. Now back to you, George, for the traffic report."

A news truck from one of the Phoenix stations was hovering in the parking lot. I wondered if it carried the same reporter who had encountered Nash this morning. He'd told her to fuck off before she finished her sentence.

As the grievers who'd been circled around the burial site began to back away and glance up at the threatening sky, Nash remained in place with his head bent and his big hands hanging at his sides.

The pastor concluded the ceremony and touched Nash on the shoulder before following the crowd. He appeared to say something but I was too far away and it didn't seem to matter anyway. Nash ignored him.

My left heel wobbled in the slippery grass as I made my way over to Nash. I avoided looking at the two caskets covered with bright flowers. I didn't want to think about what they contained.

Nash didn't look up as I approached and I couldn't see his face.

"Nash," I said as the rain intensified. "Are you okay?"

Now he looked up. A loud overhead thunderclap punctuated the moment. The expression in his blue eyes was so anguished I was tempted to reach for him. But Nash Ryan was not the kind of man who would lay his head on anyone's shoulder and weep.

"It's over," he said and seemed surprised. I wondered if he'd been listening to the service at all or if he'd been too lost in his bleak thoughts. This wouldn't be the first funeral he'd sat through, not the first time someone he loved was taken in a brutal manner.

"Yes," I said. "It's over."

That was true. At least this part was over. The authorities had mercifully released the bodies quickly and the funeral was able to proceed only four days after the fire. A lot of people in town had stepped up to help but Nash insisted on personally handling the arrangements himself. Maybe he just liked keeping his mind occupied.

Perhaps that's why he'd been too busy to spend any time with Colin.

In the short term there was no shortage of people happy to fill the void and take care of the baby but sooner or later there was a critical decision to make. I knew what Heather and Chris had wanted. My cousin had told me about the visit to Steve Brown a few months ago. The attorney was probably waiting until after the funeral to share the contents of the will.

People wondered and whispered among themselves. *"What about the baby? What will happen to him?"* And I stayed silent because I didn't have the right to gossip, especially when Nash himself hadn't yet been informed about the role his father intended him to play.

Nash's observation suddenly took on a deeper meaning. Yes, the funeral was over. But now he'd need to figure out what came next.

Nash walked silently at my side as we trailed after the sea of black-clad figures heading for the parking lot. Even though the rain was coming down steadily we didn't hurry. I held my handbag over my head to serve as an inadequate umbrella while thunder rumbled above. Nash didn't seem to notice that he was getting soaked to the skin.

We'd encountered each other plenty of times in the days since he returned to town but we hadn't been alone together or had a one on one conversation. The vibe between us wasn't awkward exactly, but it wasn't comfortable either. From what I'd seen of Nash so far, he didn't go out of his way for the sake of good manners.

"Your car?" he said, gesturing to my pile of old Ford bones that was probably a grocery store trip away from sudden death.

"Yes." I unlocked the driver's side door. "I'll see you at Nancy's house?" I asked him.

Nancy Reston, often referred to as 'Saint Nancy' had been Hawk Valley's mayor for two decades and retired last fall because she loved children and wanted to run a daycare. She had volunteered to host a gathering at her house after the funeral so the family didn't have to be bothered with such plans. Nancy herself had missed the funeral because she was watching Colin and Emma.

Nash didn't answer and was staring off into the distance so I thought he hadn't heard the question.

"There will be food," I said, feeling as if I needed to fill the silence with words. Even stupid words. "Nancy hired a caterer. It was nice of her to go to all the trouble."

Nash said nothing. He could have been a statue. A square-jawed, absurdly good looking sculpture permanently posed beside the hood of my car.

I cleared my throat. "I meant to ask what you want to do about tonight. Nancy had Colin last night but I don't know if she's up to covering two nights in a row. I can take him tonight if you want…"

My voice trailed off because I finally realized what he'd been staring at. From here the Hawk Mountains were only ragged shadows. The smell of smoke was long gone and from afar there was no hint about what kind of disaster had unfolded up there. You'd have to get a lot closer to see the scars left by the fire.

Grief flooded me. It had been a constant companion lately but every now and then the ache sharpened to a crippling pain. Heather was nine years older then I was so we hadn't been close while growing up. In my narrow opinion my perky blonde cousin was somewhat conceited and superficial. But when I returned to Hawk Valley four years ago as a pregnant college dropout who'd just exited a toxic relationship and didn't feel up to answering questions about anything, Heather glued herself to my side and became my biggest champion. She helped me find work. She was there at the hospital holding my hand when Emma was born. And when she saw a long awaited positive sign on a drugstore pregnancy test, I was the first one she called with the news.

The tears I'd managed to contain throughout the funeral were now threatening to engulf me.

"Oh god," I moaned and found myself leaning on the wet car for support.

There were suddenly arms around me, strong arms lifting me from my slumped position and pulling me against a broad chest. I wrapped my arms around his shoulders and breathed in the pine scent of his aftershave. Nash said nothing as he held me and that was fine. It only lasted for a moment and in that moment we were just two anguished people clinging to each other in the parking lot of a cemetery as a cold rain fell. I couldn't remember the last time I'd been held by anyone and I would have gladly hung onto him a lot longer. But Nash let go and backed away.

"I'll see you later," he said before heading to his truck.

I didn't have a clear idea whether he planned to show up at Nancy's or whether he needed me to take care of Colin tonight. However, I didn't feel like chasing after him for answers so I sighed and ducked into my own car. I shrugged out of my wet blazer, relieved the blouse underneath was mostly dry, before making the short drive to Nancy Reston's house.

The house was in the oldest part of town, only two streets over from the one where Nash and I had grown up. Years ago my mother had sold her old house in that neighborhood and moved into a fairly new condo across town. As for the gorgeous Victorian that Chris Ryan had spent years restoring, I would assume it belonged to Nash now. Well, Nash and Colin.

Nancy had only invited the friends and family of Chris and Heather so there wouldn't an obscene number of people to deal with. The silver haired former mayor greeted me at the door with a warm hug and produced an embroidered pink towel so I could do something about my damp hair. I was still standing in the foyer and toweling off my messy hair when the small hurricane that was my daughter sped past me.

"Hey there, missy," I said, trying to scoop the giggling girl into my arms.

Emma was not a child who liked to be contained. She wriggled away.

"Look what Grandma gave me," she announced, triumphantly holding up a five dollar bill.

The last time my mother gave Emma money, my daughter had decorated Abraham Lincoln's face with bright red crayon and then wrapped the bill around a ball of clay. The lesson should have been to avoid offering paper money to a three year old but my mother was a slow learner sometimes.

"And where is Grandma?" I asked her.

Emma pointed. "In there." She scrunched up her face and my heart skipped because for a second she looked exactly like her father. I should be used to the resemblance by now but somehow it still caught me off guard.

Emma resisted when I took her by the hand but I couldn't let her tear through the house getting into all kinds of trouble. Nancy had her hands full with the arriving guests.

My mother offered me a nod from her place by the picture

window beside Uncle Ben, the oldest living member of my family. His thin hands trembled and his face was confused as my mother yapped in his ear between bites of lemon cake.

Emma stopped trying to struggle out of my grip when I directed her to the table of refreshments and piled fruit on a plate. Emma loved strawberries the way other kids loved chocolate bars.

Jane was seated on a small sofa with a napping Colin in her arms. Her posture was rather stiff and she kept her eyes on the baby. Jane didn't often volunteer to hold her nephew and never offered to babysit. At first I thought it seemed Jane was almost afraid of the child, yet after observing she over the past few days I didn't believe that was it. Jane wasn't afraid of the baby. She was afraid of herself, maybe of her ability to hold him properly. Heather once described Jane as 'painfully fragile' and that was an accurate description. I knew the whispers about her history. The breakdowns. She'd supposedly been steady for quite some time but since the fire she seemed to be withdrawing more. Heather and Chris had come to their decision for a reason. Jane would never be up to the task of taking care of Colin.

I settled Emma on a nearby chair with her plate of strawberries and eased down on the chintz sofa beside Jane. "Do you want me to take him?"

Her nod of relief was immediate. "Yes, thank you."

Colin awoke as he was shifted into my arms. "Hey, little man," I said and he smiled. I moved him to an upright position, wondering if it was time for a bottle, but for the moment he seemed content to lay his head on my shoulder and try to grab my chunky turquoise necklace.

"He loves you," Jane said, a little wistfully.

I didn't point out that Colin was a baby and didn't know how to love anyone. Babies required things. Comfort, feedings, clean diapers, affection. They didn't yet have anything to offer in return.

Kevin Reston materialized with a thick cardigan sweater. He carefully draped it over Jane's shoulders.

"You doing all right, honey?" he asked her with such tenderness my heart seized up a little. Jane hadn't been lucky in many aspects of her life but she'd been lucky enough to find love. Many of us would search forever and only find pale imitations of the real thing.

"I'm fine," Jane said, though anyone who looked at her would have some doubt. There were dark circles under her eyes and her small frame looked slighter than ever. I doubted she was sleeping much. Or eating.

"Mommy?" Emma piped up. "Can we go home now?"

"Not yet, baby."

"I want to pet Bruno."

"He's been jailed in the back bedroom," Kevin said, referring to his mother's wily terrier. He grinned at Emma. "Otherwise he'd be jumping on everyone and stealing all the food."

Emma considered and then changed tactics. "I want to go in the backyard."

"It's raining, Ems," I told her.

She crossed her arms and looked unhappy. The days since the fire had been confusing for her.

Kevin cleared his throat. "Actually, I was just outside and the rain seems to be letting up." He winked at Emma. "What do you say? How about we rescue Bruno and let him run around the backyard?" Kevin glanced at me. "If it's okay with your mom."

"That's more than okay," I said. "Thank you, Kevin."

Kevin tried to get Jane to accompany them to the backyard but she shook her head and pulled her sweater more securely around her body.

After Emma bounced away, trailing Hawk Valley's fire chief, Jane craned her neck around.

"Where's Nash?"

I was about to admit I wasn't sure he was even coming when the doorbell rang. Nash walked in looking slightly less sodden than he had in the cemetery. I had to admit, he wore the disheveled look well.

"There he is," Jane said and a slight smile curved her lips.

Nash evaded Nancy's attempt to towel him off and then stood awkwardly in the parlor doorway, surveying the quiet gathering. His gaze landed on Colin, who was still happily installed on my left shoulder. I wished I had a window into Nash Ryan's head to see what he was thinking.

"And Steve Brown is here," Jane noticed and there was surprise in her voice. The lawyer was the kind of guy who kept to the corners of any room and was easy to miss. "I wonder why."

"Steve and Chris were good friends," I told her gently, thinking she should be aware of the fact already. "They went to high school together."

Steve Brown approached Nash. He had the look of an archetypal attorney; slightly balding, slightly overweight and perpetually serious. He'd been practicing on the upper floor of a brick building on Garner Avenue for as long as I could remember and carried the legal secrets of many of Hawk Valley's longstanding residents in his solemn, bespectacled head.

"Oh," Jane nodded. "Right. I forgot."

Through Steve's mellow murmurs I picked out the words, "Tomorrow," and "My office."

Nash seemed irritated. "Let's just talk now," he said, a little more loudly than necessary.

Steve obviously didn't like the idea but he sighed and led Nash out of the room, presumably to someplace more private.

"What's that about?" Jane wondered.

"I'm not sure," I said.

Of course that wasn't true. I knew exactly why Chris's friend and lawyer would have felt obliged to corner Nash only an hour after his father's funeral. There wasn't just the matter of the store, the house and property to deal with. Those things could wait. But a child couldn't.

Colin gurgled next to my ear and I rubbed his small back, feeling a surge of fierce maternal emotion. He wasn't my child but I loved him. I would fight to protect him.

In my head I began cataloguing everything I knew about Nash Ryan.

Loner.

Unpredictable.

Detached.

Wickedly hot.

Unforgiving.

It didn't sound like a good recipe for a parent. There'd always been a tumultuous relationship between Nash and Chris. Still, Chris would have chosen to believe the best about his eldest son. Despite everything I'd ever heard about Nash Ryan, Chris and Heather must have had their reasons for assuming he would be the best guardian.

My opinion was still up in the air. So far Nash hadn't inspired much confidence where Colin was concerned.

Jane opted to head out to the backyard after all. Colin began fussing after a few minutes so I decided to hunt down a bottle for him. Nancy likely had one ready to go in the fridge.

There was a cozy rocking chair in the kitchen so I took a seat and let Colin eagerly latch onto the bottle. The window in front of me had a nice view of the backyard. Emma looked like she was having the time of her life, running around Nancy's green grass with the hyper terrier chasing, fluffy tail sweeping back and forth excitedly. Jane was also out there now and Kevin wrapped a protective arm around her while I watched. Emma tossed a small red ball in the air and then squealed with delight when the dog leapt up and caught it. I smiled. It felt good to smile after so many sad days in a row.

A shadow in the doorway made me turn my head and I stopped smiling. Nash stood there, appearing shocked and more than a bit pale. He looked at Colin, who was happily sucking away at his bottle and oblivious to being examined.

"Do you want to hold him?" I asked. I expected Nash to refuse.

I was right.

"Not now," he said.

"Then when?" The question was sharp. I hadn't meant for it to be. But not once had I seen Nash hold the baby.

He answered the question with one of his own. "Where's Jane?"

I gestured to the window. "Out back."

Nash lowered his head and moved toward the back door.

"He told you, didn't he?" I blurted. "Steve told you about the will."

Nash looked at me. "You knew?"

"Yes." I tried to read his expression. "What are you going to do?"

But Nash Ryan had already proven he didn't answer questions he didn't feel like answering.

Maybe he didn't know the answers yet.

He left the kitchen and I watched through the window as he spoke to his aunt. Once he raked a hand through his dark hair and glanced toward the window. Our eyes met and a chill of unease traveled down my spine.

All along I'd wondered, and feared, what Nash's reaction would be when he learned he'd been named as the sole guardian of his baby brother.

From the look on his face, it seemed he wasn't handling the news well at all.

Chapter Five

Nash

"Me?" I'd croaked in disbelief. "You've got to be fucking kidding."

Steve Brown, my father's longtime friend and attorney, raised an eyebrow but tactfully confirmed that no, he was not in the habit of kidding around about child custody arrangements. My dad and Heather had actually named me as the sole guardian of my four month old brother.

"You are also the executor of the estate," Steve explained. "The largest assets are the house and the store, half of which are bound up in a trust for Colin but you will be empowered to make all financial decisions and-Nash?"

I'd left him behind to babble about trusts and other bullshit on his own and sought out one of my few remaining relatives to explain a few things.

"You seem unhappy," Jane said in the backyard of Nancy Reston's house after I gave her a rundown of the conversation with Steve Brown.

Kevin Reston kept his arm around my aunt and shot me a wary look. I couldn't blame the guy. He remembered me as the asshole teenager I'd been back when he volunteered to help coach the football team at Hawk Valley High.

"Just caught off guard," I said, noticing that we weren't the only ones in the backyard. A dog and a little girl were trampling Nancy's flowers. I'd seen the girl around enough in the last few days to recognize her as Kathleen's kid.

I tried to sort out my thoughts. "This is a lot to take in."

That had to be the understatement of the millennium. The relationship between my father and me was messy. I'd always assumed he didn't hold me in high regard. He'd told me so enough times. So why in the hell would he name me as Colin's guardian? There had to be other options.

Not my grandparents. They'd been dead for years. Heather's mother was gone. Cancer or something. Her deadbeat father was still alive but I'd heard he was living in Idaho and muttered 'stupid bitch' when called with the news that his only daughter was dead. He didn't even come to the funeral.

And not Jane. She would have been the logical choice. If only she was stable. My aunt was a nice lady but when I was in high school she streaked naked through the Chicken Delight restaurant in nearby Boland while shrieking, "Stop the carnage! Save the chickens!" Jane wasn't a caregiver. Jane was someone people took care of.

Yet I still didn't understand how I'd landed at the top of the list. Chris and Heather Ryan had lived in Hawk Valley all their lives. They couldn't walk to the mailbox without tripping over a half dozen friends. At least a few of them must be steady folks with jobs and parental instincts.

Kathleen, for example.

When I'd found her in the kitchen a few minutes ago she'd looked like a breathing advertisement for tranquil motherhood, the kind of woman who might be cast in a commercial for vegan organic baby carrots or some shit.

"You'll get to stay here in town now," Jane said and I saw the idea made her happy. She just took it for granted that I'd jump at the chance to abandon my old life and become an instant parent.

Fuck.

I ran a hand through my damp hair and tried to think. I'd never even changed a goddamn diaper.

Then I looked up and saw Kathleen Doyle was staring at me through the kitchen window. In her arms my baby brother continued to happily suck the contents of his bottle. He didn't know that he was an orphan. He didn't know that the peaceful, happy childhood his parents had imagined for him was gone.

I was a selfish person. Some might call me a dangerous one. But my heart wasn't cold enough to feel nothing for the tiny human who was now my responsibility. My father and Heather knew what kind of man I was. If they'd left Colin in my care it was because they couldn't think of a better option. And anyway, they must have figured this would never come to pass. I'd only been chosen as a precaution.

"Nash?" Jane called because I'd abruptly turned and headed back through the door to the kitchen.

Colin had finished his bottle and Kathleen was patting his back. She looked startled when I busted into the room again. I wasn't sure what she thought of me and I didn't care much. I had only one priority now and she wasn't it.

"Can I hold him now?" I asked.

A surprised eyebrow popped up and she glanced at Colin as if she wanted to hear what he had to say about the question. Then she sighed and eased up out of the rocking chair.

"Of course," she said, reaching me in three graceful steps.

I reached out but she pulled back and handed me a blanket.

"You're still wet from the rain so drape this over your chest. And wait, move your arms closer to your body. You're holding a baby, not catching a ball."

Kathleen Doyle sure liked handing out orders but I was willing to accept a little direction. If she assumed I didn't know what I was doing then she was right. I'd learn though. I'd learn everything there was to know.

Colin produced a low mewl of protest when moved from the warm comfort of Kathleen's arms to endure my awkward cradling.

I thought he'd be heavier. He peered up at me and a wrinkle formed between his brows, like he was worried about why he'd been handed over to some unshaven stranger. The hair on his head was wispy and blonde, like his mother's. I had a sudden flashback of Heather throwing her had back and laughing at something. It was something I'd said, although I couldn't recall what. I wasn't a funny guy.

If babies were capable of doubt, there was definitely doubt in this kid's eyes. He hadn't gotten those eyes from Heather. They were bright blue, like my father's. Like mine. His mouth suddenly puckered and I thought he might cry.

"It's all right," I said. "It's me. It's your big brother."

I tried to touch his cheek but he grabbed at my finger, curling his hand around it with more strength than I would have expected.

"Don't worry, Colin," I said with confidence I didn't feel. "I'm not going anywhere."

That was the truth. I really wasn't going anywhere. I couldn't take him back to a tiny one bedroom apartment beside the ocean. The life I'd led there was solitary and sometimes reckless and it was over. Colin's parents had wanted him to grow up here and there was no one else to do the job.

My life had just been irrevocably altered and I felt the need to tell someone about it. I looked up and caught Kathleen Doyle's eyes staring at me.

"I'll be staying right here," I told her, as if daring her to argue with me.

She didn't.

Chapter Six

Nash

SOMETHING WET TOUCHED MY RIGHT EAR.

I might have slept through it if not for the sharp volley of impatient barking. When I tried to roll over Roxie jumped on my chest.

"Gimme a break," I muttered, knowing it had to be pretty damn early in the morning because I was still dead tired.

Roxie smacked me with her paw. "*Woof.*"

The dog wasn't the only thing making noise. The plaintive wail of an infant reached my ears and for an instant I was confused about why there were crying baby sound effects echoing through my apartment.

Then I remembered that they weren't sound effects.

The dog's ears flattened and she whined as she glanced at the open bedroom door before jumping off the bed.

"I'm up," I groaned, blinking hard to clear my head a little. I was in my old bedroom, the one room in my dad's house that had been untouched by renovation projects. Sports pennants and half naked women still decorated the walls, frozen in time as the dwelling of a teenage boy. The room was the same as it had been when I last lived here.

All that had changed was absolutely everything else.

Roxie barked again. The translation was either, "Get that damn kid to stop crying," or, "Why are you sitting there scratching your dick instead of running to take care of the baby?"

"I'm going," I groaned, stifling a yawn.

Colin's room was on the other side of the second floor, right beside what had been the bedroom of his parents. So far I'd avoided looking in there. Even the sight of the closed door made me feel a little sick.

I had hoped they died in their sleep, the smoke from the swift moving fire overtaking them before they had a chance to react. But I'd since learned that was not the case. My father and his wife had been found beside their pickup truck. Upon waking up to discover the world was on fire my dad must have grabbed Heather and made a run for the vehicle, hoping to escape. In that final moment they would have realized it was already too late. Their hands were still joined when the rescue crew discovered them.

I paused at the doorway to Colin's nursery. When I lived here the boxy little room with grey textured wallpaper had been used to store some inventory for my father's store on Garner Avenue. Now it was an eruption of color with expressive painted animals on the walls amid happy scenes filled with balloons, smiling suns and rainbows. A teddy bear observed me from the corner rocking chair and a stuffed tiger slept at the foot of the crib where my brother paused for breath before belting out another cry.

Roxie nudged my hand like she was trying to push me forward. I crept over to the crib slowly so I wouldn't startle the kid. He didn't know me yet. Only two days had passed since the funeral of his parents.

"Hey, buddy," I said, attempting to sound soothing and self-assured. Instead my voice scraped out of my dry throat and sounded more like a growl.

Colin stopped crying, opened his eyes to stare at me for a few heartbeats, and then erupted again, kicking his legs and waving his tiny fists with impressive four-month-old fury. Roxie made a sympathetic noise from the doorway. I sighed and scooped my hands under the baby's writhing body while trying to crush a stab of unease.

There wasn't much that could scare me and I had a habit of running head first into challenges. Sometimes I even pursued the worst of them. But every time I picked Colin up there was this new and uninvited sense of fear trying to push its way to the front, sharpened by a very hostile thought.

I have no fucking business being here.

Colin was still squirming and twisting and I realized I should probably check his diaper. Sure enough, it was heavy and saturated. I had him on the changing table, trying to figure out which way the new diaper was supposed to go, when he let out a squawk, followed by a stream of piss that hit me square in the chest.

"Good aim," I muttered, managing to get the diaper secured on his body before wiping my chest off with a fist full of baby wipes.

Once he was wearing a clean diaper Colin agreed to be snapped back up into his stretchy one piece. Somehow I did it wrong because I wound up with a front snap that had no match and made the whole outfit look lopsided. But hey, the kid was clean and no longer crying so I wasn't going to make a thing out of it. I carried him to the kitchen to retrieve one of the last remaining bottles Kat Doyle had prepared. She'd given me two cans of powdered formula and a lot of very precise instructions that I immediately forgot because there was only so much information I could stuff into my head in the space of a few days. No big deal. I'd just add bottle preparation to the long list of things I'd need to figure out.

Colin began energetically drinking a bottle in the cradle of my right arm while I tried to operate the coffee machine one handed. Normally I avoided caffeine but this seemed like a good morning to make an exception. I was surprised to see that the time on the clock above the stove said 8:50 am. My sense of time was all screwed up. I'd assumed it was earlier.

The coffee machine splashed one final stream of liquid into the mug that said 'Hawk Valley Happiness'. There'd been a half dozen just like it in the cabinet. I didn't bother with cream or sugar, swallowing the contents as fast as my mouth could stand the heat.

Meanwhile, Colin finished his bottle and let out a whimper. I thought he might still be hungry so I offered him another bottle. He seemed happy to have it.

The knock on the kitchen door almost made me drop my mug of Hawk Valley Happiness. Roxie jumped up. She watched the shadowy shape outside, barked once and then started wagging her tail.

"Did you forget you're a watchdog?" I asked, flicking aside the yellow curtain covering the glass panel.

Kathleen Doyle waved to me from the other side and I didn't know whether to groan with annoyance or fling the door open with gratitude. Mostly Kathleen was all right. No longer the skinny nerd who used to follow me around, she was all grown up with a kid of her own and she was obviously grieving over her cousin's death. Plus she adored Colin and she seemed to know everything about babies so she'd been amazingly helpful. But she could also be exhausting. Kathleen was packed with high energy and extreme competence and at the moment dealing with her felt like a real pain in the ass. Still, I opened the door because she didn't deserve to see the dickhead side of me.

"Good morning," she said brightly, preparing to step over the threshold before I'd invited her in. She had her kid with her, a little girl with brown pigtails and a pouty expression. She didn't look like Kathleen. She probably looked like her father, whoever that was. I hadn't been rude enough to ask.

Colin responded to the sound of Kathleen's voice, forgetting the bottle and trying to launch himself in her direction. Kathleen cooed and plucked him out of my arms without asking. Roxie was delighted with her sudden visitors, thumping her tail against the stove and licking the kid's face.

"I like this dog," the girl announced, giggling.

"Emma," her mother warned. "Be careful about petting dogs you don't know."

Emma scowled at her mother. "But he likes me."

"She," I corrected, cracking a smile. "Her name is Roxie."

"See Mommy? It's a she. She's nice."

"You still need to be careful."

I turned to Kathleen. "Look, it's fine. Roxie wouldn't hurt a fly."

Kathleen wasn't listening to me. She was too busy fussing over Colin. "Are you hungry, angel? You want more ba-ba?"

Ba-ba??

Kathleen grabbed the bottle from me and deposited it back into Colin's mouth. She hummed and rocked him back and forth. I had to admit, the kid didn't seem bothered by all the attention. He stared up at her with infant awe and seized a clump of her curly red hair, waving it around.

"Is he getting everything he needs?" she asked and finally looked my way. What she found caused her to blink, purse her pretty red lips and return her gaze to the baby.

I was still bare chested, wearing nothing but a pair of boxers, but I wasn't going to break a sweat running upstairs for something better. Kathleen had barged in here unannounced. So if she wanted to scowl and blush and pretend like she was trying not to stare then I hoped she had a damn good time. I took another sip of coffee.

"He's fine," I said, slightly bothered that she was questioning whether I was taking care of Colin.

She checked out his crookedly snapped outfit. "Really?"

"Sure. We've been having a great time together, invited a few strippers over last night, huffed some glue and partied until the sun came up."

"Mommy, what's a stripper?" Emma asked.

Kathleen was annoyed. "Something we're not going to talk about right now."

"Why?"

"It's my fault, Emma," I said, setting my mug down. "I said a bad word. I'm sorry."

The child stopped petting Roxie and squinted up at me. "Who are you?"

"Honey, this is Nash Ryan," Kathleen said. "You've met him. He's Colin's big brother."

The little girl was doubtful. "He doesn't look like a brother. He looks like a dad."

Kathleen tried again. "He's Uncle Chris's oldest son. Remember?"

"Oh yeah," Emma said and her face fell. It must have been explained to her on some level, the tragedy of Chris and Heather. But there was no telling how much a little kid really understood about death. She probably wasn't even in kindergarten yet. I'd been a teenager when I first encountered real tragedy and I'd still been totally blindsided by the permanence of it.

But then Roxie licked Emma's face again. Emma laughed and the dark moment passed.

Kathleen cleared her throat. "Hey, Nash, can I ask you something?"

I yawned. "What's up? You want some coffee?"

"No thanks." She pointed to the empty bottle on the counter. "Did you just give Colin a bottle?"

"Yeah." I shrugged. "He just woke up and he seemed really hungry."

"So this is his second bottle?"

"Unless the rules of arithmetic have changed."

"And have you burped him?"

"No. He didn't seem like he needed it."

Kathleen exhaled a little too loudly and scowled a little. I got the feeling I'd just given her the wrong answer.

There was still a little bit of liquid left in the bottle but Kathleen withdrew it from Colin's mouth and began to transfer him back to me.

"It's okay, sweetheart," she said in a singsong high-pitched sweet voice when Colin grunted in protest. "Your big brother's just gonna burp you."

Kathleen loved holding Colin so I figured there must be a reason she was so abruptly handing him back to me. I didn't have time to think about it because during the attempted baby handover the back of my hand accidentally brushed Kathleen's shapely left breast. My neglected dick threatened to awaken and all of a sudden I was sorry I was standing there in nothing but flimsy boxer shorts.

Think of something else, anything else. Hamburgers. Dog shit.

"Uh, hold on," I said, swerving over to the sink while Kathleen continued to hold the baby out. "I've got to wash my hands."

This was fucking ridiculous. I wasn't some horny teenager drooling over the first feel of a tit. Just because I hadn't touched one in a while didn't mean I was on the verge of losing control.

"Nash?" Kathleen said, sounding exasperated.

Baseball. Road kill. Dryer lint. Anything but tits. ANYTHING BUT TITS!!!

"Just a second." I squirted hand soap into my palms and struggled to tame my impulses with completely sex-free thoughts that had nothing to do with unintentionally touching Kathleen Doyle's boob for half a second. I needed to get off as much as the next guy but this girl sure as hell wasn't going to volunteer to play hide the salami. Anyway, there were other priorities besides sex.

For the next twenty seconds I became the most industrious hand washer in the state of Arizona. I didn't rinse the soap off until I was sure my dick had calmed down and wasn't going to come popping out of my shorts.

"I'm good now," I said, shaking the water off my hands and turning back to face Kathleen.

She gave me a funny look and stuck my brother in my arms.

Colin kept squirming while I tried to pat his back. I noticed Emma was still on the floor with Roxie. She was petting the dog and whispering something while Roxie stared at her with rapt fascination. Kathleen moved to go lean against the far wall, staring at me with her arms crossed like she was waiting for something to happen.

A few seconds later I figured out what that 'something' was when Colin bobbed his head, opened his mouth, and spat slimy white baby vomit all over my right shoulder.

"Fuck," I said.

"Eww!" Emma shrieked.

Roxie barked.

Colin started to cry.

"Aw, it's okay my precious sweetheart," Kathleen said and for a weird second in all the confusion I thought she was talking to me.

She wasn't. Once again she snatched Colin away while murmuring to him in that sugary sweet tone of voice that made me want to either roll my eyes or barf. Kathleen carried the crying baby upstairs, leaving me covered in puke while her kid gaped at me.

"You need to clean that up," Emma informed me and then resumed petting Roxie.

"Thanks, I will," I muttered.

I grabbed a handful of paper towels to absorb the bulk of the mess but that didn't get rid of the stickiness. Plus I now reeked of sour milk. Not once had it ever crossed my mind that I'd end up serving as a canvas for both piss and puke in the same morning.

Meanwhile, I could hear Kathleen upstairs. She was singing some nursery rhyme about bunnies in the forest and Colin had stopped crying. I tossed the gross paper towels in the trash. More than anything I wanted to take a few minutes to clear my head in the steam of a hot shower.

"Listen, " I said to Emma, "will you be okay down here for a few minutes?"

The girl looked at me, blinked her big brown eyes and then laid her head down on the kitchen tile beside Roxie's paws. Roxie sniffed at her hair and licked her face. I took that to mean all was well so I jogged up the stairs.

When I peeked into Colin's room Kathleen had her back to me while she cleaned him up on the changing table. The blue flowery skirt she wore was loose and long and didn't hide the fact that she had a great ass. I might be a piece of shit for doing it but I stayed long enough to get a real good look at the view before retreating, then grabbed a change of clothes from one of my suitcases and retreated to hall bathroom.

The old pipes groaned as I switched on the shower but the water was blissfully hot. I felt slightly better after about thirty seconds under the spray but I was still amped up in a way that water couldn't solve. For the past week my life had been all sadness and funeral arrangements and anxiety and regret. I needed something else. A release, just something brief and sordid to refocus my thoughts. My dick twitched and then hardened when my hand closed around it. With everything going on in the house at the moment it wasn't really an ideal time to jerk off while thinking about a flower-covered ass and firm tits. I did it anyway. No one would have to know.

By the time I emerged from the shower and threw on some clothes, Kathleen had taken Colin downstairs. I found her in the kitchen, pouring some ghastly looking pink cereal into a bowl. Colin had been happily installed in his bouncer and placed in the middle of the wide kitchen table. He was clean, wearing a different outfit, and his wisps of light hair had been combed. He seemed content to swat at the colorful toys that hung from the bouncer. Emma sat on a booster seat at the table and Roxie's head was in her lap. It seemed my dog had found a new master.

"I hope this is okay," Kathleen said, retrieving a spoon from a nearby drawer and setting the bowl of cereal down in front of her daughter. "Heather watched Emma so often she tended to keep her favorite foods around."

I shrugged. "Fine by me."

Kathleen looked me up and down. I didn't know what she was

looking at. I was no longer almost naked so there was nothing to see. I wore jeans and a green t-shirt with the letters so faded I'd forgotten what they had once said.

But in case Kathleen's legendary intelligence included psychic powers I grabbed a bottle of all purpose cleaner and started spraying down the tiled countertop so she wouldn't guess I'd just jerked off to an imaginary fuck in which she'd played a starring role.

"Looks like your hand is all healed," she said, pointing.

I looked at the back of my hand. There was still some bruising and scabbed skin but there was no need to wear a bandage anymore. Still, I was reminded that Kathleen was no fool and I needed to pick my words carefully.

"Yeah," I said, keeping my tone even. "I'll be more cautious in the future."

"Nash, you can be honest with me if this isn't working."

I stopped spraying and stared at her. "What's not working?"

She glanced at Colin and looked sad. "You don't seem ready for this. You never expected to be the guardian, did you?"

I set the bottle of cleaner down a little too hard. The resulting noise was a bit loud. Roxie's head popped up and she looked at me, startled. Kathleen crossed her arms again. Emma continued eating her cereal.

I spread my palms on the countertop and tried to keep the anger out of my voice. "It doesn't matter what I expected. Heather and Chris didn't expect to die. This is the way things are. And despite what you seem to think of me, I'm not going to flake out on my responsibilities."

She raised an eyebrow. "I wasn't implying that. You just really seem to be struggling."

"Kathleen, give me a break. Two days ago I buried my father and his wife and found out I'll be raising a kid for the next eighteen years. I'm still trying to let it sink in. My life has been turned upside down."

She let out a small hiss, a sound of disgust. "This isn't about you nailing yourself to the cross, Nash. This is about what's best for Colin."

"And you don't think I'm capable of doing what's best for Colin."

It wasn't a question. She was being pretty clear.

Kathleen cocked her head. "Do *you* think you're capable of doing what's best for Colin?"

My temper was rising. Maybe it had something to do with her imperious attitude. Maybe it had something to do with the fact that she was honing in on my worst fears. The truth was I really wasn't sure I had it in me to be everything Colin needed. I didn't know if I was capable of being a good parent, or even a satisfactory one.

Or maybe I just resented the fact that Kathleen looked sexy as sin even when she was driving me crazy.

"What would have been best for Colin," I said in a tight voice, "is if his parents had never fucking died."

Kathleen grimaced. "Of course. But that's not reality."

"No, it's not reality. The reality is that Heather and Chris are dead. The reality is they chose me as the guardian for their son, who also happens to be my brother." I exhaled and lowered my voice. "So that's what I'm going to do. Be his guardian."

She didn't look convinced. "Just like that? Don't you have a job back in Oregon?"

"I'm a freelance website designer. I can do that anywhere."

"But you can just pick up and move with no notice?"

"Sure."

"There must be other things to consider."

"Like what, Kathleen?"

"Well, don't you have a life, Nash?"

I was sick of her questions. "Don't *you* have a life, Kathleen?"

She flinched. "I have a life," she said quietly and reached out to touch her daughter's head.

Emma glanced at me and then kept eating her cereal. I had the feeling I'd touched a nerve. I hadn't meant to. I appreciated everything Kathleen had done. I was glad she cared about Colin. And I really didn't know what her personal situation was, Kathleen Doyle had been born brilliant, one of those people who's expected to go out and conquer the world. But here she was back in her hometown living in a run down duplex with a little kid and no ring on her finger.

"Actually I didn't have much of a life," I said and Kathleen looked surprised. "Not really. I lived alone. I didn't go out much. I existed. So I'm not losing a thing."

All that was true. Yet it wasn't the whole truth. I didn't feel obliged to explain every thought in my head to Kathleen. She didn't need to know that something still burned inside of me, something that had ignited the day my mother was murdered by a man she trusted. Something that compelled me to creep around in the shadows and mete out small doses of justice when I found the chance. Kathleen struck me as the type who would never endure violence, even when it was necessary. If I had admitted the real story behind my injured knuckles she wouldn't understand. She might decide to cause a problem.

I stepped around the counter and approached the table. I squeezed a spongy pink pig that hung from Colin's bouncer. It made a shrill squeaking sound. He kicked his legs and smiled. I smiled back.

"I'm in this for the long haul," I said in a soft voice, talking more to my brother than to Kathleen.

"I'm sorry," Kathleen said. "I didn't mean-"

"Don't be," I said sharply. "Let's just forget it."

She nodded. "Okay."

For a few seconds there was no sound but Emma's crunching.

I decided I needed another cup of coffee so I refilled the mug.

"You look like you were on your way to work," I said. I had no idea what Kathleen Doyle did for a living, nor did I particularly care, but the conversation needed a new direction.

"Ah, work," said Kathleen, pulling up a kitchen chair and having a seat. "That's something else I wanted to talk to you about. And I'll take that cup of coffee if you're still offering."

I filled another one of the Hawk Valley Happiness mugs and handed it to her. She smiled when she saw it but I didn't know why. I watched as she tossed her thick red curls over one shoulder and raised the mug to her full, sexy lips.

"What's this about work?" I asked to keep my mind on G-rated topics.

"Yes. I wanted to discuss the store, to see what you had in mind. It's been closed for a week already, which is of course understandable. But I was wondering what your thoughts were on a timeline for reopening."

I'd given exactly zero thought to my father's store on Garner Avenue. The place had experienced a number of transformations over the years. When my grandfather bought the building it was a failing bar. He remodeled and opened up a café called Ryan's Place. It limped along for a good number of years but then my father took over when I was a toddler. Running an eatery was complicated with a slim profit margin and Chris Ryan had other ideas. He thought Hawk Valley was on the verge of a renaissance and Garner Avenue would become some kind of artisan mecca, attracting tourists and art shoppers like the places in Sedona and Scottsdale. So Ryan's Place became Hawk Mountains Gallery. It was a miscalculation. One measly gallery wasn't enough to draw the collectors to the area. So once again a change was in order and Hawk Valley Gifts was born. It was just a common souvenir shop where you could buy all kinds of kitschy crap with your name embossed in gold lettering but there was a sizeable area in the back where local artists sold their creations on consignment. At least that was how things stood the last time I was in there. I had no idea what was going on with the store these days.

Kathleen awaited my answer.

"I'll give it some thought," I said even though the store was low on my list of concerns.

"I could meet you down there this afternoon," she offered, checking her watch. "I've got to drop Emma off at preschool and then I have to meet a couple of clients but I can carve out some time around two."

I didn't know why Kathleen should care so much about the store. It sounded like she had more than enough to keep her busy.

"Maybe another day," I said, glancing at Colin in his bouncer. He was still enthralled with the dangling pig.

Kathleen was not pleased. "Nash, there are really some things that warrant immediate discussion where the store is concerned."

"Fine. Just not today." I had some other things to figure out, like child rearing. And my own work had been put on hold. There were half a dozen unfinished projects sitting on my laptop and there was probably a limit to my clients' sympathies.

Kathleen frowned. "You also have two employees to consider, you know."

Nope, the thought hadn't even occurred to me.

"Are you one of them?" I asked her. That would explain why she was so insistent, although I would have thought Kathleen and her mega brains could do much better than working at a small town gift stop.

She shook her head. "No. Well, sort of. I mean, I wasn't one of the employees I was referring to. But I've been doing the books for the last three years so I can tell you everything you need to know about the store's financial status."

"You're an accountant?"

She shook her head. "Closer to a bookkeeper. I operate independently and a number of Hawk Valley's small businesses are my clients." A sad smile touched her lips. "I have Heather to thank for that. She convinced your father to hire me when I had no degree and no experience and then she recommended me around town."

Kathleen dug around in a small brown handbag, plucked out a business card, and handed it over.

KATHLEEN DOYLE
SHOEBOX BOOKKEEPING
Serving small businesses all over Hawk County.
Let me take care of your needs!

I had to stifle a snort over the last tagline. I might go to hell for thinking it, but I'd be glad to outline a few ways she could 'take care' of my needs.

"Are you laughing?" Kathleen asked.

I shoved her business card into my back pocket. "Nope. Just had to clear my throat."

She played with a long red curl and eyed me. "So does two o'clock work for you?"

I had the feeling she was going to pester me until I agreed. Besides, I should take a look at the store and consider the options. My dad's will had left me in charge of all managerial decisions and the store was something I'd have to deal with sooner or later.

"I'll make it happen," I said. "I'll just clear my blistering social schedule."

Kathleen smiled, a real smile, not a melancholy one. She might be bossy and occasionally condescending but this girl could compete with the sun. She was beautiful.

Emma sulked when her mother told her it was time to leave. "I wanna stay with Roxie."

"It's time for preschool, sweetie. Remember, it's a special day. The class is getting a new goldfish."

Emma crossed her arms and then I saw her resemblance to her mother. "But I wanna stay here."

"Hey," I said and the kid looked at me like she'd forgotten I existed. "You can come back and see Roxie anytime. I mean that, Emma."

And I did. I'd be a cold-blooded creep if I wasn't at all moved by a little girl who loved my dog.

Emma smiled. She kissed the dog on the top of her head and reached for Kathleen's outstretched hand. Kathleen mouthed the words, "Thank you," and I nodded.

"By the way," Kathleen said before she closed the kitchen door behind her, "that white minivan parked in front of the house was Heather's. There's a car seat already in the back and the keys should be on the hook beside the front door."

"Okay."

"If you take Colin anywhere you'll need to strap him into a car seat."

Seriously? I was no baby specialist but for crying out loud l knew at least that much.

"Thanks, Kathleen," I said, a little sarcastically.

She didn't notice. "See you at two?"

"I'll be there."

She broke into another brilliant smile and waved at Colin. "Bye bye, beautiful baby boy," she said in a voice that made her sound like she'd been sucking on helium.

Once the door was closed the room felt awful empty. Roxie whined and gave me a puzzled canine look, probably wondering what I'd done to drive her new best friend away.

"Forgot to feed you this morning, didn't I?" I asked.

The bag of dog food I'd thrown in the truck before we left Oregon was almost gone. I poured the rest into a dish and set it on the floor. Roxie dove right in and my own stomach growled. There was a stack of casseroles in the fridge, all brought by well-meaning neighbors, but nothing sounded good right now. I needed to go grocery shopping today. I needed to do a lot of things.

Colin kicked his legs and waved his arms, hitting the fuzzy pink pig in the process.

"Well little guy," I said, trying to sound half as cheerful as

Kathleen and failing, "what should we do first?"

The kid made a weird face, turned bright red, and expelled an unmistakable sound; wet shit hitting a diaper.

"My fault for asking," I said.

My brother grinned at me.

Chapter Seven

Kathleen

Being here felt strange, almost intrusive. I'd never been in the shop when it was empty. Chris had given me the alarm code and a key right before Colin was born. He said it was just a precaution, just in case something came up while he was busy at the hospital. He trusted his employees and one of them had been with him for over a decade, but he wanted another backup. Someone nearby, someone reliable.

"Someone who's family."

The last time I was here was only a little over a week ago when I dropped off the monthly financial reports and handed over the payroll checks. Chris emerged from the small stockroom and greeted me with a smile. He thanked me for agreeing to watch the baby so he and Heather could enjoy a night at the mountain cabin for their anniversary.

I felt a chill even though the place was far from cold. The carefully stocked shelves and bright displays were projecting a kind of post apocalyptic feel in the dim light so I found a switch and flipped on enough lights to erase the afternoon shadows. The inventory was eclectic, everything from gaudy roadside souvenirs to handmade fine art.

After a few minutes I checked my watch again. Nash was late. I wondered if he'd show up. Part of me hoped he wouldn't. The store really did require some immediate management decisions. I hadn't made that up. But dealing with Nash Ryan might not be an easy task. He still radiated defiance, the years having done little to blunt the natural rebelliousness that once fascinated me.

That was another thing. The infatuations of adolescence hadn't faded completely. This morning I'd felt flustered and nervous under his gaze. It was a feeling I disliked, one I didn't pursue. That wasn't all due to Nash. I was thinking of my own mistakes, of realizing too late that a man who made me uneasy was the wrong choice.

As for Nash, he knew damn well how good he looked in the kitchen standing there in his boxers, a ripped monument of virility, silently daring me to check him out. I couldn't help but comply. Moreover, I had a feeling he was well aware of it.

I sighed in the empty store. As usual, I was overanalyzing. In all likelihood Nash wasn't trying to catch anyone's attention, least of all mine. He was tired and struggling to keep up with his new responsibilities. I was the one who'd busted into his kitchen without calling this morning.

I'd been driving Emma to preschool and making a mental note to give Nash a call later on today when I detoured over to the oldest section of Hawk Valley. I couldn't stop thinking about Colin. I needed to make sure he was all right after being placed in the care of a man who was obviously clueless about taking care of a baby. A man who'd always despised his father and had never shown the slightest interest in Colin's existence.

That's not fair, Kat.

I drummed my fingers on the metal bars of a postcard rack. Maybe it wasn't fair. Heather had confided in me so that I knew the relationship between Chris and Nash had been strained, complicated. But I was willing to set fairness aside when it came to Colin's best interests. If Nash proved to be an incompetent guardian then I was prepared to step in.

The door chime jarred me out of my brooding and Nash walked through the glass door, car seat in hand.

"He's asleep," Nash whispered and looked around for a place to set the baby down.

I beckoned and led him to Chris's office in the back. Nash gently placed the car seat in the middle of his father's old desk. He stopped and looked around for a second and I wondered what he was remembering. He must have been in this room a thousand times while growing up. But when he turned to follow me back to the store his face was impassive.

"Did the car ride knock him out?" I asked when we were out of earshot.

Nash nodded and leaned against the checkout counter. He gazed around the store but didn't seem especially interested in anything he saw.

"Heather used to drive him around the block over and over again to lull him to sleep," I said.

Nash scratched his chin.

I cleared my throat. "I guess it's been a long time since you've seen the store."

He pointed to the far wall. "There used to be rows of t-shirts over there."

"They were poor sellers. The store still carries some but they are higher quality."

"Do they all have the words Hawk Valley on them?"

"Pretty much."

He scoffed. "I don't know who wants to buy that garbage except for people who already live in Hawk Valley."

I argued with him. "You'd be surprised. We've had more tourist traffic through here in the last few years. The city council just voted to fund a campaign to change the town slogan to 'Discover Hawk Valley: Gateway to the Hawk Mountains.' The population in the Phoenix area continues to grow and people are always looking for weekend escapes to somewhere slightly cooler."

Nash smirked. "You sound like a travel brochure."

"So? I think Hawk Valley is a great town."

He raised an eyebrow. "So that's why you stayed here?"

No, that wasn't why. I'd always dreamed of a big city future. Things just didn't work out that way. Still, I felt defensive and irritable that Nash was knocking my hometown. There were far worse places to be.

"I like to think I can appreciate what's in front of me," I said, "instead of always hunting for something else."

Nash laughed outright.

"Shh," I warned. "You'll wake Colin up." I didn't know what I'd said to entertain him. "Why do you find me so funny?"

Nash looked at me. "I don't, Kathleen."

"That's the second time today you laughed in my face."

He frowned. "When was the first?"

"When I gave you my business card."

"I don't remember laughing."

"It was evident from your expression that you were barely holding it in."

He let out an obnoxious low whistle. "Damn, have you always been this psychic?"

"Cut it out."

"No, seriously, you could monetize that skill."

"Your sarcasm leaves a lot to be desired."

"You could rent a little hovel on Garner Avenue, hang beaded curtains in the doorway and charge people twenty bucks apiece while gazing into a glass ball and pretending to see something exciting."

"Nash!"

"Kathleen," he said, mocking my frustrated voice.

"You're exhausting," I said wearily.

"And you're easily flustered," he said and yawned.

I took a breath, trying to keep my temper and failing. "Look, my plate is full. I'm a business owner, a mother, and a student. But I've bent over backwards to help you and I don't appreciate being regarded as a joke!"

"Shhh." Nash put his finger to his lips and glanced toward the office doorway. "Now who's gonna wake the baby up?"

Nash wasn't laughing now but he was clearly enjoying himself. I was struck by how little I really knew him. He'd been a puzzle even to his family. Heather confessed that she kept hoping he'd mellow out and accept Chris's attempts at reconciliation. But that never happened because evidently Nash was still a stubborn bastard. I shouldn't be surprised. The boy who went around with a truck-sized chip on his shoulder had never evolved. He'd just gotten bigger. Stronger. Better looking.

Apparently Nash realized he'd overstepped. He sighed and his expression became almost remorseful. "I don't think you're a joke, Kathleen. Not at all. I apologize if I gave that impression."

I wasn't sure he meant it but I was willing to give him the benefit of the doubt. "Apology accepted. And you can call me Kat."

"I'll stick with Kathleen."

"Suit yourself."

Nash looked around again. "So what am I doing here?"

It was a deep question. "I know it's not ideal but Colin needs you and-"

"At the store, Kathleen. What was so urgent that I needed to come down here today?"

I had to move to the counter where I'd left my laptop. Nash watched me from less than two feet away. I flipped open the lid and examined the data I'd already memorized.

"Net income is still in the red this year. Sales were hurt over the winter when there was a ton of road construction on Garner Avenue. There's a temporary cash flow problem. It happens now and then and Chris would usually loan the money to the store out of his personal funds but the renovations he and Heather completed on the house were costlier than expected. He didn't have much to spare. Compounding the problem is the fact that the bank changed his line of credit terms. There's enough to pay utilities and meet payroll but not enough to order new seasonal inventory and with the busy summer season coming up it's essential to address the issue. Plus every day the store stays closed is a day without sales."

Nash looked at the door. "Doesn't look like anyone's beating a path to get in here."

My eyes narrowed. "The big sign that says CLOSED might have something to do with that."

"So the store is failing?"

"I didn't say that."

"You sure didn't paint a rosy picture."

"You need to reopen, Nash. And you need to address the line of credit issue and order new inventory before the summer rush."

He sighed. "For crying out loud, I don't know anything about running a souvenir shop."

"Of course you do. This is your family's business. You were practically raised here."

"No, I grudgingly operated the cash register during the summer when I was a teenager. I never knew or cared how the place functioned."

I shut the lid of my laptop. "Well, it's time to care, Nash."

He didn't agree. He again glanced toward the room where Colin slept. "Maybe it's time to let it go," he said softly.

My mouth fell open. "You can't do that."

He gave me an odd look. "It's a souvenir shop, not a national treasure. The world will be just fine without more ugly ceramic mugs."

My fists clenched. "This was your father's business. He would have wanted it to survive."

"Yeah, he probably wanted to survive himself. But as I reminded you earlier, that's not the reality we're dealing with."

"Nash," I said sharply, then bit off the next words. My mother had always warned me that bossiness was not an agreeable quality.

Actually, her words were, 'Don't be so bitchy," but the sentiment was the same. I couldn't bulldoze Nash into seeing things my way. He had a lot on his plate too.

"It's important," I said softly.

He raised an eyebrow but waited politely for me to continue.

"The store," I continued. "It's hard for small businesses to hold on in this day and age. Your family has run this place in one form or another for over forty years. It means something to the people around here, and it will mean even more to them now that your dad's gone." I scanned the back wall where paintings from artists in the area hung in expectant silence, waiting for a buyer. "Everyone wants a reason to be optimistic."

"A happy ending," Nash said but he didn't sound sarcastic now. Only sad. "I don't think it's possible in this situation."

"Maybe not a happy ending. Just a less tragic one. It would hurt to see the store close. And I don't just mean because it would be an empty storefront on Garner Avenue. Every painting you see on that back wall comes from an artist, including your Aunt Jane. There's probably not a kitchen cabinet in town that doesn't have one of those Hawk Valley Happiness cups that Heather designed. Your father sponsored a local little league team every year. The two employees are an elderly woman with a disabled husband who has worked here for over ten years and a college student studying to be a teacher. There are a lot of people, including me, who are happy to help you keep the store open if you'll only give it a try."

"That was a mouthful," Nash said when I finally stopped talking.

"Will you think about it?"

His eyes landed on a stunning landscape painting depicting the highest peak in the Hawk Mountains. I knew it had been painted by his aunt and I wondered if he recognized her style.

"I'll think about it," he agreed.

I smiled. "Good."

Nash nodded in my direction. "So what's your deal?"

"My deal?"

"You wear a lot of hats. You're an accountant, a mom, you rescue small town stores and judging from your interaction with Colin you're also a skilled baby whisperer. And did I hear you mention you're a student too?"

"Online classes but yes."

Nash studied me. "Is there anything you can't do, Kathleen Doyle?"

"Relationships."

UGH!!!

Nash chuckled. "Noted."

I was inwardly cringing. "That sounded pathetic."

He shrugged. "A little."

I rolled my eyes. "I swear I'm not begging for pity. I just meant that I don't have the time nor the inclination to deal with relationships."

"You're not the only one."

"Maybe someday my outlook will change but for now I'm better off alone."

Nash looked interested. "Bad experience?"

A chill rolled through me. "Yes."

"You're honest," he said, nodding. "I like that."

No. I'm the opposite of honest.

"He must have been Emma's father?" Nash guessed.

The subject of Emma's father was not a good one. Someday there'd be a reckoning for the things I'd done, the lies I'd told. But that wouldn't be happening today and none of it was Nash Ryan's goddamn business anyway.

"I haven't seen Emma's father since I was pregnant," I said. At least that part was technically true. I made a show of checking my watch. "Speaking of Emma, I've got to go pick her up."

A sudden cry signaled the awakening of Colin. My first instinct was to bolt down the hall and get him but Nash beat me to it. Colin was still crying when Nash returned with the car seat.

"Hold on, kid," he said. He set the baby down on the floor and hunched over, fumbling with the belt fasteners. I waited a few seconds, then bent over to help. I had Colin freed and in my arms in three seconds flat.

"He's probably wet," I said, patting Colin's bottom. "Where's the diaper bag?"

Nash blinked. "Ahh…"

"You didn't bring any diapers?"

"No."

"No?"

"No. I didn't think we'd be gone long."

"Nash, you always need to bring the diaper bag. I gave it back to you packed with clean diapers, remember?"

He was annoyed now. "I forgot, okay? I'm not used to carting around so many accessories."

"Well, you need to get used to it. Babies have a lot of needs."

"Kathleen," he said wearily and I thought he was going to say something nasty but he just exhaled noisily and took a step in the opposite direction while looking away. Colin was still squirming. I bounced him my arms a little to distract him.

"You drove here in the minivan, right?" I asked.

He shot me a look. "Is there a point to that question?"

"Yes. Heather usually kept a few spare diapers in the glove compartment."

"That's a good idea."

Exasperation was getting the best of me. "Can you please go get one?"

Nash was looking more irritated by the second but he went outside without another word. He returned a moment later with a fresh diaper. He dangled it front of my face and I grabbed it.

"You want me to change him?" I asked.

"Is there any way to stop you?" he grumbled.

I ignored the question and carried the fussing baby to the office where I set him down tenderly on the surface of his father's antique desk on top of a blanket and swiftly changed the diaper. It wasn't until I was done that I discovered it hadn't been wet after all.

Nash was leaning against the counter with his arms crossed when I returned. He watched silently as I removed my hair from Colin's chubby fists and carefully re-installed him in his car seat.

"He's probably hungry," I said.

"Probably," Nash agreed and took the car seat from me.

"I can meet again the same time tomorrow. We've got a lot more to talk about if there's a chance you're going to keep the store running. I want to show you the financials. And since your father covered the register so often you will need to hire another employee unless you plan to be here just as much."

"Stop." Nash shook his head and for a second he just looked extraordinarily tired. "Enough for now, okay?"

I was doing it again. Being pushy, overbearing, demanding.

Bitchy.

I swallowed. "Okay, Nash. I'll stop."

He paused by the door and stared at me for a few silent seconds. I didn't know what he saw when he looked at me. The resident smarty-pants who thought she'd take the world by storm and now struggled to make ends meet as a single mom in the small town she'd once sworn she'd escape.

"I'll be in touch," Nash said and then he was gone.

I took a small object from the counter and held it in the palm of my hand. It was a duplicate copy of the key to the store. I'd forgotten to give it to him.

Chapter Eight

Nash

MY EYES WERE STARTING TO BLUR WITH FATIGUE AND IT was only ten p.m. The night before had been rough, with Colin unwilling to sleep for more than an hour at a time. He was eating just fine and kept filling his diapers so according to my internet research on the habits of babies, there was no cause for alarm. I checked his gums because I read somewhere that sometimes babies can start teething early but his gums looked pink and not remotely swollen.

Kathleen probably would have snapped her fingers and known instantly what the problem was but calling Kathleen would mean I'd have to *talk* to Kathleen. Talking to Kathleen meant getting an earful about forgotten diaper bags and improper bottle etiquette. After our testy meeting down at the store the other day I figured we needed some space.

Jane and Kevin visited in the late afternoon and I was glad to hand Colin off to them for a few minutes so I could have the luxury of a ten minute shower.

But once my aunt and her boyfriend were gone I was on my own again, wearing out the hardwood floors as I walked Colin back and forth and back again because he started crying every time I put him down. I didn't know how much crying a typical baby did but it seemed this kid was shooting for a world record. He finally fell asleep about an hour after the sun went down and I would have been happy to follow his example if I didn't have a pile of work to deal with.

So instead of catching up on some much needed sleep I was at the kitchen table, rubbing my eyes in between tweaking the web page of a Portland-based steakhouse chain I'd done projects for in the past.

Roxie snored underneath the table but she jumped up when I got to my feet. I'd barely made a dent in my task list but the rest would have to wait. I stretched my fingertips toward the ceiling and heard my joints pop.

There were many evenings when I'd sat in this kitchen for hours because my dad had a rule about cleaning your plate before leaving the table. I didn't like visiting my father. My mother always indulged my picky eating habits, preparing special meals that fit my tastes. It was a different story when I came to Hawk Valley. Chris Ryan was baffled by an eight year old who wouldn't eat red meat and had no interest in catching fish at the lake up at the mountain cabin. On one of those trips I threw down my pole and told him we should leave the fish alone because they were better off where they were. He turned a cold eye in my direction and warned me to pick up the pole and start catching fish like a normal kid or else I could walk back down the damn mountain.

"Your problem is that your mother spoils you. That girl never did have any sense."

I always knew my parents didn't like each other. It must have been rough, trying to raise a child with a person you can't stand. But my mother never said a bad word about Chris Ryan directly to me. I never told her that he didn't return the favor.

That was the last time my father and I went fishing together. In an act of defiance I did pick up that pole and I stayed put until I had caught twice as many fish as he did. Then when his back was turned I dumped the ice chest full of dead fish into the muddy lake water.

He didn't speak to me for the rest of the day.

The dog let out a soft whine and I was wrenched out of old memories.

"Need to go out?" I asked and her tail wagged. She was way ahead of me by the time I got to the back door.

I watched her bound into the darkness and wondered what my dad would think about a dog living in his house. He'd always been strongly anti-pet, at least pets that weighed more than a pound, only allowing small rodents that could be caged and had limited life expectancies. The only other time I'd had a dog was at my mother's house in Phoenix. His name was Captain and he was an energetic border collie who shadowed my every move when I was home. He was killed the same night she was.

Roxie responded to my low whistle and raced back inside. I rewarded her with a pat on the head.

"Good girl."

The dog flapped her tail and accidentally knocked over a blue porcelain vase that had been perched on a low table. I watched it fall to the hard floor and crack into several pieces, wincing at the noise and then waiting for the inevitable cry from upstairs. When it came the sound was shrill and piercing, loud even for him.

I bolted into action, taking the stairs three at a time to get to Colin's room. He kept screaming when I picked him up, screamed louder when I held him close, arched his back and shrieked like a banshee when I checked his diaper. Nothing comforted him. His diaper was dry. He didn't want a bottle. He didn't want to be held. I even tried putting him in the car seat and driving him around the block but that didn't quiet him at all so I gave up and brought him back home.

"What's the matter with my favorite buddy?" I said, trying to sound all *goo goo* ridiculous like Kathleen did when she talked to him but he only screamed some more.

I tried rocking him in a living room chair but he didn't want that either. His cries were relentless, strident. The sounded full of pain and they gutted me like no other sound ever had before. I held my brother's struggling little body close and pressed my lips to his forehead.

Hot. Too hot.

Panic rose instantly. He was sick. That's why he'd been crying so much, why he couldn't be consoled. I should have known. I should have thought of it. A parent would have realized sooner.

"It'll be okay, Colin. You'll be okay." My voice was artificial, high and cheerful.

I cradled him in one arm and retrieved my laptop with the other. I searched the words 'baby fever'. I searched the words 'sick baby'. I searched the words 'sick baby fever crying'. The results were so varied they were of little use. Colin might be getting a cold or he might have meningitis. I didn't know if he'd had any shots. I didn't know who his doctor was. At some point Kathleen had rattled off that information but it was one of those times when I was tired of listening to her talk and tuned her out.

She'd also given me her phone number but I hadn't added it to my contact list. My only option was to head upstairs and dig through my laundry to find the pocket where I'd shoved her business card the other day. Luckily her cell number was listed on the bottom. She answered on the second ring.

"He's sick," I blurted out a split second after she said hello.

If Kathleen had been sleeping when I called she was awake and alert now. "Nash? Colin's sick?"

"Yeah. He's running a fever."

"How high?"

I paced the floor with the phone in my ear and my crying brother in my arms. "I don't know. He feels hot and he's been crying on and off since last night and I thought everything was fine when he fell asleep but he started crying again and when I touched his head I noticed how hot he was."

It was a jumbled babble of words but Kathleen understood.

"Okay, listen. The first thing you need to do is give him a dose of ibuprofen to get the fever down. Look in the diaper bag in his room. There should be a bottle in there with a dropper that will allow you to dispense the proper dosage directly into his mouth. Now let me ask you, has he been eating?"

I'd made my way to Colin's room and was already rooting around in the diaper bag. "Yeah, he's been eating."

"Peeing? Pooping?"

"Both."

"Does he seem listless? Lethargic?"

I set the screaming baby down on the changing table. "Does he *sound* listless?"

"Do you see a rash anywhere?"

I unsnapped his outfit and examined him. "No." The medicine was in my hand. I scanned the bottle for the dosage and wasted no time filling the dropper before depositing the contents into Colin's mouth. He scrunched his mouth up and was silent for a second, then resumed screaming.

"Should I take him to the hospital?" I asked.

"Hawk General closed two years ago so the nearest hospital is forty five minutes away. There's a brand new urgent care facility that just opened up on Cottonwood Road, right off I-95. They probably won't be busy. I'll meet you over there."

I was going to tell Kathleen that she didn't need to do that. It was late and she had a kid of her own to take care of. But I was relieved she was coming. Kathleen with her take charge, know-it-all attitude was exactly what Colin needed right now.

"Thank you," I said and snapped Colin back into his outfit.

This time I didn't forget to bring the diaper bag when I left the house. The urgent care was a ten-minute drive away and there were only two other patients in the waiting room. I was halfway finished with filling out my life story on a clipboard full of papers when Kathleen rushed in. I could admit I was damn glad to see her.

"How is he?" She sat in the yellow plastic chair right beside me and reached for Colin, unbuckling him from his car seat.

"Much calmer now," I said. Colin had fallen asleep on the drive and stayed that way even when I brought him into the brightly lit building. His head felt cooler too.

"My poor baby," Kathleen murmured, kissing his face and rocking him in her arms. It was tough to get rid of the lump in my throat when I watched her hold my baby brother. She really loved that kid. She loved him every bit as much as I did.

"I dropped Emma off at my mom's," Kathleen said, still staring down at Colin. "She can keep her overnight."

Kathleen managed to look excellent even at this time of night under the harsh lights of the urgent care waiting room. She wore a blue v-neck tee and a loose skirt that reached to her ankles. Her wild red curls spilled over her shoulders and she wore no makeup. She didn't need any. And I couldn't be sure but from this angle I guessed she wasn't wearing a bra.

I'm such a fucking dick.

This girl comes out in the middle of the night to help me out in a crisis and all I can do is check out her tits.

I stopped watching Kathleen and returned to the tedium of my paperwork. "Sorry if I woke you up."

"You didn't. I had a paper to write."

Next to a line that said 'Allergies' I wrote a question mark. "That's right, you mentioned you were doing online school. What are you studying?"

"Accounting. I'd like to get my CPA license someday."

"That's nice."

"Not really. But it's a good career that will pay the bills."

I studied her again. Colin slept on her shoulder now while she tenderly rubbed his back. "What did you want to do instead?"

A sad smile touched her lips. "It took me a little while to find my niche but I was a philosophy major."

"Impressive."

"I wanted to be a university professor. Get a PhD so I could have some fancy letters after my name, perhaps teach overseas for a while."

Those plans sounded more like the Kathleen Doyle who was hyped as the town prodigy, the girl who skipped a couple of grades and braved the halls of Hawk Valley High ahead of schedule, ignoring all the snickering over her flat chested little kid appearance.

"And yet you became a bookkeeper in Hawk Valley," I said and immediately wished I hadn't. I was thinking aloud, wondering about the fork in the road of Kathleen Doyle's life.

"Emma," she said by way of explanation and her smile was no longer sad.

I should have figured that out. Kathleen was a few years younger than me, probably twenty-three. She'd graduated early, valedictorian of my class, headed off to college with big dreams and then came back home after she got knocked up by some guy she obviously didn't want to talk about. My own parents had been young and foolish when I joined the world so I knew all about how the arrival of a kid could change a life's trajectory.

"Do you have any idea much more I could have done if you hadn't been born?"

My father had been a little drunk when he said that and we'd just had another of our infamous fights. I was probably fifteen at the time. Chris Ryan didn't apologize very often but the next day he did apologize for saying those words. He stood there in the doorway of my bedroom, his hands crossed over his chest, his eyes on the floor as he said he was sorry. He'd been angry. He'd had too many beers. He didn't mean what he said. I believed him. He wanted me to say something too, some acknowledgement of forgiveness. But I stubbornly stared down at my homework and said nothing.

"Colin Ryan?"

The nurse in purple scrubs was standing there waiting. Kathleen carried Colin while I followed with the car seat and diaper bag.

"You just have to leave Mommy's arms for a second," the nurse said when it was time to place Colin on the scale. "Fourteen pounds, two ounces."

"Is that good?" I asked, sounding as anxious as I felt.

The nurse gave me an indulgent grin. She looked young, really young. She'd probably started nursing the day before yesterday. "It's fine. You two must be first time parents?"

"No," said Kathleen and left it at that.

The nurse promised the doctor would be in shortly and left us alone. Colin was starting to fuss so Kathleen paced the short length of the room to quiet him down.

"Want me to take him?" I asked.

She started to say no, but then handed him over. "If you want to."

I was getting used to the feel of his tiny body against my chest. Holding him now felt natural.

"We'll get you feeling all better soon," I said in his little ear. When I looked up my eyes found Kathleen's. Her eyes were striking, a light green I had never seen on anyone else.

The doctor didn't keep us waiting long. I didn't remember her but she knew who I was. She lived in town. She'd been on some local charity board or something with Heather.

"Double ear infection," she announced a few minutes later after examining Colin. "That would explain the fever and the fussiness. Other than that he looks perfect so I'll write you a prescription and you can take this little guy home."

"Thank you, Dr. Crawford," Kathleen said.

"You're very welcome," said Dr. Crawford. She scribbled some notes on a piece of paper and then looked directly at me. "Once again, I'm so very sorry for your loss. I still can't believe it." Her eyes moved to Colin and her expression saddened visibly. "Please let me know if there's ever anything I can do."

It was the same sentiment repeated to me by dozens of people since the night I arrived in Hawk Valley. A useless, well meaning 'thoughts and prayers' kind of thing to say. I wished there was something they could do.

"I appreciate that," I told the doctor before she left the room.

Kathleen knew where there was a twenty-four hour pharmacy and insisted on picking up the prescription herself.

"You just get this handsome little man home," she said. "It won't take me long to fill this and we can give him the first dose right away."

"Thanks," I said. The word felt inadequate but it was all I had to offer.

She smiled. "Emma's had her share of ear infections. They clear up quickly once the antibiotics kick in."

"Seriously, Kathleen," I said as Colin let out a sleepy sigh on my shoulder. "I owe you for this."

She reached out and touched Colin's head, her fingertips brushing my shoulder in the process. "Nonsense. I'll always be there for Colin. And for you."

"I'm lucky to have you," I said, not realizing the possible double meaning of the words until I heard them out loud.

Kathleen only blushed and looked away.

I was happy to take Colin home and wait for her to show up with the medicine. It was nice, this feeling of cooperation for the sake of a child we both cared about. And it was good to have a friend. I didn't keep too many of those around and that never bothered me. But lately I was starting to feel the deficit. And yes, I did think of Kathleen as a friend.

A friend with a sinful body, sexy hair and a dazzling smile.

A friend who was kind and generous, if a little bossy.

A friend who got my dick hard if I stared at her for too long.

I liked Kathleen. I respected her. And I couldn't stop wanting to fuck her if I tried.

Chapter Nine

Kathleen

AFTER THE MEETING DOWN AT THE STORE ENDED ON A SOUR note it took every shred of my willpower not to call Nash or drop by the house the following day. When he said, "I'll be in touch," I wasn't sure if he was irritated with my pushiness about the store or if he just needed some space to figure things out on his own. I'd happily move mountains for Colin but my role was limited because I wasn't his guardian. Nash was his guardian.

I didn't expect to hear from him after ten p.m. with panic in his voice as Colin screamed in the background. Nash didn't strike me as a man who got anxious easily. He wouldn't ask for help for himself. But he'd reached out for Colin's sake. As we sat together in the urgent care waiting room I started to understand that Nash wasn't the stoic character he seemed to be. Taking care of Colin wasn't just an obligation to him. It looked more like love.

And for the first time I agreed that Chris and Heather had placed their baby boy in exactly the right hands.

"Do you need a medicine dropper?" the pharmacist asked as he bagged up Colin's medication.

"Yes, please," I said.

It was after midnight by the time I was on my way to Nash's place. After I pulled up to the hundred-year-old Victorian house that must have witnessed its share of drama and tragedy over the decades I remained beside the car for a moment and just gazed at the old house.

The streetlights cast a pale glow on the intricate trim along the gables. I'd always loved this place. Growing up just down the street I'd been fascinated by its charming gingerbread house appeal. Since Heather married Chris Ryan and moved in here I'd probably come to visit a hundred times. Part of me still couldn't believe they weren't immersed in their idyllic happy lives just on the other side of the red front door.

The door opened and Nash appeared. He must have been watching for my car. Years ago I'd been aware of the rumors about him, about Heather. At the time I assumed they weren't true. Even after Heather resigned from her office position at the high school I refused to believe that there was anything unseemly about her choice. Everyone knew Nash ran around with a variety of girls but there was no way my beautiful, haughty cousin would get involved with a teenager. Not even one who was on the verge of manhood and as sexually charged as Nash Ryan. Eventually I found out differently but by that time I wasn't shocked. By then I knew all about mistakes. And secrets.

Nash carried Colin in his arms and he raised one hand in greeting, probably wondering why the hell I was hanging out beside the curb.

I held up the white paper bag from the pharmacy and made my way over to them in the darkness.

Colin didn't like being awakened to take his medicine. After we got the first dose down his throat I took a good look at Nash and noticed the weariness in his face. He didn't argue with me when I said I'd take Colin to his room and rock him until he fell asleep again.

Nash stayed downstairs while I brought Colin to the nursery and sat in the rocking chair my mother had given Heather as a baby shower gift. I softly sang the words to "You Are My Sunshine" just like I sang to Emma every night at bedtime.

And I wished with all of my heart that his mother were here rocking him to sleep instead of me.

Colin's forehead was cool and his breathing even when I placed him in the crib and turned on the sound machine that faintly broadcasted white noise.

"I love you, angel," I whispered before I left the room because every child in the world should hear those words as often as possible, whether they understood them or not.

I found Nash sitting on the living room couch, staring at an empty television screen. His dog, Roxie, had been sleeping in a corner. She raised her head when I came downstairs, then settled down with a sigh.

"How is he?" Nash asked.

"Sound asleep." I sank down on an empty space on the leather couch.

Nash's gaze flickered over me and I realized I'd sat down awful close to him. I didn't shift away though. Neither did he.

There was a small stain on the left sleeve of his shirt. I pointed to it. "I think you were hit by the spit up train again."

He looked down, shrugged and pulled the shirt off, exposing his tattooed arms and toned chest. He raised an eyebrow at me. "Better?"

Hell yes.

I cleared my throat and tore my eyes away from six packs and pecs. It wasn't easy.

"You should get some rest," I said. "He'll probably sleep for a while and I can stick around in case he wakes up."

Nash stared at me. "Aren't you tired? It's almost one a.m."

I smiled and nudged him. "I'm a night owl." That was true. My busy schedule often required me to stay up late and operate on little sleep.

He yawned. "You probably have a million things to do in the morning."

"No. It's Sunday. And Emma's fine at my mom's house."

He leaned back on the couch with a sigh and gave me another long, searching stare. "I don't know how to thank you, Kathleen."

"You're welcome."

"I mean it. Thanks for being here for Colin. Thanks for showing up tonight even though I'm a dick."

"You're not a dick."

He thought about it. "I'm a dick sometimes."

"Sometimes," I conceded.

He grinned. He should do that more often. Nash's smile had a dose of magic in it. Then his smile faded.

"I should have known," he said and there was a raw current of emotion in his voice.

"Nash, you couldn't have known that Colin had an ear infection."

He shook his head. "No. I meant I should have known that something like this could happen, that time on this earth is never a guarantee, that you can lose people at any time."

I folded my hands in my lap. "It's impossible to predict the future."

"That's true," he said and now there was a hard tone to his words. "I can't predict the future. But I already knew that in this life there's no contract for a happy ending. I'd found that out when my mother was killed by the man she loved."

I didn't know what to say. Over a decade ago the murder of Nash's mother was big news here even though it happened down in Phoenix. Murder-suicides were still rare enough then for the case to be shocking. The story was ugly, painful to even think about. Nash's mother had been shot in the head while she slept. Her killer was the man she'd married just two months earlier. After he shot his wife the man shot the family dog. Then he shot himself. Nash was lucky he was up here visiting his father for the summer. Otherwise he would likely have been killed too.

Or maybe he saw it a different way. Maybe he thought if he'd been there he would have been able to stop the horror from unfolding. Whatever the case, the echoes of that event must torment him. Even the young girl who already adored him from a distance had noticed how he changed after his mother's murder. He spoke less and fought more. He was always popular and yet always somehow apart from everyone else. He seemed haunted back then. In a way he still did.

"I'm sorry," I said because I regretted that there was nothing I could do to ease his sorrow.

Nash grimaced and stared down at his hands. "I could have visited, Kathleen. I could have called more. I could have made things right between my and my dad, especially because I was aware of how much he wanted that to happen."

My eyes filled with tears. "Nash."

His head was still lowered. "I'm no role model for fuck's sake. Why in the hell did they pick me?"

I didn't know the answer. I could only guess, based on what I knew of my cousin and her husband. And what I'd learned of Nash so far.

"Because your father had absolute faith in you. Because he knew you'd rise to the challenge, that you'd love and protect that baby boy. Nash, your father and Heather didn't doubt you." I touched his shoulder. "I shouldn't have doubted you."

He wouldn't look up. "There's a lot you don't know about me, Kathleen."

"I know enough."

Now he raised his head. Our eyes met. His were no longer full of exhaustion. They were full of pain.

And then when I moved my hand from his shoulder to his face they became full of something else.

His jaw was rough under my fingertips, bristly with a day's beard growth. In a distant time I'd fantasized about being this close to Nash Ryan. I'd daydreamed that some day he would look at me the way he was looking at me now. With uninhibited desire.

I knew what would happen next. This had nothing to do with the past. Or the future. Or the heartbreaking circumstances that had led us to this particular moment. This was just about here and now.

And here and now we both wanted the same thing.

I moved my hand lower and proved it.

"Kat," he groaned as my hand closed around him through the fabric of his gym shorts. He was hard, thick, perfect. I boldly stroked him and he groaned again, this time with a curse. I hadn't been with anyone in a long time and a primitive need pooled in my belly then rolled lower, between my legs. Nash directed my hand inside the elastic waistband of his shorts and I touched hard, heated flesh. I'd almost forgotten how this kind of triumph felt, how empowering it was to bring a strong man to the brink of ecstasy. I started to slide to my knees, intending to take him in my mouth. But he stopped me.

"Get rid of this," he demanded, yanking on my shirt.

I obeyed, slowly drawing my shirt up and then over my head. In my haste to get out the door earlier I'd forgotten a bra. I wriggled out of my long skirt, then hooked my thumbs in my damp panties and rolled them down. As I knelt on the floor in front of him, Nash stared at me for such a long moment I started to feel self-conscious.

He seized me with no warning, his big hand fastening onto the back of my neck and pulling me in for a kiss that was ferocious, electrifying. This was what I'd been missing, the way it felt to be overpowered by a kiss. I hardly felt myself being lifted but suddenly I was in his lap. My hands roamed over the hard muscles of his chest but not for long. I was as impatient as he was, maybe more, straddling him, grinding against the feel of his skin in a desperate quest for relief.

He shoved his shorts down and looked me in the eye. "You're sure you want this?"

I couldn't talk. I just nodded.

Nash surprised me when he became gentle, easing inside of me slowly, like he feared I might break if he was too rough. My skin stretched and quivered as I took him all the way in and I couldn't stand it. I wrapped my arms around his shoulders and rode him with furious rhythm until he seized my hips and demanded to assume control. I gave it to him. I let him move me at the pace he wanted and reveled in the primal frenzy of our bodies colliding.

It didn't take me long to come and holy shit did I come hard. The orgasm was an avalanche and all I could do was get temporarily buried by it, stifling the urge to scream as the tremors wracked me in waves. Nash's arms kept me from collapsing into a spent puddle as the aftershocks kept rising and falling.

"Too fucking close," he finally gasped and withdrew from me. Dimly I realized why, understood that he was right to pull away. We'd been absurdly reckless, not even using a condom. Another few seconds and we might have had a problem.

But we weren't finished yet. I closed my fingers around his thick, unsatisfied cock and stroked the solid length, teasing the tip until he shuddered, moaned my name again and came in my hand.

We were both sweating, gasping, panting as hard as marathon runners. I slid off his lap and onto the couch, trying to catch my breath and figure out what should happen next.

Nash recovered first, swiping his shirt off the floor and carefully mopping the evidence off my hand. He watched as I gathered my clothes and held them to my chest in a rumpled heap.

"I should let you get some sleep," I said.

Nash brushed the back of his right knuckle across my arm. My shiver was involuntary.

"I'm not tired," he said.

"Even after all that?"

He thought the question was funny. "Especially after all that."

I swallowed. "I think I should go."

"No you shouldn't."

I pulled my panties on because I was starting to feel ridiculous sitting on the couch butt naked. Nash, on the other hand, didn't seem troubled at all. He looked as relaxed as I'd ever seen him.

"What should I do then?" I asked, adding a playful note to my voice.

"Nothing." He slid down to the floor, opened my legs and pushed my panties aside before treating me to a brief exploration of his tongue as I gasped and arched my back.

"Don't do a goddamn thing just now," he ordered in a gruff whisper and the feel of his bristled jaw against my sensitive inner thighs was almost as wickedly good as his tongue. So I followed his orders. I didn't do a goddamn thing.

Chapter Ten

Nash

My first thought when I woke up was about Colin. I tensed for a second and relaxed when I remembered that Colin was fine now. I couldn't hear any crying so he must still be sleeping. The antibiotics were already working their medical magic.

My second thought was that I felt good. Really fucking good. Clear headed and restored.

Then I looked beside me and didn't feel so good anymore.

Kathleen was curled up on the edge of the bed. If she rolled over half an inch she'd fall right off. Her red curls covered her face but her breathing was deep and she didn't stir when I extricated myself from the tangle of blankets. I managed to tug the sheet away in the process and the view of her smooth, bare skin was stimulating in ways I didn't want to be stimulated right now.

I dug a clean pair of gym shorts out of one of my suitcases because I still hadn't unpacked. The room's décor hadn't changed but the old dresser in the corner of the room was filled with arts and crafts supplies that must have belonged to Heather. I couldn't recall my dad having much use for glitter and yarn. At some point I'd need to do something about the fact that the closets and cabinets all over the house were filled with personal effects belonging to my father and his wife. I couldn't think about that yet though. The idea of pawing through the abandoned possessions of the dead still hurt too much.

Kathleen let out a soft sigh and then started to roll over, which would have sent her crashing to the polished hardwood floor. I dove in to scoop my hands underneath her and roll her back to safety. She still didn't wake up. I stood there for a few extra seconds staring at her.

Fuck, she was sexy.

That didn't mean I was proud of myself for drilling that hot body in a dozen different ways last night.

I hadn't been thinking. Kathleen didn't strike me as a bed hopping type of girl. She might expect things. Things I didn't have available to give to her right now. Probably not ever.

I left the room and quietly closed the door behind me. The Kathleen quandary would have to wait until later. In the meantime I could admit that getting my brains fucked out last night had done wonders for my mood.

Down the hall in the nursery, Colin was awake and waving his little arms around, trying to reach for the stuffed monkey mobile over his crib. I took it as a good sign that he no longer shrieked in pain and when I put my palm on his forehead I was relieved that it was cool.

"Come on, kiddo," I said and he actually gave me a little smile as I lifted him out of the crib. Not for the first time I wondered what was going on in his baby brain. Was there any part of him that understood how his life had been turned upside down? I hoped not.

Colin wriggled around when I was changing him and resisted being snapped back into his outfit so I just carried him downstairs in his diaper. The sun was shining outside and the house was warm. Summer was almost here.

Roxie was waiting at the bottom of the stairs, tail wagging. I let her out through the back door and she immediately dove into a cluster of birds that had been pecking in the grass.

Yesterday evening I'd measured out powdered formula and made a couple of bottles to stow in the fridge. Colin drank one down eagerly and then emitted a substantial burp when I held him upright.

"Good boy," I said. I realized I was praising another human for the routine feat of belching. The thought didn't faze me a bit.

This morning Colin was more agreeable about swallowing his medicine and he seemed downright cheerful when I set him in his bouncer. He immediately made an effort to grab the colorful objects hanging from the bouncer's toy bar but only succeeded in flailing his arms around. I flicked the silly pig toy he liked so much and the way he smacked at it with such enthusiasm made me smile. I was getting the hang of this baby stuff.

"Good morning," said a voice and I turned to see Kathleen standing in the doorway.

She was fully dressed in last night's clothes. That was a minor disappointment but I couldn't realistically expect her to strut around my house naked. In fact it wasn't even a good idea for a variety of reasons. Although the view would have been fucking epic.

"Good morning," I answered, keeping my voice neutral and glad she wasn't throwing herself into my arms. In fact she seemed a little uncomfortable, crossing her arms over her chest as she leaned against the wall while failing to look me in the face.

Kathleen brightened when her eyes landed on Colin. "Hello, sunshine," she said, coming right over and unfastening the bouncer restraints that I had just fastened. "How's my boy today?" She cuddled him and kissed his face and made a bunch of nonsense sounds that delighted the baby.

"I gave him his second dose already," I said. "I think he's feeling better."

Kathleen nodded and then continued with the *wee wee ga ga* shit. I wished I knew the right thing to say the morning after you fucked your new friend and kind of wished you hadn't.

I switched on the coffee machine. "Want a cup?"

"So you've become a fan of caffeine after all," Kathleen said in a teasing voice and when she looked at me she smiled.

I relaxed a little. Maybe this didn't have to be so weird after all. "Yeah, I've discovered its useful properties." I removed two identical

Hawk Valley Happiness mugs from the kitchen cabinet. They seemed to be multiplying. "So do you take cream and sugar?"

"Neither," said Kathleen. "But I've got to get going. My mom loves Emma but her patience for a precocious three-and-a-half-year-old only has about a twelve hour window."

Kathleen carefully replaced Colin in his bouncer while I searched my brain for a way to end the conversation diplomatically.

"My cock thanks you."

No. Definitely not diplomatic.

"Come back anytime."

Sounded sarcastic as shit.

Kathleen finished fussing with Colin and cleared her throat. "Nash, I hope last night didn't wreck anything."

Listening to her voice made me recall the distinct breathy squeal she made every time an orgasm hit her. But I kept a straight face. "Not at all."

Her face was anxious. "You think so?"

"Yeah. You're great. Last night was…great."

"It was." She nodded. "And it wasn't the best idea."

"Probably not."

She lifted her chin and leveled her gaze at me. "Just so you know, this is not something I do regularly."

"Me neither."

Her raised eyebrow said she didn't believe me but she obviously didn't want to start an argument.

On the other hand, I kind of felt like starting one if it put the truth out there. "You seem unconvinced."

"It's none of my business."

"Of course it's not."

"Then I won't ask."

"But I think you should."

Kathleen sighed. She crossed her arms again. She did that a lot. "You want me to ask if you're the type of man who screws anything with tits?"

This was getting fun. "Yes."

She was blushing. "So are you?"

"Am I what?"

"A player."

I filled both mugs with coffee and gave her one even though she'd said she didn't want any. She had to uncross her arms when I handed the cup over and I noticed that the fact that I was taking my time about answering the question was making her squirm. I kind of liked making her squirm.

"The last girl I was with was one I dated for five months last year," I said. "I don't bang random chicks for the hell of it. I'm no player, Kat."

She digested the information. She looked confused.

"Why'd you think otherwise?" I pressed, wondering what kind of gossip was floating around about me in Hawk Valley ever since I left.

Kathleen set her coffee on the table and there went her arms again, crossing her chest and hiding the ripe, generous shape of her breasts. But not before I noticed her nipples were hard. The observation was interesting.

"I guess I shouldn't have been so presumptuous," she said. "It's just that I remember what you were like in high school."

"What was I like?"

She was thoughtful. "Noncommittal I suppose. You were attached to a different girl every other week and none of them appeared to matter to you for very long. I never heard you refer to a single one of them as your girlfriend."

"You must have paid a lot of attention," I said.

Now I was messing with her. I knew she had a colossal crush on me back when she was all knees and elbows. Every time I looked up I'd see her pale little face peeking around a corner and then she'd dart away as if she thought I hadn't noticed.

Kat blushed. "I've always been very observant."

"A good quality in a stalker."

Her lips pursed. "I didn't stalk you."

"I thought we were being honest."

She let out an exasperated breath. "Well, perhaps I was a little more intrigued by you than I should have been."

"And why not? I'm an intriguing guy."

Kathleen cocked her head and studied me. "You were a heart-breaker back then. I figured you still were. People don't usually change. And anyway, just look at you."

I mulled that over. "I don't understand."

"Yes you do."

"Humor me, Kat."

"You are sexier and more mysterious than ever. And you know it."

"Maybe."

She rolled her eyes. "Oh shut up. It's obvious you're absurdly good looking and you seem to have nothing but contempt for adult concepts like relationships and love. I'm not saying I was right about you, but that's the reason I made certain assumptions."

I was bothered. Kathleen obviously had some baggage, given the crack she'd made once about sucking at relationships but I didn't know why she figured I held love in contempt. Love was probably great or people wouldn't be falling all over themselves to find it. Just because I'd never known the feeling firsthand didn't mean I lurked around in the shadows casting the evil eye on happy couples.

"So do you assume *all* single guys who don't break the looking glass are unrepentant manwhores?"

She held my gaze. "No. I just thought *you* were."

I snorted.

"You wanted honesty," she reminded me.

"I did. And in the interest of honest disclosure, let's just say I've learned from my mistakes."

She was silent for a moment. She had to realize what I was talking about.

"I guess that's all we can do," Kathleen said slowly. "Learn from our mistakes and try to be better versions of ourselves than we were."

It was kind of an odd, introspective thing to say. She twirled a piece of hair and looked troubled, suddenly lost in her own thoughts. I figured that whatever was swimming through her brain right now probably had nothing to do with me.

I drank my coffee and watched Colin pursue the prize of the pink pig, oblivious that anything else was going on in the room.

"By the way," I said, suddenly arriving at a decision. "I'm going to give the store a chance."

Kathleen's eyes snapped to my face. "You are?"

I nodded and she positively beamed at me. In fact she looked so happy you'd think I'd just promised her a cruise to the Bahamas.

"Nash, that's great. This will mean so much to the community. And you can count on my help."

I felt like kind of a heel for accepting even more help from Kathleen but I was glad she offered.

"So what do I need to do first?" I asked.

She immediately became businesslike and started ticking off her fingers. "Well, for starters you need to reopen the doors as soon as possible. I'll call Betty and Hayden, your employees, and work out a schedule. We talked about hiring another cashier to fill in the gaps, didn't we? Yes, I think we did. I'll place some ads on job sites and I can take care of the interviews if you want. Or you can do it. Just let me know. Oh, and you need to order more inventory. I recommend a visit to First Valley Bank where your accounts are. You'll need to extend the store's line of credit and meeting your account manager might help."

"One thing at a time." I held up a hand. My brain couldn't keep up with all the chores she'd just rattled off. "Let's start with the cash flow issue. I've got some money. I can arrange to have it wired from my bank today. And Steve Brown had mentioned something about life insurance funds so I can probably peel some of that off after I put away the bulk for Colin."

"This is good." Kathleen bobbed her head with eagerness. "This will work, Nash. I know it will."

"Then I'll borrow some of your optimism and agree."

Colin enhanced the moment by swatting the pig and squealing.

Kathleen glanced at the clock above the stove. "I really do need to go."

"Okay. I'll let you."

"You can call me later if you want to talk in more detail about a plan of action for the store."

"Will do."

She leaned over and kissed Colin. "Good bye, sweet face. Glad you're feeling better." Her handbag was on the kitchen table. She must have left it there last night before getting sidetracked by orgasmic amusements. She shouldered her bag and headed out. "I'll talk to you later, Nash."

"Talk to you later, Kat."

She had her hand on the door and suddenly spun around. "What changed your mind?"

"About the store? I don't know, I guess some of the things you said made sense."

"I'm glad to hear it but I meant something else. What changed your mind about calling me Kat?"

"You said your friends all call you Kat." I raised an eyebrow. "Isn't that right?"

She grinned. "Yes, that's right."

When Kathleen left there was an instant void in the room. Even Colin stopped waving his limbs around and just sat still with a thoughtful expression.

"Just you and me again, kid," I said and I could swear he raised an accusing eyebrow.

"No judging, little brother," I warned and picked him up out of the bouncer.

Chapter Eleven

Kathleen

It was Tuesday morning when I ran into Jane Ryan wearing a bohemian dress in peacock colors and frowning over a pile of heirloom tomatoes at Windom Grocery on Garner Avenue.

"Kat!" Jane's grimace vanished and she appeared delighted to see me. She had the classic Ryan family thick black hair and deep blue eyes, like her brother and her nephew. But where Chris's hair had started to show streaks of gray hers was still lustrous and uniform.

"Hi Jane." I hugged her.

When I was a kid Jane babysat for me a few times when my mother began dating her soon-to-be third husband (later to become her third ex-husband). Jane's babysitting career ended the day we found a lost puppy at the park. Jane wrapped the struggling creature in her jacket in a misguided rescue effort. When we returned to my front yard the angry ball of fur leapt out of her jacket and fastened its teeth to my left arm. I screamed. Jane screamed louder. One of my neighbors heard the noise and jumped over a hedge to get to us. After he pulled the 'puppy' away it ran off and he asked why the hell we were playing around with a coyote. Jane hyperventilated and I needed to get a series of rabies shots. My mother was not amused.

"Nash told me what happened," she said and I dropped the two boxes of cereal I was holding.

I bent down to scoop them up and regain some composure because I was sure my face was as flaming red as that tomato in Jane's hand. I hadn't thought of Nash as a hapless blabbermouth who would gossip to his aunt about his sexual escapades but I'd been wrong about people before.

"I'm so glad Colin's okay," Jane continued. "Kevin and I were over at the house last night. Thank you for everything you did for him. And for Nash. I know my nephew's not always the easiest man to get along with. I'm so grateful you were there."

I breathed easier. Nash had just told her about the midnight trip to urgent care. Not the after party.

"I was happy to come," I said, nearly gagging over my words because they were true in more ways than one.

Jane studied me. "You look beautiful today."

I touched my hair. "That's nice of you to say."

"Radiant." Jane nodded.

"What?"

"You're radiant. There's this aura of gratified serenity surrounding you."

"New skin product," I said, hoping that would put an end to this particular conversational thread. It didn't.

"No." Jane frowned at me the same way she'd frowned at the inadequate tomatoes. "That's not it. This is a glow that comes from within."

I was bad at keeping a poker face. Jane was still scrutinizing me as if my forehead was tattooed with letters she could read.

And they'd say: I fucked Nash Ryan. And I liked it.

"The store is reopening this week," I said as if that explained everything.

Jane blinked. "What store?"

Honestly, I loved Jane but sometimes the woman was daft. "Chris's store. Hawk Valley Gifts."

Instantly I wished I hadn't brought up the name of her dead brother. Jane's expression changed. "Right," she said softly. "It was once my dad's store. He used to keep a jar of penny candy sticks on the counter."

I hugged the boxes of Emma's favorite cereal to my chest. "The reopening is Friday morning," I said. "I'm sure Nash would love it if you'd stop by."

Jane cheered up. "Will you be there?"

"Yes. For a little while anyway. I've been helping Nash get all the details sorted out. He's going to reach out to some of the local artists who have work for sale to see if they have anything new. Have you been painting?"

"Not really." Jane's gaze wandered out the glass door. "I used to always look at the mountains for inspiration. I can't do that anymore."

I looked where Jane was looking. The Hawk Mountain range had always been a permanent friendly backdrop to anyone who lived here. I guess I wasn't alone in suppressing a shudder every time I gazed at them now.

I couldn't stick around and talk to Jane for very long. I'd only stopped in here to pick up Emma's cereal before my scheduled meeting with Nash. Garner Avenue was a long, narrow strip that ran through the center of town. Hawk Valley Gifts occupied a space way at the other end but I chose to walk, inhaling the honeyed promise of early summer.

There was a new sign on the shop door, right above the one that said 'CLOSED'. The bold typed letters read, "Hawk Valley Gifts will be reopening Friday, June 8. Thank you for your support." Nash must have put it there.

He leaned against the checkout counter, elbows resting on the polished wood in a way that suggested he'd been waiting for a few minutes. I wasn't late. Nash was just trying to prove he was on top of things.

"Where's Colin?" I asked as some basic part of me performed an involuntary somersault. I'd spoken to Nash a couple of times since we parted on the great Morning After but this was the first time we'd been in the same room together since I walked out of his kitchen two days ago feeling fabulous and faintly sore. If I appeared as radiant as Jane insisted then I had Nash to thank although I'd rather lick the Garner Avenue asphale than admit it to him.

"Nancy's watching him," Nash said. His eyes skimmed over me with slow precision. His blue polo shirt was a step above his usual attire and his black hair was carefully combed instead of tousled and wild. I could smell his aftershave from here, a scent of spicy masculinity that had been designed to make ovaries quiver.

"Is that breakfast?" he asked, pointing to the boxes I was accidentally crushing.

"No." I set them down on a nearby half empty shelf. "Emma's a challenge when it comes to food. Sometimes this is the only thing she'll agree to eat and I ran out this morning. Wait a minute." I thought of something. "How'd you get in? I forgot to give you the key."

He shrugged. "I found another one."

"Where?"

"My father's safe."

"How'd you get into the safe?"

"He left the combination with Steve Brown as part of his will instructions."

"You saw Steve Brown again?"

"How many questions are you going to ask me this morning, Kat?"

"I don't know. How many are you willing to answer?"

Nash moved away from the counter and took a step in my direction. He was looking at me again. He was looking at me in a way that made me forget things like decency and common sense and the fact that I was a single mom who shouldn't take chances. The truth was I was ready to rub one out on his hand if he extended it.

"You look beautiful today," he said in the husky tone that told me more than his words did.

I smoothed down my knee-length swing skirt. "I've had this

outfit for years."

"It's nice."

"Nash." I swallowed. "I thought we agreed this wouldn't happen again."

"You don't like compliments, Kat?"

He was three feet away, surveying me with intense interest. He knew what was on my mind. He knew I wanted him and he was going to make me admit it.

"I like them," I whispered.

Nash was pleased. "What else do you like?"

"I think you've figured out one or two things."

He agreed. "Or more."

My mouth twitched. "You know, I came here for a meeting."

"What a coincidence. So did I."

I took a calming breath. I had to remember my reasons for concluding I shouldn't have screwed Nash Ryan. "I guess we need to lay some ground rules."

Reason 1: I don't have the time or inclination to be involved with anyone right now.

"I guess we do," Nash said.

"We didn't really talk about it the other morning."

Nash crept even closer. His preppy polo shirt was at odds with the ink running riot all over his strong arms, which he crossed over his broad chest as he observed me. "Let's talk about it now."

Reason 2: We're friends. I think.

I forced my face to look serious. "Okay, Nash. You like honesty so I'll give it to you. I'd do anything for Colin and I really do care about you too. But right now I don't have room in my life for a relationship."

He grinned. "I didn't ask you for one, Kat."

Reason 3: This could end badly and impact Colin. And Emma. And me.

"Fair enough," I sighed. "I really value your friendship and the other night was incredible. But my priority is Emma."

"And my priority is Colin."

"So we're on the same page."

He closed in. "Yes we are."

"Then there's nothing else to say."

Nash was inches away. He touched the top button on my blouse, pushed his fingertip into the buttonhole crease. "No, there's nothing else to say."

My breathing hitched. He had to have heard it. "What are we going to do, Nash?"

He captured the button, twisting until it popped off. "Whatever you want, Kat."

Reason 4: None of the above reasons mean shit.

"You know what I want," I admitted and flattened my hand against his chest, reveling in the hard feel of the muscles beneath the fabric. "No hassles, no complications."

He unfastened another button from my blouse, this time without tearing it off. "I can give that to you. I'm not a fan of hassles *or* complications."

My hand traveled lower, settling on his belt. "This is just about two people who know how to make each other feel good. I think we both need that right now."

Nash moved my hand down so I could feel how hard he was. "I think you're right," he whispered.

"There's nothing wrong with it."

"Nothing at all."

I kept my hand where it was while he made short work of the rest of my buttons. Then I paused and shrugged out of the blouse. Nash checked me out and gave a low whistle.

"Have I mentioned yet that you're totally fucking gorgeous?" Then he smiled in the manner that threatened to melt my heart if I had any intention of allowing my heart to be melted.

I tugged on his belt, relishing the way he looked at me, enjoying how bold I suddenly felt.

"I want to see you too," I said. Then I gasped and turned around. "Wait, is the door unlocked?"

He had his hands on me, unhooking my bra and nudging me in the direction of the counter until I bumped into it.

"Probably," he growled and now he was at my back, pushing my skirt up and my panties down. My breasts spilled from my open bra and briefly found their way into Nash's hands before they were flattened against the counter when he bent me over. My legs were jelly, threatening to collapse underneath me as Nash pulled his pants down and teased my ass with his cock. This was ridiculous, downright perverted. I was about to get nailed across the counter at a goddamn souvenir shop in broad daylight and I couldn't think of anything that would feel more fucking fantastic.

I bucked against him and he said, "Fuck," and pushed my hair aside, sucking at my neck while his hands worked to roll a condom on. Meanwhile I throbbed so hard a faint breeze across my clit would probably send me into oblivion. I needed to come so badly I was about to reach down and deal with the problem myself.

But that wasn't necessary. Nash nudged my legs father apart, found the right angle and drove himself in deep. He was instinctive the way he knew when to slow down and when to pound without apology. He was teaching me that not all orgasms were created equal. The powerful spasms I experienced with him had little in common with the sweet waves of pleasure I'd known before. No wonder why I had no willpower where Nash was concerned.

The pace of his thrusts became faster, frenetic, our bodies pulsing together in sin and sweat. I felt him come with a groan and a shudder and a smile of victory spread across my face. It was still there when we separated and started gathering our clothes.

"You look amused," he remarked, sliding his boxers on first.

I hooked my bra. "I like having the power to send the great Nash Ryan over the edge."

He eyed me. "I didn't know I was great."

"My vagina thinks so."

He laughed. "You crack me up, Kat."

"Why?"

Nash pulled his shirt over his head. "You're all things at once. Prim and dirty and careful and careless."

That summed me up better than he knew. "Just trying to keep you guessing, Nash."

"I'm not complaining. It's a hot combination."

I pulled on my skirt and watched him zip his fly. He caught me looking and his expression changed. "You sure all this is okay with you? Seriously, I appreciate everything you've done. I like you and I'd hate to think I'm messing you up in any way."

I picked up my blouse. The top button was gone, plucked away by Nash's fingers and tossed somewhere unseen. But I buttoned the rest and tucked the shirt into my skirt.

"I'm pretty sure the only thing that's been messed up so far is my hair." I made a show of smoothing my unruly curls into place.

Nash finished getting his clothes in order and leaned against the counter in exactly the same position he'd been in when I got here. "You still want to have this meeting?"

"Of course." I picked up the bag that doubled as a purse and laptop carrier and opened the computer on the counter beside him. "Let's take a look at the inventory reports and go from there."

Chapter Twelve

Nash

THE REOPENING OF THE STORE WENT MUCH BETTER THAN I thought. Half the town showed up and everyone who set foot in the place bought something, even if it was just a pack of gum. Kat was right about the support from the locals.

I stuck around for the whole day, shaking hands and greeting people who'd come down with their families to let me know they were glad this place was back in business. Even people I'd gone to high school with showed up, including a few former flames who'd cursed me back in the day for one reason or another. But all of them had known my dad and if their memories of me were less than wonderful they weren't holding grudges anymore. Normally I wasn't the social butterfly sort but it felt good to be a part of this, part of something positive.

A few people anxiously asked, "How's the baby? How's Colin?" and I assured them the baby was fine, that he wasn't here because after a recent illness I didn't think it was smart to expose him to a lot of people. They'd nodded approvingly at the answer and I felt like I'd done the right thing.

All the time my eyes kept searching newcomers for Kathleen. She'd already mentioned she'd be running around to meetings and whatever all day but I looked for her just the same.

Even though it would have been an inconvenient time to pop a boner the way I did whenever she walked in the room.

I'd really intended our first hot night to be a one time thing, a lapse of judgment instigated by the emotional roller coaster I'd been riding lately. But working out my inner demons with the help of Kat's sexy body brought me a sense of calm. I just hoped she was telling the truth when she said she wasn't looking for more than a friend with benefits. With all the obligations I was juggling that was all I could offer her.

Kathleen never did drop by but Kevin Reston made an appearance. Since I'd arrived back to town he was always friendly enough, maybe for Jane's sake, maybe for my father's, but I got the impression he didn't know what to make of me. I understood. After some district cutbacks, he used to volunteer to help coach the Hawk Valley High football team and once he broke up a brawl between me and Travis Hanson, the school quarterback. Kevin earned a black eye and a busted nose for his efforts.

"You just missed Jane," I told him. "She was here a little while ago."

He nodded. "I know. We met for coffee down the street."

"Did she order you to stop by?"

He grinned. "Yeah."

"Well, I'm glad you did."

Kevin cleared his throat. "You know, I was also thinking we could go out and grab a beer tonight. Your dad and I used to meet up at Sheen's the first Friday of every month."

I didn't drink much these days. But I knew Kevin had been my dad's friend for many years and felt his loss acutely. Plus I was sure this invitation had been extended to make Jane happy and anyone who tried this hard to make my gentle aunt happy deserved to be met halfway.

"I'd have to find a sitter for Colin," I said. "He's with your mom today."

Kevin waved a hand. "And you know she would love to watch him for a few hours longer. There's nothing my mom would rather be doing than taking care of babies."

It was true that Nancy Reston had insisted over and over that anytime I needed a sitter I should keep her at the top of the list. Accepting favors from kind people was still a new concept to me.

"All right," I said. "I'll give her a call and if she's cool with watching him you got yourself a beer buddy."

Kevin flashed a grin. "Meet you at Sheen's around eight."

"You got it." I swiped a Hawk Valley Happiness mug off a nearby shelf. "And have one of these on the house."

Kevin accepted the ceramic cup. "Thanks. Can never have too many."

Nancy Reston actually sounded delighted when I called to ask if she could keep Colin until around nine p.m. She told me to take as much time as I wanted. I ended the call feeling a little guilty. Imposing on Nancy and Kathleen and whoever else offered to help wasn't a permanent solution. I'd have to make a regular daycare schedule if I was going to manage the store the way my father had. It was also going to be impossible to juggle two careers plus child rearing. I'd already put the word out to my clients that I was no longer accepting new work.

"You need to put in more hours at the store. Someday the place will be yours, Nash."

"Oh fuck that. I'd rather cut off my right hand than hang around here and be a washed up Hawk Valley lifer."

Memories are funny things. They can hibernate deep for a decade and then hit you like a punch in the gut, a long forgotten nugget that flashes through your mind out of nowhere and leaves you wondering if it was real.

"Excuse me," said a voice. It belonged to a small silver-haired woman who was covered in some silky shawl thing that looked expensive. "Who can help me with buying that painting over there?"

She pointed to a sunrise watercolor of the Hawk Mountains. One of Jane's paintings.

"I can help you," I said.

The store closed at seven but I stuck around to thank the employees and take care of a few tasks. Finally at a quarter to eight I locked the doors and headed down the street to Sheen's.

It was the same dim, hole-in-the-wall bar I remembered walking past a thousand times when I was a kid. Because this was Friday night it was pretty crowded with a bunch of people watching the baseball game on the screen above the bartender's head. Others played a game of darts. The game seemed like a bad idea given the human density in the place.

Kevin hailed me from a table. He was sharing it with another person.

Son of a bitch.

Travis Hanson, former high school quarterback and all around cocky asshole hadn't crossed my mind in years and yet today he was occupying all kinds of space in my head.

He was also occupying the seat beside Kevin.

I pasted a smile to my face and took the remaining chair. Back in the day Travis had been a prick who liked to hurt people smaller than he was but maybe he'd changed. That happened sometimes.

"Nash," he said, fist bumping me like we were BFF's instead of former archenemies.

"Hey, Travis. How's it going?"

There was a despicable smugness in his grin. He spread his arms. "I own this place now."

"No kidding."

"Yep. My dad fronted me the cash last year when old man Sheen retired and moved down to Tucson. I harassed him into giving me a hell of a deal too." Travis snapped his meaty fingers and a cute brunette in a short denim skirt came scurrying over.

"Hey, sweetness, you remember Nash Ryan, right?" he said as his hand rested on the girl's ass.

'Sweetness' didn't seem bothered by the attention. She nodded. "I remember you, Nash. You were a senior when I was a freshman."

"Right," I said. I couldn't recall having laid eyes on this girl in my life.

Travis snorted. "As if he was keeping track back then. Nash never cared if they were too young or too old. The boy got around, that's for damn sure."

The comment was in unbelievably poor taste. It was more than a dig at me. It was a veiled reference to old rumors. I'd never confirmed anything but that didn't matter in a small town. Kevin shot me an apologetic look.

"I'm so sorry about what happened to your family," the waitress said. "My mom knew Heather so she was at the funeral. She was still crying when she got home, said that earth had lost an angel when Heather was taken."

Taken. That made the situation sound slightly hopeful, as though the possibility existed for Heather to return. But there was no way Heather would return. She'd died on a mountain with the man who loved her. For a long time I'd been furious with both of them. But it was possible now to remember things I hadn't thought about in a long time, like how Heather used to pay off delinquent lunch accounts for kids during her brief career working in the front office of the high school. And the time she bought flowers for a classmate who was distraught after the girl's dog was hit by a car.

"Thanks," I said. "She's missed."

The waitress offered a gentle smile. "So what can I get for you?"

"Anything you've got on tap would be great." I didn't plan on taking more than a couple of sips anyway. I was tired, I wanted to pick up Colin and the bar scene was never my hangout of choice.

Travis openly leered at the waitress's backside as she walked away "That's mine," he said proudly as if he was talking about a car.

"Good for you," I said with sarcasm.

He smirked. "And let me tell you, there's one tight pussy in there to go with that sweet ass."

I didn't want to hear about it. I caught Kevin's eye. He looked uncomfortable.

Travis wasn't done talking though. "Likes to mouth off on occasion though so I've got to keep her in line." He belched.

My dislike for the guy instantly swerved from mild to severe.

"Careful someone doesn't decide to keep *you* in line," I said slowly.

Travis peered at me, the layers inside his thick skull evidently trying to decide whether or not I was kidding.

"That wouldn't go well," he said. "Thought you learned that lesson once already, Ryan."

My hand curled into a fist beneath the table. "From what I remember you bled pretty hard that day, Hanson."

Kevin coughed. "Pretty sure I bled harder than either of you," he said good-naturedly. "My nose has been crooked ever since."

"Sorry about that," I said, keeping my eyes on Travis, who stared back with the flat look of a man who had a few screws loose.

"It's okay," Kevin said. "My lady says it makes me looks rakish."

The waitress returned and set my beer down on the table.

"Thanks, sweetness," Travis said, giving her another obnoxious feel.

I was tired of this guy, tired of being here. If I stuck around too long I'd get into trouble. Luckily the bartender showed up and quietly said something to Travis about the whiskey supply.

Travis frowned. "Everyone's fucking helpless," he grumbled, rising from his chair. "Gotta go deal with this."

"Take your time," I said and Travis fixed his gaze on me.

He was obviously weighing the idea of telling me to get the hell out of his place. I wouldn't have been upset if he did.

But he just offered a cold grin and said, "Good to see you Nash." His tone implied the opposite.

"What an asshole," I said when he was gone.

Kevin chuckled. “He is a piece of work.”

“Can’t believe Sheen sold the bar to that guy.”

“Yeah.” Kevin made a face. “Listen, sorry I dragged you out here. I forgot that old feuds can still be raw.”

Kevin wasn’t trying to be profound. He was just talking about the fact that Travis and I still despised each other. But I was thinking of my dad. We’d never gotten along. We were unpleasant mysteries to one other and after my mother’s death that sentiment only festered.

With Travis out of the way, Kevin and I were able to have a pleasant conversation. He knew a lot about what I’d been up to since leaving Hawk Valley and I could only guess he’d come by that information from my father. I found myself wondering what my dad would think if he saw me here in his old stomping grounds, having a beer with his buddy and discreetly checking my watch because I wanted to be on my way to pick up my baby brother.

When nine o’clock approached I stood up and dropped some cash on the table.

“You got to get going?” Kevin asked.

“Afraid so. Colin’s an early riser.”

He held out his hand. “Hey, thanks for hanging out for a little while.”

“Thanks for asking me.”

He grinned. Back when he helped coach football and I was a linebacker with a shitty attitude, Kevin Reston had seemed old and about as interesting as an unpainted wall. I was wrong. Kevin was really a great guy. I was glad he and Jane had found one another.

As I left the table it looked like Kevin was going to stick around for a little while and nurse the beer in his hand.

“Chief,” someone bellowed over by the dartboard. “Why don’t you come over here and show us how it’s done?”

Kevin picked up his beer and headed over. “On my way.”

Before exiting I took a detour to the men’s room. I’d barely touched my beer but my bladder was full from the bottle of water I’d swallowed before heading down here.

I was washing my hands off in the sink when I thought I heard a shout. I turned the water off and listened. There, unmistakable beneath the bar music and the brash voices of its customers, was the sound of a man's voice shouting in anger. It was coming from the other side of the wall and I could pick out a few words.

"Fucking told you (mumble) fucking pay (mumble)."

The responding voice was smaller, higher pitched. A female. "Sorry. I thought I ordered more."

"It was your damn job!"

"I'm sorry!"

"Bitch."

There was the sound of a thump followed by a sharp cry and I'd heard enough. I barreled out of the bathroom and through the nearest door, where I found the waitress from earlier sobbing into her hands while a red-faced Travis Hanson loomed over her with his neck veins bulging.

And even though I knew it was Travis, for a blurred second of blind rage I didn't see him. I saw the man I always saw in my waking nightmares, the man who wasn't satisfied just to rid the world of his own life so he had to take more. I saw my mother's husband.

I didn't think. I lunged. Travis's face had time to register a look of surprise before I grabbed him by the throat and shoved him into a nearby wall hard enough to crack the surface.

"The fuck," he sputtered and the girl screamed.

I was ready to do more, to pound him fucking bloody but suddenly there were arms around my waist, yanking me backwards while voices exclaimed in the background.

"Nash, cut it out!" Kevin yelled and that made me stop trying to rip free.

Travis, meanwhile, had recovered from his collision with the wall and was about to charge. The waitress bravely put herself in the middle, casting horrified glances my way and then back at Travis.

"Please stop," she said and she wasn't just talking to her boyfriend. She was addressing both of us.

Kevin hadn't let go of me yet. "You calm the fuck down."

I was bigger, stronger, and could have easily shaken him off but I didn't. I nodded and Kevin released his grip.

"What's this about?" Kevin asked in a commanding voice, a voice that was used to getting his questions answered.

I looked behind me and saw a few curious faces peering in the doorway. Kevin noticed them too and waved them away.

Travis glared. "My employee screwed up. I got a little loud about it, that's all. And then this bozo comes charging in here like he's on a fucking roid rage and starts smashing up the place."

"You're still a lying sack of shit, Hanson," I spat.

"Enough!" Kevin turned to the girl and his voice became kinder. "What really happened, Alyssa?"

Alyssa touched her reddening cheek, most likely the place where Travis had smacked her. She avoided my eye and glanced at Travis. "I forgot to place an order for the whiskey," she said. She swallowed. "Travis was right to be pissed and sometimes he yells."

"Is that all?" Kevin prodded.

"Yeah."

"He hit you," I said.

She shook her head but still wouldn't look at me directly. "No."

"The only one acting like a psycho around here is you," Travis growled. "Now get the fuck out before I decide to be unforgiving and press charges."

Alyssa's eyes met mine and then quickly shifted. She might be frightened. Or she might have a bad habit of making excuses for a guy who'd fooled her into thinking he cared. Either way I couldn't be angry with her for lying.

Kevin snapped his fingers and exited the room. "Let's go, Nash." His tone indicated there was no room for argument.

Travis smirked. Alyssa looked at the floor.

I was about to give up and follow Kevin out when I changed my mind and approached Alyssa.

"This is what he does," I told her in a quiet voice. "His type doesn't stop."

"Get the fuck out now!" Travis shouted.

I might have been happy to take him on again if Kevin hadn't returned and bodily shoved me out the door, down a dark hallway and out a back door that led to an alley behind Sheen's.

"All right," I grumbled, breaking free of his grip.

"What the fuck was that, Nash? Revisiting old rivalries?"

I faced him. "He hit that girl."

"That's not what she said."

"But it's true."

"Did you see it happen?"

"No," I admitted, "but it sure sounded like he belted her pretty hard."

Kevin exhaled noisily. "So this is still what you do? Swing first, think later?"

"I couldn't do nothing, Kevin."

"No, you never can."

I started to walk away in the direction of the street where I'd parked.

"Nash!"

I kept walking. "I've got to go pick up Colin."

"I don't think that's a good idea right now."

I spun around. "Are you fucking kidding? You make excuses for Travis the Prick but you've decided *I'm* dangerous?"

Kevin held up a hand. "I think you should go home and cool off."

"I'm cool."

He looked down. "Your fists are clenched."

I did look down. So fucking what if they were clenched? I relaxed them.

Kevin sighed. "Nash, it's late and you're not in a good frame of mind. Why don't you just leave the baby with my mom tonight and start over tomorrow?"

I paused. Colin had to be asleep already. Maybe it was in his best interest to let him be for the night instead of jarring him out of a sound sleep.

"Fine," I said, rather stonily.

"Good." Kevin nodded. "I'll text my mom and let her know."

"Thanks."

Kevin regarded me silently in the darkness. A sports car sped down Garner Avenue and some teenager whooped loudly out the window.

"What the hell got into you back there anyway?" he wanted to know. "I thought you'd fucking grown up a little."

I had no answer for that. The words wouldn't have stung so much if they'd come from a man I respected less. I left him standing there, found my truck and left the small world of downtown Hawk Valley behind. I got all the way home before realizing I was too keyed up to enter an empty house and stare at my balls all night. Instead of cutting the engine I pulled away from the curb.

The duplex where Kathleen lived wasn't very far. I cut the headlights when I was still a few houses away and set the truck in park. There was a light on in Kathleen's front room. The clock was closing in on ten p.m., not a polite time to knock on anyone's door, let alone one where a little kid lived. But I remembered Kathleen saying she was a night owl so I pulled out my phone and was about to shoot her a text when I saw movement behind the kitchen curtain.

I pocketed the phone and jumped out of the truck, approaching the door and getting a sense of déjà vu. The one and only time I'd been to Kathleen's place was the night I arrived in Hawk Valley, when I was still numbed by a new and terrible loss.

I rapped on the door softly in case her kid was sleeping. The second I did it I realized showing up this time of night might be taken the wrong way. I hadn't come here for some drunken late night booty call. I just wanted someone to talk to.

But suddenly the door opened there was Kathleen staring at me in surprise.

No, I didn't just want to talk to *someone*. I wanted to talk to her.

"Nash." She looked at my empty hands. "Is everything okay? Where's Colin?"

"He's fine," I said. "He's with Nancy."

Kathleen moved back a step. "Come in." She was wearing a soft grey shirt that she probably slept in and came halfway to her knees. I wondered if she was wearing anything underneath. From the way her soft curves were outlined beneath the fabric I kind of doubted it.

"Sorry to show up so late," I said, taking a look around at the small but comfortable surroundings. "I like your place."

She shut the door. "You've been here before."

"I know."

Kat looked around and made a face. "I'll be moving soon. The landlord just informed me that he intends to sell the property at the end of the summer."

I stuffed my hands in my pockets. "That's too bad."

"Nash," she said, "what's wrong?"

There were so many things wrong. And I shouldn't be dumping them all over the person who might be the best friend I had right now.

I stood in the middle of the room and stared at a small square painting of an empty winding mountain road. It was Jane's style and sure enough there was her distinctive signature in the corner.

"I hope I didn't wake up Emma," I said.

"You didn't," Kathleen confirmed and sat on the couch with her legs tucked under her. "I'm sorry I didn't make it down to the store reopening today." She rubbed her eyes. "Everything was crazy. I had a big project due, three client appointments and I had to pick Emma up early from preschool because she had a stomach ache."

"Is she okay?"

"She's fine. I ran her over to the pediatrician just to make sure." Kathleen studied me, probably because I was still standing awkwardly in the middle of her living room at ten p.m. "Sit down."

I planted myself on the edge of the couch. It was tempting to lay my head down on Kathleen's lap. She waited for me to say something. Somewhere in the apartment a clocked ticked the seconds away.

"I hit someone," I said.

Her eyes widened. "Who?"

"Travis Hanson."

She grimaced, as if the sound of the name hurt her ears. "Why?"

"It doesn't matter. He deserved it but that's not the point. I handled it badly. I've been handling things badly for a long time." I paused and thought about what I wanted to say. "I never told anyone this, but there were signs, Kat. Things I should have picked up on."

"What do you mean?"

"I mean sometimes she'd drive me to school and I'd notice bruises on her arms. Or she'd be late picking me up from somewhere and her eyes would be red from crying. She'd always tell me it was nothing. She made up stories about watching a sad movie or getting banged up on some exercise equipment at the gym. I should have done something. But I did nothing."

"Oh." Kathleen touched my shoulder. "You're talking about your mother."

I blew out a breath and allowed the memories to come flooding back. "She started seeing Paul only a few months before they got married. I remembered thinking there was something off about the guy but I didn't put the pieces together, didn't think anyone would listen anyway. I was a cranky teenager with a shitty attitude so of course I disliked my mother's new husband. I was so used to being the center of all her attention. It was always just the two of us. Sure I spent summers and vacations with my dad but we had never been close."

Kathleen didn't say anything. She just kept her hand where it was on my shoulder, a kind gesture to remind me she was here, that she cared.

"Chris Ryan was not a man who saw much value in sitting around and talking about feelings but in the beginning, after it happened, he tried to get me to open up. He said the anger could eat me alive if I let it. He was right. I never allowed anyone to get too close. You remember what I was like, how often I used to fight in high school. I'm still fighting, Kat. I never stopped."

I looked up to find her staring at me with worried eyes that swept down to my hands. I knew what she was thinking of. The night I came to town my knuckles were still bruised and raw from dispensing my own brand of vigilante justice. But I wasn't ready to tell her about that. I'd already told her more than I should have.

I stood up, feeling the sudden need to get the hell out of here, away from Kathleen's scrutiny before she saw more than I wanted her to see. She tugged on my arm, urging me back down to the couch. I relented, reclaiming my seat and then did the thing I wanted to do the most, the thing I didn't do with anyone. I rested my head against her soft body and allowed her to comfort me.

"I thought you'd fucking grown up a little."

I couldn't stop hearing Kevin's words. He was right and I needed to do better. I had a little boy to raise and protect. It was time to acknowledge that in some ways I *hadn't* grown up. In some ways I was still that fourteen-year-old kid wracked with guilt and grief because in my mind I'd failed. I'd failed to defend the person who meant the world to me. I couldn't live with that kind of failure again.

Chapter Thirteen

Kathleen

BEFORE I FOUND NASH AT THE FRONT DOOR MY PARANOIA had gotten the better of me. I felt jumpy, ill at ease, plagued by the consistent thought that I was being watched, though the curtains were closed and the only sound in the apartment was the ticking of an old mantle clock.

Emma had been crying when I picked her up early from preschool. Like any mother, my child's tears were like a knife straight into my heart. But today there was something about the way she was crumpling up her little face that left me feeling more anxious than usual. She looked too much like her father when she cried.

I took her to the doctor although there was no medical mystery. One of the children had brought in donuts as a birthday treat and Emma had eaten more than her fair share. She wound up vomiting all over the crayon table but she was already feeling better by the time we got home. I gave her some ginger ale and plain toast and we watched episodes of her favorite cartoons.

Hours later, after she was asleep, the uneasy feeling wouldn't leave me and I knew it had nothing to do with Emma's stomach incident. This afternoon I'd nearly deleted an email to my business account from an address I didn't recognize. I thought it was spam but then opened it on a whim.

Kat,
It's been a long time. And I need to talk to you.
Harrison

Dread can surge through the bloodstream in an instant. My stomach dropped and my heart began pounding. I stared at the email and then deleted it. The writer had no claim on me and he knew it. We were finished even before I did something that would sound unforgiveable if I told the story. There were only two other people in the world that knew and one of them was dead. The other hated me. The feeling was mutual.

But it wasn't just the shadow of worry gnawing at me as I roamed the quiet rooms of my apartment.

There was also a ghost. Years ago he'd befriended and consoled and assured me that I deserved better than a guy who cheated and treated me like dirt. He did all that even though he was crumbling under the weight of his own demons.

As she grew, Emma looked more and more like her father. Sometimes when I saw my daughter's face it was like he was begging to be acknowledged. I had never acknowledged him or even spoken his name since the day of his funeral. I'd been telling the same lie ever since returning to Hawk Valley. My mother didn't know. I hadn't even told Heather.

I was aware that most lies possess a shelf life. I was aware that someday Emma would ask about her father. And then I wouldn't be able to lie any longer.

I'd been pacing around the living room, lost in my own jumbled thoughts, when the soft knock startled me. With some wariness I looked out the peephole and then breathed a sigh of relief when I recognized the person on the other side. He was the one adult I wouldn't mind dealing with right now.

There was something wrong with him tonight. I saw it right away and was thankful it didn't have anything to do with Colin. But

I was unprepared for the things he said, for the way he allowed me to collect him in my arms and hold him.

Nash Ryan wasn't a man who shared his feelings eagerly. The story he told me about his mother was heartbreaking. To carry that burden of inescapable guilt for so long had wrecked him on some level, had led him to pursue an isolated life where he was still fighting battles that only existed in his head. Nash had revealed to me the most vulnerable side of himself and I didn't know why, but I still had the sense he was holding back.

I lost all sense of time as we stayed on the couch with our arms around each other. But the sound of small steps shuffling into the room ended the embrace.

"Mommy?" said Emma, rubbing her eyes as a stuffed duck named Mr. Ford dangled from one hand.

Nash had already moved to the other side of the couch. I smoothed my nightshirt down and gently addressed my daughter.

"What's wrong, baby? Your tummy still hurt?"

"No." Emma planted herself on the couch between Nash and me. She kicked her bare little feet and frowned. "I had a dream."

"A bad dream?"

Emma shook her head and pushed her wispy brown hair out of her face. "In my dream I had a dog."

"A dog?" I touched my daughter's head and smiled. Emma had been obsessed with getting a dog ever since meeting Roxie. "That sounds like a nice dream."

"It was," she said and yawned.

Nash was watching her in silence but I saw he was amused.

Emma noticed him suddenly. "Why are you here?"

"Emma," I said, clearing my throat to stall for time. I never brought men around to meet Emma, which wasn't usually a problem because my dates tended to cap out around twice a year. "Nash just stopped by to say hello."

"Is that why you were hugging him?"

Nash caught my eye. “I was sad,” he told Emma. “Your mom was being nice, trying to make me feel better.”

“Do you?”

“Do I what?”

She sighed and crossed her arms, a gesture she'd gotten from me. “Do you feel better?”

He was trying not to laugh. “Yeah. I feel much better.”

“Why didn't you bring Roxie?”

“It's late. She was tired.”

“Hey.” I circled my arm around her small shoulders. “Speaking of tired, aren't you tired, little miss?”

“No,” said Emma but she yawned again. She wrinkled her nose and peered up at Nash. “You should have brought her. She could have slept in my bed.”

Nash smiled. “Roxie would have enjoyed that.”

Emma nodded. “I miss her.”

“I think she misses you too.”

“Mommy, can I go see her now?” She looked up at me with a beseeching expression that was tough to resist.

“Not now, Ems. You need your rest.”

“Tell you what,” Nash said, leaning forward as if he were telling a secret, “you can come over and see her anytime.”

“Tomorrow?” Emma said hopefully.

“Uh,” Nash said, glancing at me. “Fine with me if it's okay with your mom.”

“Are you working at the store tomorrow?” I asked him.

“No. I can go over the new merchandise orders at home while taking care of Colin. I promoted Betty to assistant manager and the new guy you found on short notice looks like he'll work out to fill in the gaps part time.”

That reminded me of something. “Thanks for hiring Todd by the way,” I said. “He's the son of my mom's friend. People don't always give him a chance because they think he's on the slow side. But he's a hard worker and he'll do a good job for you."

"I'm sure he will."

"What time?" piped up Emma.

When we looked confused she let out another one of her 'can't believe you adults are so dense' sighs and hugged her stuffed duck. "What time can I come see Roxie?"

Nash grinned. "We'll work it out."

"What does that mean?"

"Emma-bear," I said, nudging her off the couch. "Let's talk about it tomorrow, okay? Right now you need to get back to bed."

Emma resisted for a few seconds but then she jumped off the couch and started to walk back to her room.

"I'll just be a minute," I said to Nash.

I followed Emma back to her bedroom and tucked the covers around her as she yawned and closed her eyes.

"Sweet dreams, angel face," I said, kissing her smooth forehead.

"Of dogs," she said in a whisper and a few seconds later her eyelids began fluttering. She didn't often wake up in the middle of the night and I was confident she'd stay asleep now.

My little girl didn't see me blow her a kiss from the doorway before I closed the door behind me but I liked to think she could somehow feel the love even when she was dreaming.

Nash was still sitting on the couch right where I'd left him. I wasn't sure he would be. His eyes swept over my body with such bold heat my nipples tingled. I didn't even know a reaction like that was possible from a two second glance.

"I should go," he said, standing.

I leaned against the wall. "You don't have to."

He paused, then peered in the direction of Emma's room and headed for the door. "Why don't you shoot me a text when you and Emma are ready to stop by tomorrow?"

"I'll do that."

Nash turned and stared at me. "Thanks, Kat."

I didn't want him to leave. But the words got stuck on my tongue. "There's nothing to thank me for, Nash."

He still stared at me. His hand was on the doorknob and suddenly he grinned. "You know, I was thinking something earlier. Something that might be a little pathetic."

"I'm sure it's not pathetic."

"You might disagree if you knew what it was."

"Try me."

"I was thinking that these days you just might be my best friend."

That statement could be a sweet tribute. Or it could be an intoxicatingly sexy thing to hear in the right circumstances. These happened to be the right circumstances.

"And you might be mine," I said.

Our eyes locked. Nash hesitated, then nodded as if he'd just come to a reluctant decision.

"Good night," he said and exited abruptly.

Now it was my turn to sigh. I had no right to feel disappointed. Maybe Nash thought tonight's mood had become too intimate and we'd end up blurring the lines beyond physical pleasure, beyond the closeness of a fairly new friendship.

I went to confirm the door was locked, checking the peephole out of habit. The distorted glass showed me that Nash hadn't left. He was standing just within the harsh glare of the porch light, his back turned as if he was studying the street.

He didn't move when I opened the door and joined him outside, silently closing the door behind me.

There was a chill in the air, a remnant of a cool breeze that sometimes rolled off the mountains and lingered before giving way to summer humidity. I stood in front of him barefoot and raised my arms, wrapping them around his broad shoulders. I had never been short as a child. In adulthood I wasn't small boned and petite. Many men were smaller than me. And every time I'd been with Nash I'd been fascinated by the size of him. He was about six foot four, layered with muscle, and it was intoxicating when he wrapped his powerful arms around my body. The way he was doing now, surrounding my waist, pulling me against him, forcing me to suppress a moan when my nightshirt rode up and I felt him through my panties.

"Kiss me," I whispered.

Nash pulled me out of the glare of the porch light first. I felt my back make contact with the wall on the far side of the kitchen window and his mouth crashed into mine with demanding hunger. I knew this area was dark, that we would be unseen. My elderly neighbor lived on the other side of the building. The street was quiet. There was no one to witness the way I urged his hands to keep exploring beneath my thin nightshirt. No one could see how I rubbed my sensitive core against him with a shameless rhythm that would send me over the edge if I kept it up. My panties had to be damp when he peeled them over my hips and loosened his belt. I would do this. I had no will to pull away. I would eagerly open my legs for him right here against the side of the freaking building like a sex-crazed lunatic. I wanted him that much.

But then I came with my legs around his waist, bucking against him like a wild animal rutting in the cool night air and shamelessly getting off by using the friction of his clothes, the pressure of his hands kneading my flesh and the tantalizing feel of his hard cock that was still trapped in his boxers.

"Does that offer still stand?" he challenged when I was still trying to catch my breath.

"What offer?"

"You said I didn't have to go."

I planted soft kisses along his jaw. "It still stands."

"You want me to stay?"

"Yes."

"Yes what?"

"Yes, I want you to stay."

Nash had more sense than I did. He didn't screw me out here

within sight of the street. He took me to my bed, stripped everything off and put his mouth all over the place until I shook and quivered and was struck with another overpowering orgasm. I was still writhing in its intense throes and trying to stay quiet when he rolled on a condom, lifted my hips and pushed his way inside. I'd already learned something important about him. Nash never fucked exactly the same way twice. He'd been slow and gentle before, teasing at other times, and then there was this, the way he slammed into me with ferocious passion. I loved it. I loved having him inside of me, losing himself, gasping as he came.

Afterwards he kissed my breasts, rolled his tongue along my belly and then pulled my quilt up over my naked body before folding me into his arms.

"Will you spend the night?" I asked, wincing over the question. I didn't want him to hear how much I hoped the answer would be yes.

"I'd like that," he said and kissed my forehead. "But I'll leave early before Emma wakes up. Sleep now, beautiful Kat."

But I didn't sleep right away. He fell into a calm slumber long before I did. I was too busy staring at the dark ceiling and trying to sort out the warring thoughts in my head.

I was no longer thinking of ghosts and enemies of the past. I was thinking of something much more practical.

When Nash and I first started down this path I'd sworn to myself that my heart wasn't up for grabs. But in no time at all he had come perilously close to capturing it anyway. He just didn't know it.

I wondered if I'd ever tell him.

Chapter Fourteen

Nash

"I MIGHT NEED A FAVOR," I SAID, ZIPPING MY FLY.

Kat tossed me a mocking look. "I believe I just swallowed your most recent favor."

I chuckled. She always managed to surprise me. Kathleen Doyle was a perfect blend of wit and beauty.

"I meant a favor that doesn't involve skin and orgasms."

"That doesn't sound fun."

"It might not be. And feel free to say no."

She buttoned her blouse. It was a shame. The view was much better when it was unbuttoned. "I'm intrigued."

"I've got to go back to Oregon and clean out my apartment. Most of that shit can get pitched into the nearest charity bin but there are some things worth keeping."

"And you want my help loading the moving truck?"

I rolled my eyes. "No. I'm planning on flying out, doing a quick clean and pack before driving back here in a UHaul. It should take me less than forty-eight hours but it's not really a trip suitable for an infant."

"So you're asking me to watch Colin."

"Yeah, if you can take him for just a couple of nights that would be great. I'm already taking way too much help from Nancy when it comes to daycare. I didn't want to ask her to keep him overnight too."

Kathleen finished buttoning up and put her hands on her hips, surveying me with a puzzled look. “Nash, I thought you knew you didn’t even have to ask. I’m always ready to help with Colin.”

“And Roxie,” I admitted.

She raised an eyebrow. “Your dog?”

“It would be easier and faster if I could leave her here. She’s well trained. Just feed her, walk her and give her a place in the corner to sleep.”

“Emma would love that,” Kat said, smiling. “The problem is my landlord doesn’t allow pets. I know I’ll be moving out soon anyway but he’s kind of a dick and if he finds any evidence of pet hair he’ll smack me with a mammoth cleaning fee.”

The solution was simple. “Stay at the house for a few days then.”

When Kat didn’t instantly jump at the option I realized she might be thinking I’m one big dictatorial asshole.

Watch the baby. Take care of my dog. Stay at my house. It’s not like you have your own life, right? Right??

Kathleen did have her own life and more responsibilities than I could keep track of. I wished I’d never brought up the subject.

“Look,” I said. “It’s okay. I should have guessed it was an imposition. Maybe Jane can-“

“No.” She interrupted, shaking her head. “It’s really no hassle.” Her pained expression said something a little different.

I sat on the edge of the desk in the office that had been my father’s and my grandfather’s before that. This summer Kat and I had developed a regular routine. Twice a week we’d meet to meet at the store before it opened and do some real dirty work before discussing financial matters. But our interactions weren’t exclusively about naked games and money. Whenever she had the time I took her out to lunch. She and Emma stopped by the house several times a week, Kat to see Colin and Emma to see Roxie. And we talked and texted constantly, about everything from Colin’s new ability to sit up to miscellaneous local news. Aside from Colin, Kat had turned out to be the most important person in my life.

But I couldn't deny that I seriously loved fucking her. This morning I had taken my time peeling her clothes off and teasing her while feeling triumphant over how easy it was to get her to come on my hand. Then she got on her knees and sucked me off like a champ with my hands tangled in her thick curls, thrusting my cock between her lips to set the pace.

Yet now the mood had grown serious so I needed to forget about how soft her mouth was for a few minutes.

"You don't seem thrilled," I said. "Forget about it, this is on me. I really shouldn't have asked you to drop everything and come oversee my life."

She waved a hand. "Nash, stop. I'm always happy to spend time with Colin and you know Emma will be ecstatic to have a dog for a few days."

I studied her. Kat wasn't the brooding type. It's one of the things I appreciated about her. People knew where they stood with her. If something was up she wouldn't keep quiet about it for long.

"Then what's wrong?" I asked gently, drawing her to me and tipping her chin up so I could see into her troubled eyes.

"I was just thinking about the last time I stayed in that house." She sighed and rested her head on my shoulder before continuing. "I was between apartments and Emma was still a baby. I had two weeks until my new lease began and the idea of staying with my mother was enough to induce an ulcer. So Heather insisted that I stay with her and Chris. She cooked homemade meals for me, wouldn't allow me to lift a finger to help with housework and watched Emma so I could get some much needed rest." She raised her head and now she smiled. "I slept in your old room. I bet you didn't know that."

"I didn't."

Her smile fell away. "I miss her."

"I know you do," I said. I planted a quick kiss on her lips and moved over to the desk.

Kathleen watched me as I sat down and began examining an

inventory report. "We've never talked about her. Not really."

"Who?" I knew damn well who. I just didn't want to have that particular conversation now. Or ever.

"Heather."

I hit a computer key harder than I needed to and squinted at the screen. "You asking if all the old gossip is true?"

"No. I already know what's true and what isn't."

My eyes sharply swung back to her. "She told you?" I'd suspected as much. That didn't mean I wanted to talk about it.

"Yes, she told me."

I exhaled noisily. "It was a long time ago. Things got ugly."

"Love triangles usually do."

I snorted. "Love triangle. Makes it sound like a fucking soap opera." Then I paused, wondering what Heather's side of the story had been. "Heather and I got closer than we should have. I was eighteen and already no angel but nothing really happened. I liked being with her. A lot. And I thought I could trust her. Then I found out I couldn't."

Kathleen winced. "Heather felt truly terrible about what happened. She cared about you but she was in a bad place in her life at the time, had just suffered through a really crappy breakup. She made some dreadful choices but she was vulnerable and she was young."

"She was twenty-five," I pointed out. "Younger than you are now."

Kat nodded but looked uneasy. "And she always blamed herself for the rift between you and your father."

"She didn't help. But my dad and I didn't need any assistance when it came to grabbing each other's throats." I grimaced, remembering occasions when furious words flew between us like carelessly flung knives. My father wasn't to blame for all of it. I'd said things I wished I hadn't and found it impossible to take them back.

"The two of us had been sitting on a powder keg for a long time," I admitted. "All we were waiting for was someone to light the match."

"Heather never wanted to be that someone."

"I'm sure she didn't." The sarcasm in my voice hadn't been planned.

Kat became defensive. "It's true, Nash. When Heather realized the magnitude of what she'd done and how she was getting between you and your dad she stayed away from both of you, even left and took a job in Flagstaff for a while. You'd already gone off to college and she felt like too many people here were still talking about her. But then her mother got sick so she came back. Chris was a friend to her while she held her dying mother's hand. She didn't mean to fall in love with him. And I'm sure he didn't mean to fall in love with her either."

Her face was earnest. She wanted me to say that all was well, that I completely forgave Heather and Chris. But the taste of betrayal is bitter. It lingers. Kathleen wouldn't understand that because she was as close to perfect as anyone I'd ever met.

"You know what I admire about you, Kat?" I asked abruptly.

She cocked her head. "What?"

"You think everyone is as honorable as you are."

She looked down and bit her lip. Maybe she figured the comment was mocking. I hadn't meant it that way. People everywhere should aspire to be like Kathleen Doyle, full of honesty and hope, rather than riddled with guilt and cynicism like me.

Kathleen's phone buzzed and she reached into her handbag to retrieve it. A shadow passed over her face when she stared at the screen and she stuffed the device back into her bag without answering.

"You okay?" I asked because all of a sudden she was alarmingly pale.

"Fine." She plucked a rubber band from my desk and used it to tie up her hair. "So, the conversation took a detour but what days were you thinking about making the trip?"

"This weekend if that works for you."

"It works just fine."

"In that case I'll leave Friday afternoon and be back by Sunday morning. Betty can take care of running the place in the meantime."

Kat checked her watch. "Speaking of the store, you need to open the doors in twenty minutes."

I leaned back in the thick, cushioned desk chair and reached for her hand. "Twenty minutes is enough time."

"For what?"

I unzipped and extracted my dick. "For this."

She was amused. "I thought I already took care of that."

I ran my hand up and down the hard muscle because I knew she liked watching me stroke myself and having her eyes on me just made me harder. "Take care of it again. Different position this time."

Kat stepped out of her skirt and pulled her panties down. She wasn't the only one who liked to watch things. I groaned when she inserted two fingers inside. So fucking sexy it was ridiculous.

"What position did you have in mind?" she asked sweetly and I saw the way her cheeks were flushed, heard how her breathing quickened. She was so into this, nothing at all prim and proper about her.

I wasted no time locating a condom in my wallet and getting it in place. "Get that shirt off again right now. Bra too."

"Full of demands," she muttered but obeyed with a grin. "Now what?"

"Now I'm going to suck those sweet tits while you ride me."

Kat was gloriously naked when she straddled me. The chair creaked underneath our combined weight but it would hold. I grabbed a fistful of her hair, kissing her hard, and with the other I guided my cock in. She was so goddamn ready it almost killed me to hold out until she climaxed with her tits trading places in my mouth just like I wanted.

"Oh god," she moaned, still riding the wave. "You're so good."

I teased her nipple. "How good?"

"Amazing," she whispered, hips still bucking as she finished her moment.

"You've never been fucked this good by anyone before, have you?"

"Yes."

"Say that."

"Nash."

"Say it!"

"There's no one who fucks better than you."

I gave in and let myself come while urging her to ride hard right up until the end. The desk chair finally succumbed to all this abuse and the back came off, sending us toppling to the floor.

"Shit, you okay?" I asked but she laughed.

"We broke the chair," she giggled.

"We did." I tossed a wrecked piece on the desk. "We broke the fuck out of it."

She was still giggling while she gathered her clothes. I noted the time and realized there were now only three minutes until the store opened. Normally Betty would have been here by now, briskly straightening anything that looked even slightly askew on the shelves, but luckily she had a doctor's appointment this morning.

Kathleen once again finished buttoning her blouse and I regretted that it would need to stay that way.

"I have to get going," she said.

I pulled my shirt over my head. "Busy day?"

"Moderately."

I kept my eyes on her. Watching Kat had quickly become my favorite pastime. "Come here."

"Nash," she warned, "there's not enough time for a third round."

"Then give me a kiss."

She smiled and allowed me to pull her close. She liked to be kissed slow and deep and I could feel her melting in my arms. Sometimes I enjoyed these sweet moments even more than the kinky ones.

"I wish I didn't have to go," she whispered with her arms still wrapped around my shoulders. Then she averted her head, as if she was embarrassed that the words had escaped her mouth.

I tugged at a lock of her long hair that had escaped the rubber band. "I'm picking Colin up around five. I could grab some pizzas on the way home. Why don't you and Emma come over for dinner? I mean, unless you've got too much work to do."

The invitation delighted her. I could tell by the way her eyes lit up for a split second although she seemed determined not to show it. "I don't think I'll have too much work. So we'll be there."

"Good." I pinched her ass. She had a great ass. I could be sitting around and thinking about how many stupid Hawk Valley Happiness coffee mugs I needed to order when I'd remember Kat's ass out of nowhere and get so hard my balls ached.

But at this point I really did need to open the store and Kat really did need to get to a client appointment. I released her with some reluctance. It seemed like every time I held her I felt that way a little more, that I just didn't want to let her go.

"I'll see you later," she said happily and I was really glad I'd invited her over tonight. We didn't do things like plan outings and dates. We didn't talk about the future or refer to ourselves a couple. And part of me was starting to wonder if we were going about this all wrong.

"You want any toppings on your pizza?" I asked.

"Pineapple."

"You're kidding."

"Why would I kid about pineapple? There's nothing funny about it."

"Except for the fact that it has no business being on pizza."

"I didn't know you were a food snob."

I grinned and puffed out my chest. "Turns out there's more to me than my ability to fuck you better than anyone else."

She rolled her eyes and opened the door to the office. "I shouldn't have told you that."

"But you did tell me. And you'll tell me again."

She blushed. "Whatever."

I was still smiling long after she closed the door.

Chapter Fifteen

Kathleen

NASH WAS PREPARING TO LEAVE FOR HIS SHORT BUT necessary trip to Oregon. From the moment I showed up at his house he kept handing out instructions like a nervous new mommy but I didn't mind. In fact it was rather adorable.

"He's got six bottles in the fridge. And there are plenty of diapers in the nursery but in case you need more there's a stockpile in the hall closet. And I just did all of his laundry so there's a bunch of those stretchy little outfits in his room. Oh, and if he gets too gassy the bottle of drops is in the hall bathroom upstairs."

"Got it," I said, trying not to smile. Nash had come a long way in a short time. It was hard to believe only two months had passed since the morning I watched him get covered in baby vomit right here in the kitchen after he haplessly overfed Colin.

Over in his bouncer Colin babbled and grabbed for the toys hanging overhead. His chubby fingers latched onto the fuzzy pink pig and he emitted a squeal of triumph.

Nash tickled the baby's foot and looked anxious. "I'll miss you, kid."

I ran my finger over Colin's smooth cheek and he gave me a drooling grin. "I promise I'll take good care of him."

"I know you will." Nash raked a hand through his hair. "There's no one on earth I'd rather leave him with. It's just the longest I've been away from him so my stomach's all tied up in knots." He let out a hoarse chuckle. "Listen to me. I sound like an uptight jackass."

"No," I argued, elbowing his ribs. "You sound like a parent."

He looked at me and his eyes were serious. "Thanks, Kat."

"You're welcome."

The serious expression left his face and was replaced by something else as his eyes swept over me. The weather had turned very hot this week and I wore a red tank top and shorts, my hair loose and flowing.

"I like the idea of you sleeping in my bed," he said softly because Emma was in the next room.

"I like the idea of sleeping in your bed too."

Nash reached out and swept the hair off my left shoulder, his fingers brushing across my skin. It was amazing how the briefest touch from him could produce such a powerful shudder of desire. He slipped one finger under the strap of my tank top and his voice became gruff.

"I'll be thinking of you there. In my bed. Doing things to yourself and wishing I was there to do them for you."

"What kind of things?" I whispered, feeling as if I might swoon. The physical chemistry between us was magnetic, irresistible. It grew stronger every day.

"Mommy!" Emma shouted and Nash stepped away from me a split second before she came barreling into the kitchen with Roxie on her heels.

"What the matter, honey?"

Emma stuck out her lower lip and her eyes filled. "I forgot Mr. Ford," she wailed.

Roxie licked her hand and let out a sympathetic whine.

"Who's Mr. Ford?" Nash wanted to know.

"It's this stuffed duck my mother had given her at Easter," I said.

"You need to get him," Emma said, nodding over her own solution. "Or he'll be sad."

I picked up my purse. "Is it okay if I leave her here while I run back home?"

"Sure," Nash said. He picked Colin up out of the bouncer. "Hey Miss Emma, let's take Roxie in the backyard so she can show you how well she catches a Frisbee."

"A what?"

"A Frisbee."

"What's that?"

I smiled. "I'll be right back."

Nash was already heading out of the room. "Take your time."

The drive back to my place only took a few minutes. Emma had left Mr. Ford sitting on the kitchen table. His black embroidered eyes regarded me placidly as I picked him up.

I was locking the front door when a shadow startled me into dropping my keys.

"There was a man," said Mrs. Sofia Fetucci. She was eighty-seven, the widow of a former national boxing champion and she rarely left her unit on the other side of the duplex. Last week I'd run into her daughter who confided that she was moving her mother to an assisted living facility down in Scottsdale, closer to where she lived.

"Are you okay, Sofia?" I asked, bending down to retrieve my keys.

The tiny old woman peered at me, her faded blue eyes covered with a milky layer of cataracts. I wasn't even sure how much she could see at this point.

"There was a man here," she insisted and the whole incident was beginning to feel a little spooky. I wondered if she was talking about Nash but to my knowledge he hadn't been here today.

"He was at your window," she said, pointing a bony finger at the kitchen window.

"When?" I asked, looking around and feeling more uneasy than ever. Sofia might seem lost in her own personal cloud sometimes but I'd never known her to hallucinate.

"I don't know," she said.

"But you saw a man looking through my windows earlier?" I

asked for clarification.

She nodded. "Yes."

"What did he look like?"

She scrunched up her face. "Tall," she said. "Maybe."

"Do you remember anything else?"

"No. He might not have been tall."

Well, that narrowed it down. I wouldn't even know what to tell the police.

"My elderly half blind neighbor might have seen a nondescript possibly tall man near my kitchen window at some point."

"Did you see where he went?" I asked. I wasn't completely sure the man was real but that didn't stop the hair from standing up on the back of my neck.

"No," she sighed and I saw her hand trembling. She seemed upset and unsteady so I offered her my arm for stability and then walked her back over to her place. Sofia's daughter had hired a maid, a meal delivery service and also a nurse to check on her mother several times a week but there was no one in the neat little apartment now. Her rooms were a mirror of my place, except all the furniture was covered with crocheted blankets and there were cat cross stitch pictures all over the walls. When I was satisfied that Sofia had everything she needed I left, making a mental note to find her daughter's contact information and share the strange encounter.

I got behind the wheel of my car feeling bothered, nervous. Sofia had probably just seen a solicitor or maybe one of the missionaries who would frequently canvas the neighborhood searching for people to spread their religion to. And her cataracts were so bad I wasn't even certain her version of events was correct.

But still, the flames of my anxiety were sufficiently fueled and I kept glancing in my rearview mirror. For a few blocks I thought I was being followed by a silver car. It remained a good twenty yards behind me and when I reached Nash's street the vehicle turned in the opposite direction.

Nash's car to the airport was already idling by the curb when I returned. There was a small municipal airport forty miles away where he'd catch a plane to Phoenix and then take a flight to Portland from there. I'd offered to drive him myself but he adamantly refused.

"Colin's napping upstairs in the crib," he said.

"I'll kiss him goodbye for you."

Nash flashed a grin. "I'll get to Portland this evening," he said, tossing a small carry on bag into the waiting car. "Then I'll rent the truck, drive out to the coast, pack up, maybe catch a few hours of sleep and be on my way back here as soon as I can."

"Don't worry about Colin," I told him, clutching Mr. Ford and still feeling a little rattled over the whole Man at the Window mystery. "Between Emma and me and Roxie he'll be well taken care of."

Emma suddenly burst through the front door and ran to me, claiming Mr. Ford and hugging the toy in a rapturous reunion.

Nash paused before sliding into the backseat of the car. His face searched mine. "Call me anytime, Kat."

"You do the same."

We stared at each other and he started to take a step toward me. I wondered if he planned to kiss me goodbye. I wanted him to. In spite of the fact that we were just good friends who gave each other incredible orgasms I wanted him to give me one gentle kiss before he left.

But Nash looked over at Emma, who was dancing around the front yard with her stuffed duck, and backed off. He winked at me before getting into the car.

I watched the car disappear and felt sad for some reason. Or maybe it wasn't sadness. Maybe it was because I needed Nash Ryan more than I'd ever intended to.

I held out my hand to Emma and returned to the house where Roxie awaited with her tail wagging. Emma introduced her to Mr. Ford and didn't appreciate when the dog tried to chew on Mr. Ford's soft beak.

After checking on Colin, who still slept soundly as the crib mobile rotated slowly overhead, I returned downstairs to the kitchen, washed the handful of dishes in the sink and checked out the contents of the fridge. Nash had urged me to help myself to whatever I found and I wondered if Emma and I would be eating old cheese and stale bread for dinner. I really didn't want to embark on a grocery store adventure unless it was necessary.

But surprisingly, Nash's fridge was well stocked. I scanned the contents and planned to make a salad and spaghetti for us solid food eaters while Colin would be pleased enough with his formula and canned peaches.

Emma was talking animatedly in the next room. I listened for a moment and couldn't figure out what she was up to so I went to go see.

I found a haphazard tea party in progress. Emma was lying on her belly on the floor while Roxie crouched beside her and Mr. Ford stared serenely at the sofa. As I was watching, the stuffed duck did a face plant although Emma was quick to reach out and right him.

"Sit up, Mr. Ford," she scolded. "Don't you like your tea?"

That's when I noticed the 'tea' was being served on Heather's carefully acquired antique china.

"Emma, where'd you get that?" I exclaimed, getting down on the floor and plucking a one hundred year old cup away from the curious snout of Roxie. "These are not toys."

My daughter rose to a sitting position and pouted as I started stacking up the pieces. "I can play with these," she argued.

"No honey, I told you to always ask first before you take something from here and start playing with it. This isn't our house. What happened to your coloring books?"

"Heather said I could play with it!"

I bit my lip. "Emma, you know Heather couldn't have told you that."

"She did! She showed me where they were in that brown thing."

Emma pointed to the old curio cabinet in the corner of the room. "And she said I could play with this tea set any time I wanted and I promised to be careful."

I stopped stacking the tea pieces. "When did Heather tell you this?" I asked gently. Emma was an imaginative child. She might have made up the entire scenario. But my discomfort from earlier returned and I wondered if there was any such thing as the supernatural.

Emma scrunched up her face in the same way Sofia Fetucci had. "I don't know."

I swallowed. "It wasn't today, was it?"

She looked at me as if I'd just asked the most ridiculous question ever. "No. It was the day I came here and made red hearts."

"Valentine's Day?" I asked and Emma shrugged.

I sighed, understanding now what she meant. Valentine's Day had been a Saturday and a new client, a custom furniture maker who lived up in the mountains, had begged for some emergency help because his ex-wife had sabotaged all his files. Heather offered to watch Emma and keep her overnight if I was too tired to pick her up. I'd accepted gratefully, though I felt a little guilty because my cousin had only given birth three weeks earlier. Heather had set up an assortment of paper crafts on the kitchen table and promised Emma they would have a special day. She was holding Colin when I turned back to see her waving at me from the kitchen window. I waved back and then faced the drive up to the mountains on a bitterly cold morning.

"Where are they?" Emma asked in a hushed voice and I saw she was staring at a photo of Chris and Heather on their wedding day.

I thought I'd cried all my tears for them already but no, I still had more. I tried to blink them away so Emma wouldn't see and get upset. "They're gone, baby."

Emma considered the answer. Heather and Chris had been important to her too. Hopefully she would keep some memories of them and be able to tell Colin someday.

"I wish they weren't gone," she said and her lower lip trembled.

I set the teacups down and opened my arms to her. I stroked her hair, soft and dark brown, remembering how I'd once stroked hair just like it while a man I cared about cried on my lap and begged me to tell him when his agony would end. Emma would never know him. But I remembered him every time our daughter looked at me with his solemn eyes.

Emma's sad mood didn't last long. Roxie trotted over to kiss her face and she started giggling. Colin awoke from his nap and I sat holding him in the backyard while Emma played in the grass with Roxie. Nash's dog always impressed me. Despite her size she was astonishingly gentle and enchanted by any attention Emma was willing to give her.

The afternoon passed quickly with no more troubling shadows. It was rare for me to take a complete day off but while sitting outside, listening to my daughter's laughter and Colin's happy squeals, I decided to take a break from whatever work awaited on my laptop. It would still be there tomorrow.

After an early dinner and quick baths we settled down in the living room to watch *Beauty and the Beast.* Colin nodded off on my shoulder and Emma let out a sleepy yawn as she rested her head against my arm. I thought about what a sweet moment this was. The only thing that would make it more perfect was if Nash was here to share it.

Now that I was thinking of Nash, I checked the time and figured out he must be in Oregon, probably on his way to that coastal town where he used to live. I spied my phone on an end table three feet to my left and reached for it while trying not to disturb the baby. Nash deserved to see this calm, happy scene just in case he was worrying about Colin. I would snap a quick photo and send it to him.

About two seconds after the photo finished sending to Nash a call came in. It wasn't Nash.

"Where are you?" my mother demanded to know.

"I'm watching Colin for the weekend so Emma and I are staying at Nash's house. I told you this the other day."

"And where did that Nash character go?"

I sighed. "He had to go to Oregon and pick up the rest of his stuff. Mom, I already told you that too."

She made a few more passive aggressive comments that I chose to ignore and then cryptically stated she needed to talk to me about something.

"Can it wait?" I asked, shifting Colin around because my shoulder was getting numb.

"Fine," she huffed. "I'll talk to you tomorrow. Give my baby girl a kiss from Grandma."

"Good night, Mom," I said, barely even curious about what kind of dire subject she needed to discuss. My mother meant well but she had a flair for drama. Perhaps she was feuding with the public library staff again over late fees.

I'd been planning to go to sleep early for once instead of burning the midnight oil. But once Emma and Colin were tucked away in bed I found that I was not even slightly tired so I wandered around the house.

The old house had a different feeling after the sun went down. The wooden floors creaked under my weight and every corner was thick with shadows. Old buildings possessed a certain kind of heaviness, as if burdened by the weight of all the human experiences lived within their silent walls.

I paused in front of a closed door. Nash always kept it closed. I expected when I opened it I'd find the room in exactly the same condition it had been in when its former occupants slept within. I was right.

Everywhere I looked there were signs of life interrupted. A woman's pink sandal that had been dropped near the closet. A half empty bottle of water on a bedside table. And pictures, so many pictures. Pictures of the two of them, and far more pictures of Colin as if they'd been anxious to seize every moment of the painfully short time they'd been a family.

My throat felt thick with unshed tears.

I understood why Nash avoided this room, why he'd taken no steps to sort through any of its possessions.

I backed out and closed the door with a sigh and headed downstairs.

Nash's dog was already curled up in her comfortable bed in the corner. She raised her head when I appeared and then lowered it when she saw I was alone.

My phone was still on the end table and when I looked at it I saw Nash had texted while I was roaming around upstairs.

Got the truck all packed. Will sleep for a few hours then will hit the road. Expecting twenty hours of driving. Thanks for the picture.

The words were informative and unsentimental. Somehow that bothered me. I shouldn't expect more and I was pissed at myself for feeling any frustration. Nash and I had a clear understanding. There were no requirements except mutual friendship, respect, and mind-blowing sex.

"Nothing complicated about that," I muttered, opting not to return the text since he mentioned he planned to get a few hours of sleep. I noted the time was a quarter to nine. Assuming he'd sleep for three or four hours and depart by one a.m., he'd be here around this time tomorrow if he drove straight through.

An ominous low growl sent sudden chills up my spine. Roxie had bolted from her sleepy corner and was now prowling beneath the living room window, teeth bared, hair visibly standing on end. Despite Nash's claim that the German Shepherd was a good watchdog I'd never seen her react like this before.

"You hear something, girl?" I whispered, switching off the table lamp before approaching the window.

I pushed aside the eyelet curtains and saw nothing except the yellow glow of the old fashioned street lamp shining on my car where

I'd parked it beside the curb. The porch lights of the house across the street were on but I saw no one there nor was there anyone passing in the street. A gust of wind rattled the high branches of the box elder tree in the front yard but there was no other movement.

"Must have just been a cat," I assured the dog, patting her head. Roxie looked at me with doubt.

I double checked the front door lock while Roxie paced back and forth. Another growl rolled out of her throat and she bounded toward the kitchen. I found her staring at the side door and the noise escalated from a growl to a sharp bark.

"There was a man."

My throat was dry and I was clutching my phone in my hand, prepared to call 911. Sofia Fetucci's earlier warning kept playing in my head.

Roxie's barking died down and she let out one final soft growl before sitting on her back haunches and looking at me as if to say, "I swear there was something out there."

It took a fair amount of my courage to approach the door and push the curtain aside to peer through the glass panel. There was nothing out there.

Roxie nudged my hand with her wet nose.

"Good girl," I praised her, scratching behind her ears. I watched for another few minutes but did not see or hear anything to be alarmed about. The dog's senses were far more acute and in all likelihood she had sensed some passing night creature. A coyote, or maybe a flock of bats.

Roxie yawned and I checked the lock on the kitchen door before retreating. I offered the dog a biscuit from the box Nash kept in the pantry and she chewed happily. There was no noise from upstairs so apparently Roxie's brief outburst had not awakened Colin or Emma.

All the doors and windows were checked one more time. Roxie returned to her bed and watched me with sleepy eyes. I patted her head once more before heading upstairs.

All was silent except for the soft noise of Colin's crib mobile. The kids were both sound asleep. A sudden weariness overcame me and I raided my overnight bag, quickly changing and brushing my teeth. Nash's room was tidy, his bed neatly made. He'd finally stopped living out of his suitcases and placed his clothes in the closet and chest of drawers. I slipped between the cool sheets, inhaling the spicy and familiar scent of Nash's aftershave that clung to the sheets. It was like inhaling the scent of sex itself and my hand traveled between my legs as I thought of him, wishing he was here doing the things that I was doing to myself.

Sleep came quickly after that although my dreams were a puzzling collage of past events that left me feeling disturbed in the morning.

Chapter Sixteen

Nash

Two months. That's how much time had elapsed since I last got behind the wheel intending to drive straight through several states to get to Hawk Valley.

Back then I'd only known that tragedy had found me for the second time in my life. I didn't know that once I reached Hawk Valley it would be impossible to leave.

The ten foot van I rented was larger than what I ended up needing. There wasn't too much I wanted to take with me. Most of the furniture was unnecessary since I didn't feel like finding a place for it in my dad's house.

Dad's house.

When I was a kid, being told I was going to 'Dad's house' would often be met with a groan and a complaint. I preferred my mother's small Phoenix condo to the sprawling old Victorian house with a view of the mountains. My father was never abusive. Just perpetually exasperated. And openly relieved when it came time to return me to my mother. It must have been a shock for him to go from part time dad to round the clock caretaker of a troubled teen.

Sometimes even now just before I dozed off I would jerk awake and bolt upright, positive that someone was shaking my shoulder in the darkness. There was never anyone there because it was only a memory. On that night, the night my world shattered, my father had awakened me shortly after two a.m. and the most shocking thing was that he was crying.

"Nash. Wake up, son. Something's happened."

The moments after that have been blocked out of my mind. I remembered seeing broken things around the house and hearing that I was responsible because after I heard my mother had been killed by her husband I began screaming and running around the house shattering everything I could get my hands on until my dad managed to physically restrain me. By that time I had to go to the hospital to sew up the hand I'd sliced open on a smashed window pane.

Chris Ryan didn't know what to do with me. Our time together had always amounted to less than two months a year. Now suddenly he was a full time father to an incredibly angry kid. In the beginning he tried. He dragged me to a therapist. He encouraged me to make friends, to go out for sports. I found that I liked sports, that slamming into big guys on a football field or running around on a basketball court helped channel my aggression into something that didn't involve blood. But friends were an enigma to me. Plenty of people wanted my company and it seemed like the more uncooperative I was the more they sought me out. Especially girls. I couldn't be proud of the way I'd treated girls back then. I was a jackass.

But that didn't mean I was willing to accept criticism from a man who'd kicked my own mother to the curb and then entertained a revolving door of girlfriends ever since I could walk. Chris Ryan could howl over my bad behavior all he wanted. I didn't give a shit.

When I was sixteen he came barreling into my room after taking a furious phone call from a city councilman. The man's teenage daughter had been sobbing in her room for three days because I'd told her I was both bored with her and screwing her best friend.

"Damn it, kid," my father roared, throwing the door open so hard it left a dent in the wall. "Who the fuck ever told you it was okay to treat females like disposable objects?"

"Like father, like son," I replied coldly.

His eyes narrowed. "You can't go through life acting like a selfish piece of shit."

"Why not? It's always worked for you."

We glared at each other. My fist clenched. If he came at me I was prepared to hit him. I didn't want to. But I would. However, my father wasn't a violent man. He was arrogant, thick-headed, rude and stubborn but not violent. Another fundamental difference between us.

"Figure out your own fucking dinner," he said wearily and retreated from my doorway. "I'm going out."

By my senior year I had plans. They didn't involve remaining in Hawk Valley and struggling to sell shitty souvenirs. I had good grades and I was a decent athlete. A small college in Oregon had given me a scholarship. As my high school career drew to a close I was biding my time, aware that my father was both disappointed and relieved that I'd be leaving Hawk Valley behind. I just needed to keep from getting expelled for fighting in the meantime.

Meanwhile, the front office of the high school gained a pretty new employee when Heather Molloy started sitting at the reception desk. The guys all talked shit about what they'd do to that blonde pussy if they got close but Heather wasn't really on my radar. I was juggling enough options as it was and she was older, in her mid twenties. But it was nice how she would always smile when she saw me coming.

"Oh no, what did you do this time, Nash?"

"Nothing I'm sorry for."

She laughed. "What are we going to do with you?"

Then came a morning in early spring when I witnessed the neurotic tie-wearing class president shove his girlfriend into a locker so hard she cried out. I couldn't take it. I clocked the guy, broke his nose. It was supposed to be my last straw. But Heather Molloy happened to be walking by and spoke up about the circumstances prompting my outburst. And so I was given a reprieve for stepping in to defend a fellow classmate. Thanking anyone for anything was never easy for me but I thanked Heather. In halting, awkward words I told her how much I appreciated her intervention. Heather smiled at me and touched my hand.

And that's how it started.

We'd meet at the Hawk Valley State Park, five miles outside town. It wasn't real popular with the locals. If people wanted to go hiking, fishing or sightseeing they'd drive up into the mountains, not picnic on a shallow hill beside a stagnant stream. Technically we weren't breaking any laws but the situation wouldn't mean good things for Heather if we were seen together. In the beginning we just talked. Most of the girls I knew saw me as some kind of wounded walking tragedy, something they aspired to fix. But Heather never pushed me to answer questions. That's probably why I chose to open up to her.

For the first time since my mother's murder I felt like I could breathe, like I could relax. And when I stepped over the line and kissed Heather she didn't discourage me. She kissed me right back. But no matter how many times we'd remain out there in each other's arms until long after dusk she never let things go much further.

"Nash, this shouldn't be happening."

I wasn't used to being turned down and I was growing frustrated. I ran a finger up her arm and felt triumph over the way she shivered at my touch.

"It's not illegal, baby. I'm eighteen and school ends in a month."

She was breathing hard, her resistance crumbling as my fingers snuck under her shirt, exploring her smooth skin. "That doesn't make it right."

I eased her back on the blanket and covered her with my body. "I want you Heather. You want me too."

She closed her eyes. "Maybe."

We didn't have sex. We hovered around second base and never advanced.

Then one day I walked into the store to work a shift behind the register. I hated the store but I needed a part time paycheck and my dad insisted that I couldn't get it anywhere else.

He was there. So was she. I saw them through the glass, standing close together and talking earnestly and it was weird. My dad was a good thirteen years older than Heather. Hawk Valley was a small town but I'd never even realized they knew each other. Heather threw her head back in laughter and I wondered what the fuck they were talking about that was so funny. The only thing they could possibly have in common was me and I hadn't said a word to him about her.

"Nash!" Heather stopped smiling and seemed startled to see me. "I just stopped by to say hello. I haven't been in here in so long."

I looked around the store. "Not much to see."

"Right." She tossed her blonde hair over one shoulder and looked down. "I should get going. Bye Nash. It was nice catching up with you, Chris."

"Good to see you, Heather," my father answered and I saw the way his eyes lingered on her ass as she walked out the door. It made me want to puke.

"What was that about?" I demanded.

He was whistling. "What?"

"If you need a new conquest don't look for one in Heather."

My dad was amused. The bastard even grinned at me. "Sounds like someone has a crush."

"You're such an asshole."

"Forget it, son. She's out of your league."

"And you're about a decade too old to be in hers."

Sometimes he liked getting under my skin. This was one of those times. Maybe he thought of it as payback for all the times I'd gotten under his.

Chris Ryan smirked at me as if I was nothing more consequential than a first grader chasing the girl he liked with a bunch of dandelions in my hand. "You can't compete with me, little boy. Don't even try."

"Go to hell."

I stalked out with the sound of his laughter trailing behind me.

Heather started coming up with excuses about why she couldn't meet. Graduation loomed so I had other things on my mind anyway. Besides, what was I supposed to do, pack her in my suitcase this fall and bring her Oregon with me? But still, I passed the front office more than I needed to just for the chance to receive a smile from her and felt my heart flex every time it happened.

My dad and I weren't talking much but that had been the case for so long I wasn't bothered. We were just trying to get through the next few months and put this experiment behind us. Someday things might be different between us. We just couldn't live under the same roof together.

On Senior Ditch Day I made plans to go up to the mountains overnight with a bunch of my classmates. My dad even gave me his blessing and the keys to the family cabin up there. He just told me to keep the place in one piece if possible.

There were plenty of hot girls running around and I tried to get interested in them. But even when Amelia Horton started to suck me off as I leaned against a pine tree and smoked a cigarette I couldn't keep my mind straight. I didn't want to fuck some random girl. I still wanted Heather. There wasn't love and marriage on my mind but I felt a connection with her that I hadn't found with the girls my own age. That had to mean something.

I left the senior class to do whatever they wanted and drove back down to Hawk Valley after midnight. But Heather didn't answer when I called and there were no lights on in her apartment. The idea of returning to the party was depressing. I figured I'd be better off just going home to crash in my own bed and jerk off to my fantasies.

I opened and closed the front door with care, not really caring to have any kind of interaction with my father. He might be out drinking away pieces of his liver or he might be snoring upstairs. Either way I just wanted to be left alone.

I didn't hear any noise until I was almost at the top of the stairs.

There was moaning, the sound of a woman in pain. Or the opposite of pain…

They'd left the light on and hadn't bothered to shut the door. She was flat on her back on the bed, shirt and bra pushed all the way up so her perky tits were bare, along with the rest of her. Her legs were spread wide and her body arched, rising and falling to the rhythm of my father's tongue in her pussy.

"Oh god, Chris. Oh god!"

His shirt was off and he was kneeling, his face buried between her legs while Heather moaned his name and clutched the bed sheets as he got her to come.

I was frozen, staring at the woman I had wanted, the woman I had trusted, getting her pussy licked by the last man on earth I could stand to see her with.

They didn't hear me. They didn't see me. They didn't know anything was wrong until I picked up an antique crystal decanter that had belonged to my grandparents and threw it against the far wall, shattering it into a thousand unfixable pieces.

"Nash!"

Heather wasn't moaning with pleasure anymore. She was gasping with horror, struggling to cover her body as if it made any fucking difference. I couldn't look at her. I didn't want to hurt her. I just wanted to never ever see her fucking face again.

"Get out."

She cried. "Nash I'm sorry."

"GET THE FUCK OUT!"

My father stood. He was pale, wide-eyed. He swallowed, touched the weeping Heather on the arm and nodded.

"Please go, Heather."

We faced off, father and son, listening to the sound of Heather bounding down the stairs and fleeing through the front door.

My dad swallowed, his face a mask of remorse. "Son, I'm so sorry. We didn't plan this."

I choked out hoarse laughter. "The battle cry of lying fuckers everywhere."

"No, I swear it."

"You knew," I accused.

He lowered his head. And he didn't deny it.

"She told you," I whispered. "Or you guessed. But the bottom line is, you knew about me and her and you went after her anyway."

He regretted everything. I could tell from the look in his eyes. I just didn't care.

"I didn't mean to do this," he said.

"I get it. Your mouth just kind of fell on her pussy."

"I'm sorry! Fuck, I had too much to drink tonight."

"Bullshit. What was this, some kind of sick contest to prove that you're the number one alpha male around here?"

He looked stricken. "Nash, tell me what I can do. I'm so ashamed. I'll do anything to make this up to you."

"Never see her again."

He nodded eagerly. "Yes. Done. I'll never see her again."

I turned to leave the room but I had one more thing to say to him.

"By the way, Dad, I fucking hate you."

While my mind had been preoccupied with the past, I'd crossed a state line and darkness had lifted. I had to add sunglasses to my face to fend off the highway glare.

My stomach was growling so I stopped at a roadside diner to grab some breakfast and a coffee. The coffee made me think of Kat and her affection for anything caffeinated.

My legs wanted to stretch for another minute before getting closed into the driver's seat so I hung out beside the truck. I pulled out my phone and looked again at the photo Kat had sent me last night. She'd turn the lens on herself and captured the serene image of Colin asleep on one shoulder while Emma rested on the other. Kat had a small smile on her face, that wild hair of hers unbound and spilling out beyond the frame. Her beauty was more than sensual. I couldn't think of a single other woman who could hold a candle to Kathleen Doyle.

With reluctance I pocketed the phone, wishing it wasn't too early to call or text. I'd call her the next time I stopped, though I would have liked to hear her voice right now to chase away the brooding gloom that had been consuming my thoughts during the drive. It wasn't just old hurt feelings that were bothering me.

"By the way, Dad, I fucking hate you."

I was certain I'd said many other things to him after that devastating sentence. I remembered other conversations, other words that were spoken. But for some reason, ever since his funeral the last ones I'd said to him that long ago night were the ones that had remained the loudest in my head.

Chapter Seventeen

Kathleen

THE DAY WAS SHAPING UP TO BE A PERFECT SPECIMEN OF summer. With Colin babbling in his high chair in the kitchen, Emma chattering to Roxie in the living room and bright sunlight streaming through the window, it seemed impossible that I'd ever been uneasy.

Then the sharp knock at the side door made me jump. I relaxed when I saw that the shadow outside the door was in the shape of my mother. Usually I tried to consume at least twelve ounces of caffeine before dealing with my mother's inevitable censure but coffee would have to wait.

"I wasn't expecting you, Mom," I said with as much cheer as I could muster.

She stared at me through her dark oversized sunglasses. They added a bug-like quality to her face. "I told you last night that I needed to talk to you, Kat."

I sighed. "All right."

She was about to step into the house when she suddenly frowned. "What's that?"

"It's the kitchen door. And I'm holding it open. So please come in before the flies do."

"No." She touched the door right beneath the rectangular glass pane to show me something I hadn't seen before.

When I did see it my blood froze.

"I meant that."

It was a small miracle my fingers didn't shake when I plucked an item off the door that had been affixed with a blue square of masking tape. It was nothing, just a piece of paper. And yet it rattled me to depths of my soul. The photo had been printed out on regular computer paper and I was confronted by my smiling eighteen-year-old self, flanked between two impossibly good looking guys. I remembered exactly when it was taken, at a party right after a winning homecoming game. My life had felt like a fairy tale at the time; small town ugly duckling goes to big city university and attracts the interest of one of the football gods. He was a king in that world, he and his brother, both players on a champion college football team. He could have had any girl he wanted and I was in awe. In the beginning anyway.

Due to my early academic successes I was only sixteen when I started college. After two years of constant study I finally lifted my head out of my books and wondered what I was missing. At the start of a brand new semester I allowed myself to be dragged to my first college party where I kept to the sidelines and sipped warm beer until something unexpected happened.

"Come out of the corner, little mouse. You're with me now."

He was hot and fun and exciting. I'd never even had a real boyfriend and there I was, eighteen and claimed by the twenty-one year old golden gold of college sports. He and his brother were only a year apart, equally gorgeous and talented. They were royalty. Everywhere we went other girls examined me with thinly disguised jealousy, wondering what the hell I had that they didn't. And I enjoyed it. Worse, I thought I loved him. I thought so even when he suggested that I change the way I dress, the way I speak. I thought so even when he insisted that I spend less time on my studies and laughed when I grew distraught over my falling grades. I thought so right up until I learned he wasn't faithful. In the year we were together he had never been faithful and when I assumed otherwise I'd just been kidding myself. What I did next might have been partly revenge. It didn't occur to me at the time. I thought I was trying to help a friend. But later I wondered if a much uglier motivation was there beneath the surface.

"Kathleen?" My mother was standing in the kitchen now and she was wearing a rare expression of worry on her face. "Isn't that a picture of-"

"Grandma!" Emma had been lured away from her cartoons by the sound of her grandmother's voice and ran into the kitchen, colliding with my mother's legs.

"Hello my sweet girl." My mother smoothed her hair and held out a small paper bag. "Look what your grandma brought you for breakfast."

"A chocolate cupcake!" Emma squealed as she peered into the bag.

Normally I would have been irritated but my head was still spinning. I balled up the piece of paper in my fist.

"Ems," I said, surprised that my voice sounded so calm, "here's a plate. You can take that in the living room and watch cartoons with Roxie."

Emma didn't question what strange turn of events prompted me to encourage her to eat in front of the television. She scuttled out of the room.

My mother was staring down at Colin as he kicked his legs in his high chair and played with a teething toy. "He looks more like his mother every day," she said sadly.

"I know," I said, sinking into the nearest chair. The picture was still crumpled up in my hand but the image was seared into my mind. It depicted a moment when everything had seemed perfect, before I learned of betrayal and inflicted it myself, before one of the two brothers at my side would fall into a downward spiral that couldn't be stopped, before I made a careless mistake that would alter my life irrevocably and yet gave me the best thing that would ever happen to me.

Emma laughed in the next room.

And I was aware that my mother was talking, saying something that she wanted me to pay attention to, but I was having trouble concentrating on her words.

"Kathleen Margaret," she said with some sharpness. "Do you even care about what I'm telling you?"

"Mom." I stood up. "I'm not feeling very well. I'll call you later, okay?"

"Are you kicking me out?" she huffed.

"No. But I'm distracted so I'm afraid I'm not a very satisfactory conversational companion right now."

She exhaled unhappily. "When are you going to start talking like everyone else?"

It was an old complaint, one she'd been using since I was six and informed her that she needed to 'stop projecting your own insecurities on others'. So I repeated the same answer I'd been giving her for years.

"I didn't know it was a crime to be smart."

"Kat, sit back down. I'm talking to you about something serious."

The ball of paper weighed heavily in my hand. As I sat I discreetly dropped it on the floor underneath the table so my mother wouldn't be reminded of its existence. I definitely couldn't handle an interrogation right now. As far as my mother knew, Emma's father was a cheating, emotionally abusive creep and Emma was better off without him in her life. That gave me a reason for opting not to seek child support. It also gave me an excuse to hide from the truth. My own father had taken off when I was two and other than occasionally sending a random check, I hadn't heard from him much while I was growing up.

"Can I make another cup of coffee if we're going to get into serious topics?" I asked.

"Kat, I don't care. Drink all the coffee in town if it'll make you pay attention for five minutes."

I sighed and moved to the counter beside the sink to refill my Hawk Valley Happiness mug.

My mother pounced as soon as I sat down. "So don't you want to know the details?"

Emma trotted in with a face full of chocolate cupcake icing, snatched her favorite plastic cup and accepted a kiss on the cheek from her grandmother before she returned to the living room.

I waited until she was out of earshot to inquire, "What details?"

"About his record."

I rubbed my eyes. "Whose?"

"Nash."

Colin was abruptly sick of sitting in his high chair. Or else he didn't like hearing gossip about his big brother. He let out a wail.

"What are you talking about?" I asked, not really caring to know. Colin rewarded me with a big drooling grin as I pulled the tray away, unsnapped the safety belt and lifted him.

"An assault charge in college and another one last year. The first time the charge was dropped but the second time he got whatever it's called where you get a warning and don't have to go to prison."

I frowned. "Probation?"

She shrugged. "I guess."

Nash had gotten into a lot of scrapes in high school. I remembered that clearly. There were always rumors that he was on the brink of expulsion yet somehow he managed to skate through with no lasting consequences. I'd just assumed he'd gotten past his tendency to lash out. I'd certainly never witnessed that kind of aggression from him.

"I hit someone."

No, whatever happened in that scuffle didn't really count. Travis Hanson was in perpetual need of a good thrashing and I was sure he'd deserved whatever Nash's reaction had been.

But there was also the deal with his knuckles, the way they looked bruised and cut the night he came to town and he fed me some nonsense about scraping them during a tire change.

Still, Nash had never mentioned any legal trouble back in Oregon. On the other hand, there were plenty of things I hadn't mentioned to him to so it was entirely possible. He wouldn't have had any reason to mention minor problems with the law. I'd never asked.

"How did you come by this information?" I wanted to know.

She was smug. "Retta from church has a son who is a private detective down in Phoenix. His name is Freddie and he can find out anything about anyone."

The idea was alarming. My brand new goal in life was to never become one of Freddie's projects.

"Why were you looking into Nash anyway?" I asked, bouncing Colin in my lap as he chewed on a teething ring.

She threw me a knowing look. "I'm your mother, Kathleen. Do you really think I can't tell what's going on here?"

"How about you enlighten me then?"

Her mouth pursed. "You're involved with him. You've been suckered into taking care of everything. His business, his house and even that baby."

I didn't want to yell. Emma would hear. I kept my voice low but insistent.

"Colin is Heather's child. He's our flesh and blood, your grand-nephew. He's not just 'that baby' so don't refer to him that way."

She relented, looked away. "No, of course not. You know I care about what happens to Colin. That's why I was so concerned about handing him over to a man like Nash Ryan."

"That was a decision for Heather and Chris to make," I said flatly. "They made it."

"But-"

"You know," I said, "you might have come around more often to help instead of digging up dirt behind the scenes. If you had then you would have seen that Nash takes very good care of Colin. What's even more essential is that he loves Colin with all of his heart."

One eyebrow arched. "I noticed you're not denying having relations with him."

My voice was cold. "What do you want to hear, Mom? You want to hear me admit that we have earth-shattering sex? Fine, I admit it."

She reddened with embarrassment. "Don't be vulgar, Kathleen."

"Then don't pry into subjects you don't want to talk about."

She tilted her head and looked a little hurt. "I'm only prying because I care. I care about you and about Emma and Colin too."

Emma returned with Roxie at her side. The dog appealed to my mother with a wagging tail but my mother ignored her so she turned to me for a pat on the head.

"Are you fighting?" Emma asked.

"No, honey," I said. "Why do you think that?"

"You look mad."

"I'm not mad."

"Nobody's mad," my mother insisted and held out her hand. "Now come give Grandma one last kiss before I leave."

Emma still had some chocolate on her face and she managed to smudge some onto my mother's cheek.

My mother blew a kiss to Colin before she left. For me she had only a few stern words of warning.

"Remember what I told you, Kat."

I turned my head and pretended to be looking at something fascinating out the window until she was gone.

"Me and Roxie are bored," Emma announced.

I picked up a napkin and cleaned the chocolate off her face. She resisted, wrinkling her nose and shaking her head.

"Can we go in the backyard?" she asked.

I shook my head. "No honey, let's just play inside today."

"Why?"

"It's hot out."

That wasn't a lie. But it wasn't the complete truth either. Someone had been watching me, possibly following me, even finding me here at Nash's house. I knew who it was, the same person who'd called and emailed at least a dozen times this smmer. I'd deleted every message and email, sometimes before listening or reading. He had no place in my life, no place in Emma's life. But things had escalated and I needed someone to confide in. Steve Brown maybe. Someone who could objectively tell me what my legal options were in case it was time for me to be confronted by my own lies.

"What are we supposed to do in the house all day?" Emma pouted.

I stood and heaved Colin onto my hip. "When I was a little girl I used to build forts. We could do that."

"What's a fort?"

"It's like a little clubhouse and we can build one right in the living room with some chairs and blankets."

Emma was intrigued. "Can you show me?"

I smiled. "Sure."

Twenty minutes later we were all relaxing in the makeshift living room fort. Emma and I were lying on our backs and staring up at the yellow blanket that served as a roof while Colin enjoyed some tummy time between us. Roxie sat guarding the entrance, our ever faithful sentinel.

"I like it in here," Emma whispered.

"I do too," I whispered back.

My phone rang. I'd been keeping it close, just in case I needed to dial 911 in a hurry, though I was pretty sure Roxie would go ballistic if anyone actually tried to get into the house.

I felt a flood of relief when I saw the caller was Nash.

"How's the drive?" I asked him.

"Long. Dull. How's my boy?"

I glanced at Colin. "He's fine. He's trying to lift himself up."

"Tell him I miss him."

"I will."

There was a long pause.

"I miss you too, Kat."

My eyes closed and a fleeting second of happiness surged through me. It was exactly what I've been wishing to hear from him. Some hint that there was more to us than a practical arrangement. My heart wanted me to respond, to tell him how much I missed him too. I wanted so badly to feel his arms around me, to hear the comforting thud of his heartbeat as I rested my cheek against his chest after we finished enjoying each other's bodies.

My eyes opened. I couldn't say it. Not now. Saying it would expose me to a potential level of hurt that I wouldn't be able to bear. Because Nash knew nothing of the most important story I had to tell and how I'd been hiding from it for so long, lying for so long, I wasn't sure how to do anything differently. He wouldn't understand. Nash had little patience or forgiveness in his heart for duplicity of any kind. Nash assumed I was upstanding and honorable because I'd never given him any reason to believe otherwise.

No, of course he wouldn't understand. I was on my own.

"I guess I'll see you later tonight," I said.

I thought I heard a sigh of irritation on the other end. "I guess so."

"Drive safe."

"Bye, Kat."

Emma sat up in the little structure we'd created and stared at me. "Mommy, are you crying?"

I swiped at my eyes. "No, Ems. There's no reason for Mommy to cry."

Chapter Eighteen

Nash

THE DRIVE WAS MONOTONOUS, THE MILES AND LANDSCAPES bleeding into each other. I'd been driving for more hours than I cared to think about and now I was somewhere in Nevada, a dry, brown segment of the state. The scenery reminded me of Phoenix, the place I was born and hadn't returned to in over a decade.

A rest stop exit beckoned and my bladder demanded some relief so I pulled off the highway and toward the squat building that housed bathrooms and vending machines.

The trucker who'd just finished using the facilities acknowledged me with a quick nod. I took care of business, tried to extract a soda from the broken vending machine, then paused to take in the barren landscape. The long drive was playing havoc with my thoughts. When I wasn't brooding over bad memories I was bothered by my earlier call with Kat. There was a tone in her voice, like something was wrong. She sounded sad, distracted. I knew her well enough to detect the change. Usually Kat was full of words and questions but this time she'd been quiet, not even responding when I told her I missed her. I hadn't said it with the intention of applying pressure. I'd said it because she'd been on my mind so much, almost as much as Colin, and I thought she'd be pleased to hear it.

Maybe I was wrong. Maybe she wanted to keep me at a distance after all.

I ended my break and climbed back into the truck. The sun was starting to hang low in the sky. I'd started this journey fourteen hours ago and this would be the last leg of the trip. I was making excellent time and expected to be back in Hawk Valley before eleven p.m.

A yawn fought its way out. It wasn't my brightest idea to tackle this exhausting trip on three hours of sleep. The last time I made the drive I'd had no sleep but then I was running on shock and adrenaline. Now I was just weary and wishing for home.

Home.

Funny how I'd resisted thinking of Hawk Valley as home during the years I'd lived there. I thought of it as my father's town, my father's home. I convinced myself I didn't belong to the quirky little place that seemed suspended in time at the foothills of the mountains. I belonged to it now. I just wanted to get back there and kiss Colin good night. I wanted to hold Kat and try to figure out where her head was. I knew where my head was. Somehow this trip had made it clear. There was nothing casual about what we had, not for me. I didn't want her to be my friend and fuck buddy. I wanted her to be mine.

Once I was back on the road my thoughts veered in a less cheerful direction. During this trip I'd been thinking too much about bitter topics. The things that happened between my dad and me. And Heather. The messy conclusion that possessed a Greek tragedy quality. But it hadn't ended with Heather running out of the house and my brutal words to my father.

After that night he was so remorseful it was almost pitiful. He bought all my favorite foods, stayed home every night in the hopes I'd say more than two sentences to him, opened his wallet to buy way more crap than I'd actually need to bring to college. The truce between us was tense but at least it existed. He hugged me on the day I left for college and I let him.

Heather had resigned from her job. I didn't see her around and didn't care to. We must not have been as invisible as we thought while making out on a blanket at the park because someone had seen. The rumors reached me and I refused to confirm or deny them. In fact I refused to participate any conversation that included her name.

Heather was more than just some girl I'd messed with. She might have ended up meaning something to me.

Or maybe not.

Maybe I would have just fucked her and tossed her aside to go chase something better a thousand miles away. Either way my most significant memory of her now was what she looked like lying naked on my father's bed. I couldn't forgive her for putting that in my head. She left me some voicemails of the 'blah blah never meant to hurt you' variety until I blocked her number. On graduation day I thought I caught a glimpse of her blonde hair on the edge of the crowd but when I looked again she was gone.

Once I was in Oregon I didn't think about her much. I had plenty to keep me busy. There was no shortage of girls around and sometimes I'd meet one I kind of liked. But I was finished with being careless with girls' feelings. I finally knew how it felt to be discarded and I didn't want to inflict that on anyone. I tried out a few relationships and discovered I wasn't good at them. They accused me of being closed off, detached, unwilling to let go, unable to let anyone in. They said I was a stone cold motherfucker who had nothing to give. I didn't argue. And still I refused to talk about the furious fire that burned inside of me, how it led me to seek out violence even though I despised violence. I would never cause hurt just for the pure hell of it. But the sight of anyone being mistreated, especially a woman, set off a chain reaction that ended with my fists.

There was therapy. There were support groups. Court ordered anger management. But it was all a waste of time because there was no mystery behind my actions. Every outburst had been preceded by a situation that in my mind was tied to the murder of my mother.

On the plus side, as soon as I moved to Oregon my relationship with my father took a turn for the better. It was easy to get along with someone you hardly saw and spoke to maybe twice a month.

In the fall of my third year of college my dad asked me if I was coming home for Christmas. I hadn't the year before, preferring to remain at school. The truth was the holidays bugged the shit out of me, all that tinsel fakery and phony smiles. But my dad sounded really earnest and over the last year I'd only visited Hawk Valley for a total of three days over the summer. He was pleased when I said I'd be there.

"There's something I want to tell you in person, Nash. Something that I hope will be okay with you."

His words were odd but I didn't dwell on them. Maybe he was throwing in the towel and closing the store. As far as I was concerned it would be about time. In any case I was determined to get along with him. I could make that happen for a few lousy days.

Within an hour of arriving in Hawk Valley I changed my mind.

"You're doing what?" I couldn't believe what I'd just heard.

He was nervous, kept staring at his hands. But he met my eye when he confirmed the news. "I'm marrying Heather Molloy."

My brain struggled for a reaction but no words came out so Chris Ryan saw this an invitation to keep talking.

"She moved back here about six months ago to take care of her mother. We got to be friends. Then it turned into more. Nash, this doesn't have anything to do with past mistakes. We both still feel awful about that. But what we have now, the people we are now, this is different. I hope you'll understand."

"I understand there's something really fucking wrong with both of you. That's what I understand."

"Nash, please."

"Please what?"

"She cares about you. She wants to be your friend."

I thought that was funny. "Oh Jesus, that's rich."

"She wanted to be here to talk to you. But I thought this needed to be between us."

I paced the floor of the living room, disgusted. "Of all the women around, that's the one you pick."

He stood his ground, remaining where he was. "I love her."

"Fuck that. You don't love anyone."

He looked hurt. "That's not true. I love you. I've loved you since the day you were born."

I stopped pacing. "You sure picked a special moment to say that for the first time."

"I thought you knew." He ran his hand through his hair. He'd hit his fortieth birthday this year but his hair was still thick and black, like mine. "I was just never good at saying it. I should have been better at making you feel loved. I should have been more like your mother."

I whirled on him, practically snarling. "Don't you fucking dare talk about her!"

"We should have talked about her more. That was my mistake."

"You always hated my mother."

My father was shocked. "No, son. I didn't hate her, not ever. Your mother gave me so much. She gave me you."

"Yeah. And I figured that was what you hated her for the most."

I hadn't seen my dad cry since the night he woke me up to tell me the person I loved the most was dead. A tear slid down his cheek now.

"No," he repeated hoarsely. "I loved her for that. We never got along but I always loved her, if for no other reason than because you were part of her."

I didn't want him to say these things. Not when I was hell bent on being furious.

"You've got to stop, Nash," he said. "You've got to stop blaming yourself, for feeling guilty about something you never could have prevented. You've got to stop the way you lash out, thinking you can right all the wrongs in the world. You weren't built for violence and it takes a piece of you every time. It will destroy you if you let it and my son, my beautiful boy, you are so much better than you pretend to be. Someday you'll wake up and understand that."

I didn't want to listen. "Strange words from a man who spent so much effort tearing me down."

He flinched. "I wasn't always the best father. I said and did things I shouldn't have. I own that completely. I'm asking you to forgive me."

I picked up the duffel bag I'd left by the door when I walked in here only a short while ago. "I don't want to hear it. Go on. Marry her. It doesn't fucking matter to me. We're done."

"Wait!" He stood up and covered the distance between us. My hand was already on the door.

"I want you to stay," he choked out. "I want so badly for us to start over. But I won't stop you from going if you need to. I'm just asking, no I'm begging, please don't cut off all contact. Please, Nash."

Instead of answering his plea I slammed the door in his face.

Until two months ago, that emotional Christmas Eve was the last time I set foot in Hawk Valley. Fortunately some of my father's words had sunk in. It took me some months to cool off but eventually I did pick up the phone and call him. I wouldn't go to his wedding or come visit or even welcome a visit from him but I did what he asked. I stayed in contact.

When Colin was born I was sorely tempted to visit. I'd always hoped and wished for a brother when I was a kid and now I had one. My dad sent photos every week and I found myself looking at them often, wondering when I'd meet my brother, what he'd think of me.

I never would have guessed even in my worst moments of dread that it would happen the way happened.

But that was the random fucked up nature of things in this life. Things happen that we couldn't possibly plan for. And fate can deal a cruel and unforeseen blow no matter what we intend, no matter what we want, no matter how much we wish for more time.

Chapter Nineteen

Kathleen

NASH HAD TOLD ME HE'D BE HOME BEFORE ELEVEN. AFTER I put the kids to bed I couldn't sit still so I embarked on an overzealous cleaning spree throughout the entire first floor of the old house.

All day my thoughts had been battling with each other and I still had no clear plan. Steve Brown was a family friend and a capable lawyer but I hesitated to involve him. Or anyone. Returning to Hawk Valley pregnant, alone, and without a degree had caused a ripple of gossip. I was Kathleen Doyle after all, the goody goody brainiac who left here with every intention of making a name for herself.

Instead I returned with nothing but a vague story about a failed relationship that didn't begin to touch the truth. Emma was given my last name and I refused to list the father on the birth certificate. It wasn't until I received a copy in the mail when the baby was six weeks old that I learned my mother had paid a visit to her friend in the county vital records office and changed my response.

The name Harrison Corbett stared back at me in bold typed letters.

"Stop howling, Kat. I was trying to protect you and Emma. You might change your mind someday and want child support."

She meant well so I couldn't be angry. She had no idea that the explanation I'd given her was missing some key elements, the largest of those being the name of Emma's real father.

Cleaning was therapeutic. Getting on my knees and washing the hardwood floors by hand succeeded in calming the turmoil in my head. Roxie seemed offended when I booted her out of her corner so I could clean there. She watched me with puzzled doggy eyes and then plopped down in a huff when I set her soft bed down on a different area of the floor because it was already dry.

In the kitchen I discovered the crumpled piece of paper that had disturbed me so much this morning. It was exactly where I'd dropped it underneath the table. All day I'd avoided retrieving it because I knew I'd be unable to resist the pain of smoothing out the creases and looking at it again.

The three people in the picture were so young. Impossibly young. They hadn't yet been touched by anything terrible and it showed in their arrogant smiles.

"Randall," I whispered, touching his face and wishing I had the power to step through the web of time and warn him he only had a year to live. The game he played in that night was the last one before his knee injury. After that came the surgeries, and the addiction to pain medication, the desperate and futile effort to reclaim his life, and finally the fatal overdose.

I was about to tear the paper into tiny pieces so I couldn't look at it anymore when I saw something in the bottom right hand corner. A phone number had been neatly written. It was probably the same one that had been left on unheard voicemails and listed at the bottom of discarded emails.

I snatched my cell phone and dialed before I had a chance to reconsider. The three rings took eternity and my heart thudded the entire time. He picked up on the fourth ring.

"Kathleen. About goddamn time you called me back."

Hearing his voice after all this time immediately summoned a feeling that was something like being kicked in the chest.

"I'm only calling to order you to stay away from me," I said coldly. "There will be legal consequences if you don't."

He sighed. "Can't do that. I told you we needed to talk."

I struggled to keep from shouting. I couldn't wake up the children. "We do not need to talk! Stay away. Stop stalking me or I'll have you arrested."

He chuckled. "No you won't."

"The hell I won't."

"We're not doing this over the phone, Kat. I'm here in town, staying at The Hawkian Hotel on Garner Avenue. You don't need to tell me where you are. I already know. Expect me there in ten minutes."

He ended the call, leaving me standing there in the kitchen, dumbfounded and staring at my silent phone as if it were a venomous snake. I could make good on my threat. I could call the police, claim he'd been stalking me, file a restraining order. But that would turn into a very ugly spectacle.

A car pulled up to the house ten minutes later. I wished I'd taken a moment away from my inner turmoil to throw on something more substantial than a long nightshirt with no shorts but it was too late. The moment was here. The only thing to do was to meet it head on.

I stepped out into the summer night to head off a knock on the door that would cause Roxie to erupt into a flurry of barking that was sure to wake the kids.

Even under the streetlights I could see that Harrison Corbett was as devilishly handsome as he was the night he pulled me out of a corner at a crowded party and made me his. But the joke was on me all along. To him, I was just one piece of a collection.

Harrison came around from the driver's side and noticed me at standing on the cement walkway.

"Hi Kat," he greeted me smoothly, as if we were friends instead of enemies.

"Stay there," I warned, brandishing my cell phone from ten feet away as if were something else. Like a sword. Or a cattle prod. Something that would hurt if it touched him. "If you give me any reason to call the police I won't hesitate."

"Oh please," he scoffed. "Enough with the fucking hysterics."

"I don't know what you want after all this time," I told him. "But you're not getting it."

He laughed. "You think I'd make all this effort for you?"

"I don't know what to think."

"I don't want you, Kathleen. You're not among my favorite memories."

"Likewise, asshole."

He didn't care about the insult. He looked up at the house. "Whose place is that?"

"None of your business."

"I know it's not your house. You've been ignoring all my calls and emails so my only option was to come up here to deal with you in person. I was waiting for you at your apartment yesterday but when you finally did show up you didn't stay and drove here instead."

I remembered the creepy feeling I had on the way over here yesterday, that I was being followed. I took a step back.

"Is she in there?" Harrison asked and I went cold.

"Who?"

"The kid. Her name's Emma, right?"

"Don't you talk about her," I whispered. "She is *my* daughter."

"And what are you going to tell her when the day comes when she asks about her father?"

"Shut up."

He advanced. "What are you going to tell her, Kathleen?"

"Shut up!"

He was right in my face now. "WHAT ARE YOU GOING TO TELL HER?"

I pushed him, just to get him away. He was too close. If he'd been trying to intimidate me he'd succeeded. But Harrison wasn't expecting me to strike out physically. He tried to step aside but lost his balance, grabbing onto my arm, perhaps on instinct, as he fell down on the front lawn. I fell with him. We landed in a pile of limbs and my nightshirt rode up over my waist, my bare legs slipping in the grass that was still wet from the automated sprinklers.

We were only sprawled there for perhaps two seconds but it was enough time for an overpowering spotlight to materialize out of nowhere and freeze us there on the lawn where we'd fallen.

I couldn't tell where the light was coming from at first. Then the glare cut out abruptly and I blinked, seeing the shape of a moving truck in the street.

"Kat!" Nash roared and it seemed like he hurtled out of the truck, vaulted over the sidewalk and landed at my side in the space of a heartbeat.

I was still too stunned for words as he hauled me to my feet, inspecting me in the dim light with panic written all over his face. When he was satisfied I wasn't bleeding and in one piece his panic morphed into rage. He turned it on the man who was now standing ten feet away.

"This is just fucking great," Harrison muttered.

Nash shoved him. Much harder than I had. Harrison made a legitimate 'oof' sound and stumbled toward the sidewalk. The moment would have been comical if it weren't so terrifying.

Harrison straightened up. Once a wide receiver on a university football team, he was still a physical force to be reckoned with. But given the muscles coiling in Nash's arms and the murderous glint in his eye when he glared at Harrison, I'd put my money on him.

"Who the fuck are you?" Nash growled.

Harrison exhaled noisily. "I didn't come here for this kind of trouble."

"You have no idea what kind of trouble you just ran into, motherfucker."

"Nash," I said but he ignored me, keeping me behind him.

Harrison laughed. "I get it. You're Kat's pet guard dog."

"I asked you who the fuck you are."

"Nash!" I pulled on the sleeve of his t-shirt to get him to look at me. "This is Harrison Corbett. We, um, I mean I knew him in college."

Realization dawned on Nash's face. "He's Emma's father, isn't he?"

"Aw hell," Harrison swore. "You don't stray very far from your lies do you, Kathleen?"

Nash snapped his fingers. "You shut your goddamn mouth."

Harrison wouldn't be silenced. "But she is known to stray from a man's bed so be warned."

"You bastard," I hissed.

"You two-faced sneaky bitch," he shot back.

Roxie barked from inside the house. It was a wonder none of the neighbors had heard all the racket yet.

"Get out of here," I said. "Get out of here, Harrison, or I swear I'll make sure you spend the night in jail."

"Personally I'd rather make sure he spends the night in the hospital," Nash growled.

I thought it was a small miracle that the two of them hadn't come to blows yet. But this situation was ready to explode. I needed to get them apart before something did happen.

"I mean it," I said and pointed to my phone as if I was getting ready to dial 911.

Harrison let out one last sigh. "We're not done," he warned, then got back into his stupid sports car and left.

Nash waited in a tense pose until Harrison's taillights had turned the corner before reaching for me. "Are you okay?'

"I'm fine."

"What the fuck happened?"

"We were having an argument."

"And he just happened to knock you down?"

"No. That was an accident."

Nash paused, put his hands on his hips and studied me with an expression I couldn't read in the dark. "What the hell was he doing here? I mean, you haven't seen him in years, right?"

"No, I haven't seen him in years. He's been trying to contact me for weeks and weeks though. Calling, emailing. I ignored him so he decided to come to town and confront me in person."

"Because he wanted to see Emma?"

"I doubt it."

"Then he wanted to see you?"

"No. I don't think that's it either."

"How do you know?"

"Because he hates me."

"Why?"

I lowered my head. "I screwed his brother."

"What?"

I raised my head and said in a clear voice, "I screwed his brother. Randall was his name. That's why Harrison hates me."

Nash said nothing. He just stared at me.

I laughed suddenly, aware that I sounded like a maniac. "But that wasn't the end of it. I got pregnant with Randall's baby. And then he died. He was battling an addiction to pain meds, trying to get clean. I thought I could help him. But no one could help him and one night he swallowed too many pills and he fucking died!"

I had to stop because I couldn't breathe properly. There was a pain in my gut, the memory of a wrenching grief that I'd never dealt with properly. And I wasn't laughing anymore. Tears coursed down my cheeks now.

"I didn't know what to do, where to turn. So I forgot every plan I ever had and came back here because I had only one thing left that mattered. Emma. I never told anyone the truth. Even Emma's birth certificate is a lie. I'm not who you thought I was, Nash. And I know you think I'm repulsive now, that I'm this lying, scheming bitch and you're right." I sank down to the grass, gasping between sobs. "You're right."

"Kat."

I heard his voice but I couldn't respond. I was lost in the collapse of my own carefully constructed shield. I was broken. I couldn't be fixed tonight.

"Kathleen."

He was right there on the ground with me and I did not resist at all when I felt his arms pulling me toward the solid warmth of his chest. I stayed there until I was finished gasping out agonized sobs.

Chapter Twenty

Kathleen

Hanging out on the front lawn all night was not an option. After about ten minutes of falling apart all over Nash's t-shirt while the wet grass soaked through my panties, he urged me to get up.

"Let's get inside."

He acted like he was prepared to carry me but I was embarrassed enough as it was so I got to my feet and walked across the front lawn while my wet nightshirt stuck to my thighs.

I opened the front door to find a very perplexed German Shepherd waiting but her confusion switched to tail wagging joy when Nash appeared behind me and held out a hand in greeting.

I stood at the bottom of the stairs. "I don't hear the kids. They must have slept through all that."

Nash finished petting Roxie and eyed me while I wished passionately for mind reading skills.

"I'll go check on them," he said and nodded to my grass-stained wet pajamas. "Why don't you take a minute and get cleaned up?"

His voice didn't sound cold or angry although the great Front Lawn Revelation must have shocked him at least a little. It still shocked me and I was the one who'd revealed it.

I took his advice and sought a change of clothes while Nash looked in on Emma and then visited Colin's room. The baby monitor was beside the bed in Nash's room so I could hear him in there while

I pulled a tank top and loose shorts out of my overnight bag.

"How's my favorite little guy?" Nash said softly. "Missed you, kid." A few seconds later I heard the music of the crib mobile and then Nash's footsteps heading this way.

He appeared in the doorway, crossed his arms and leaned against the doorframe. He looked tired. And damn good, although this wasn't the moment for me to be noticing that. He must not have shaved since he left the other night. The dark scruff all over his chin suited him.

"Do you know how many nights I would lie awake in this room wishing I was anywhere else?" he asked.

I sat on the edge of the bed. "No."

"A lot. And now I can't remember why. It's a nice room. A nice house. A nice town." Nash rubbed his eyes. "Do you want to wait until tomorrow to talk about it?"

"No."

Nash stared at me. I wondered what he saw now, if it was completely different than what he'd seen the last time we were together.

I stood up. "I can go sleep on the couch."

"Kat."

"Or I can just wake Emma up and go home."

"Stop it." He stepped inside the room and closed the door. Then he reached around to his back and pulled his shirt over his head before dropping his pants. We were in the midst of something serious but I couldn't help getting turned on.

Nash pulled the covers of the bed down, got settled and patted the sheet. "Get over here."

He curled his arm around me immediately and I snuggled close to him. He smelled like soap and sunshine and I sighed as my cheek landed on his chest.

"I'm sorry," I said, my voice catching. "I didn't tell you the whole story because I didn't tell anyone. My relationship with Harrison was never great. He was unfaithful and controlling and by the time we broke up I despised him. But Randall…"

My voice trailed off as I thought about the gentle half of the Corbett brothers. Randall was a year older and didn't have Harrison's arrogant brand of charm. He was quieter, more serious. Everyone thought he had one of the best chances on the team to go pro. Then a knee injury after a hard tackle sent him to the sidelines and a string of surgeries left him unable to kick a painkiller habit. I didn't have any romantic feelings for Randall, not then. My focus, my infatuation, was entirely centered on Harrison. But Randall and I were friends. I worried about him. I urged his brother to worry about him but Harrison only brushed aside any concerns with sarcastic comments.

When Harrison and I broke up it was ugly. Messy. Shattering. I'd foolishly made him my world without asking myself if he deserved the honor. My once promising academic career had been seriously damaged. My pride was in tatters. I reached out to the guy who'd always been my friend and found he was in far worse shape than I'd guessed. I wanted him to get help. I wanted to comfort him. I held him and offered him my body because we needed each other, because I thought it might give him a reason to get clean, because I selfishly wanted to feel something even a little bit real.

And it was real all right.

I really had sex with my ex-boyfriend's brother. I really got pregnant. I really woke up one awful morning to the news that Randall Corbett was dead from an overdose. And I really ran back to Hawk Valley with my tail between my legs to hide from the fallout.

I heard myself telling all of this to Nash. He didn't say anything. I appreciated that. All I really needed was to feel his arms around me while I poured out the words that had been rotting inside of me for far too long.

He remained silent when I reached the end. I had no idea what would happen next. If he wanted to tell me he was disappointed, that he could never excuse the kind of deception I was capable of, then I'd have to find a way to live with that. I'd have to find a way to live without him.

"I can't imagine what you think of me," I said, feeling the words catch in my throat. "I'm sorry I'm not the kind of person you thought I was."

He mulled that over and then sighed. "Give me some credit. I'm not judging you, Kat, if that's what you're afraid of. Things happen in life that are complicated and unexpected. If anyone knows that it's me."

I traced the muscles of his chest. "Was your life in Oregon complicated?"

He was puzzled by the question. "Not really. I lived alone beside the ocean with my dog. Why do you ask?"

I figured I ought to tell him someone had been sniffing around in his past. "My mother knows some friend of a friend who's a private detective."

"And?" he prodded.

"The guy did some digging on you. Found out you were under probation for assault charges."

Nash nodded. "I see."

"I wasn't spying on you."

"I know."

"My mother was just concerned. And I wouldn't even have brought it up except I don't want there to be any secrets between us."

"And there won't be." He picked up my hand and kissed the palm. "I used to think of myself as some kind of self-styled vigilante, getting small scale justice, taking action to protect the innocent from an even more violent outcome."

I smiled. "You sound like a super hero."

He snorted. "Not even close. Nothing good comes from seeking out violence, from burying your own agony by drawing blood. My dad knew it. He understood me better than I thought. He told me I wasn't built to live that way, that it would take a piece of me every time. It took me a long time to understand he knew what he was talking about."

"So what now?" I asked.

"Now I'll find a better way to battle the Travis Hansons of the world without resorting to my fists. I have to. For me and especially for Colin."

"Nash," I said gently and he looked at me. "Your parents would be very proud of you. Both of them."

He smiled and I saw how much the words meant to him. In the end we always wanted to make our parents proud, even if we didn't admit it.

"So what about this Harrison dipshit?" he asked. "He must know he's not Emma's father."

"Yeah, he knows." I winced. "In fact I recall he had some choice words for me the last time I saw him."

Nash tensed. "He better not come around again."

I sighed. I had no idea what Harrison was after but it couldn't be good. "I'll go talk to Steve Brown tomorrow. He'll have some ideas about what to do."

Nash refused to drop the subject. "He's been following you, right? He's up to something. I think you and Emma should stay here until he's dealt with."

"Nash, I don't want to overreact."

"I'll overreact for the both of us then." He was scowling and I could tell he wouldn't tolerate an argument. "You're staying here. I can't handle the idea of you and Emma alone and unprotected across town."

I smiled. "If he shows up again I'll just bop him over the head with my frying pan."

"I'm serious, Kat."

"So am I. That sucker is cast iron. It can do some damage."

"Knock it off. You're staying."

I relented. "All right."

He tightened his arms around me and I listened to his heartbeat.

He hadn't given me any ideas about what he thought of all the baggage I'd laid out for him.

"You didn't hide," he finally said.

I pulled away so I could see his face. "What?"

He reached out and pushed a strand of long hair out of my face. His striking blue eyes were gentle. "You didn't hide, Kat. You didn't go to some unknown place where nobody knew you and pretend to be someone else. You came home. You dedicated yourself to your daughter and surrounded her with love in the place you knew best. That's not hiding."

My eyes filled with tears. "I've never figured out what I'm going to tell her. She's young now. But someday she'll have questions. I'm afraid of what she'll think of me when she hears the answers."

He drew me close once more and kissed my forehead. "You *will* figure it out though. I see how you are with Emma. You don't hold back from letting her know how much she's loved. She'll never have any doubts about that."

I felt shy when I reached up to touch his lips. "I missed you."

He raised an eyebrow. "I wondered."

My fingers traveled over his collarbone, brushing the muscled skin and I planted a kiss there. "What else did you wonder?"

"If you had any fun in this bed without me."

"Not really."

He abruptly changed positions, gripping my hips and sliding my body down until I was flat on my back. "You want to have some fun now?"

"You just finished driving for twenty hours, came home to a virtual brawl on the front lawn and then patiently listened to me cry out my shameful past for an hour. Aren't you tired?"

Nash didn't hesitate. He shoved his boxers down and directed my hand to his dick. "Does that feel tired to you?" he demanded.

I stroked the hard length of him. "No."

"Then stop talking and do something about it."

I started to wiggle out of my panties. Nash became impatient and yanked them off.

"No shirt either," he said gruffly and practically tore it off me.

I locked my knees on either side of him, anticipating that tonight he'd want it rough and hard because he was in such a hurry to get there. That was fine with me. I was ready to take it. I braced myself for the first invasive thrust that would make me gasp and arch my back and urge him to go even deeper.

But Nash paused. I felt him against my belly, so thick and solid, and I ached to feel him closer, inside, connected.

"What's wrong?" I asked because he was looking down at me with a grave expression I wasn't used to seeing.

Nash kissed me in response. His tongue slid between my lips and he we kissed slow and deep. His two day beard scraped against my skin and I closed my eyes, losing myself in the intoxicating feel of being kissed in the all consuming way heroes kissed in stories. I was still lost in the feel of his lips when his body shifted and he pushed inside, taking what he wanted. I was happy to give it to him. We rocked together in perfect sync. It had never been this slow before with us and I loved it. I came with his weight on top of me, our mouths still locked in a heated dance.

I think I love you Nash Ryan.

Our skin was sweaty and our tongues intertwined when Nash pulled out and ended in a hot spurt on my lower belly.

"Kathleen," he groaned when the kiss finally broke and he buried his face between my breasts, both of us spent.

I stroked his damp hair and kissed the top of his head. Part of me wanted to say the words that had been rolling through my head like a bold marquee. I didn't just suspect it was true. I knew it was true. I was totally in love with him.

Nash raised his head, reached over and switched off the lamp on the bedside table. He yawned and flopped back down on the pillow.

"Good thing I brought my bed back," he grumbled. "This little mattress doesn't cut it."

I found my panties and shirt in the darkness and pulled them back on, just in case I needed to jump up in a hurry if the kids cried.

He kissed me once more. "Get some sleep, sweet princess."

"Good night," I said, reluctantly rolling to my side. I closed my eyes without telling him what I was thinking.

Chapter Twenty-One

Nash

KAT TOOK COLIN FROM HIS CRIB IN THE MORNING AND LET ME sleep in. I could hear them downstairs; Emma chattering away about teacups, Kat's soft laughter, Colin's high pitched squealing. They were all happy sounds that chased away the heavy emotional toll of the previous night. My heart was hurting the whole time Kat's story spilled out of her. To think she'd kept all that bottled up for so long and that she'd been afraid to tell anyone, even afraid to tell me, believing I'd think less of her or something. She'd made mistakes and they were messy. But she'd made them out of love. That had to count for something.

Plus I was crazy about her, messy past and all.

I threw on a pair of sweats, made a pit stop in the hall bathroom and headed down to the kitchen.

Emma was sitting at the table, barefoot in a pink nightie and giggling while Roxie licked the surface of the fancy teacup she was holding.

My dog was the first one to notice me. She let out a short bark and wagged her tail, but was in no hurry to leave Emma's side.

Kathleen was leaning against the counter with Colin on her hip while she sipped from a Hawk Valley Happiness cup. Her hair was sticking out in six directions and she'd thrown on one of my old t-shirts over her tank top. She was nothing short of breathtaking. I could just stand here and watch her all day.

"Looks like I'm the last one up," I said.

"Hey you!" Kat set her mug down and beamed at me, which was incredible. But the truly incredible moment came when Colin swerved his head at the sound of my voice, widened his eyes and tried to launch himself out of Kat's arms to get to me.

My brother's toothless drooling smile was a mile wide when I took him from Kat and planted a kiss on his chubby cheek.

"Big brother's home now," I said in his ear, wondering at what point I'd become such a sappy motherfucker that I was on the verge of womanly tears just from the weight of an infant's warm little body in my arms and the sight of his goofy baby grin.

"Aw, look at you guys," Kat marveled. "If you heard a pop that was the sound of my ovaries spontaneously detonating."

"Before anything else detonates, can I persuade you to make me a cup of coffee?"

She handed her cup to me. "Take this one. Although I feel guilty for turning you into an over caffeinated fiend."

"Thanks." I accepted the cup and sat down at the table across from Emma.

Kat's daughter regarded me with curiosity. "Where were you?"

Colin tried to stick his hand in my coffee cup when I set it down on the table. I pushed the cup away. "I had to go to Oregon," I told her.

"What's that?"

"It's another state."

"Why?"

"Why did I have to go there?"

"No. Why is it a state?"

"Why is Oregon a state?"

"Yes."

"I don't know."

"But you're tall."

"Yeah." I looked to Kathleen for help, unsure why my height meant I should be well informed about the specifics of the state of

Oregon. Kat was laughing, her hand cupped over her mouth.

Meanwhile, Emma was earnestly waiting for an answer.

"Hey, Emma," I said, changing the conversation. "I wanted to thank you for taking such good care of Roxie while I was gone. I can tell you did a really great job."

Emma was pleased. "I love her very much."

"I see that."

"So can I have her?"

"Ems." Kathleen finally intervened. "Finish your cereal, sweetheart. We need to get going. You've got preschool this morning."

"Then can I come back here and be with Roxie?"

"No. I was going to ask Grandma if she could watch you after I pick you up from preschool because I need to meet with someone important."

"Why?"

"It doesn't matter."

"Then can I come with you?"

"No honey, it's a serious kind of meeting."

Emma wrinkled her nose. "That sounds yucky."

"You can bring her here," I said. "I'd already told Betty not to expect me at the store today and I was going to unload the moving van while Colin naps. I don't mind keeping an eye on her until you're done with your meeting."

She looked surprised by the offer. "Thank you, that would be great." She paused and pulled at a strand of hair. "I'm going to see Steve Brown."

"I figured."

"Who's Steve Brown?" Emma asked.

"A lawyer," I told her.

The little girl gave me a charming smile. "Why?"

Kat needed to take a quick shower so it was my job to persuade Emma to finish her breakfast. When I told her nothing made Roxie happier than watching people eat, she nodded as if this made perfect sense and spooned the rest of the cereal into her mouth. I felt like it was a triumphant moment.

Kat quickly got ready, convinced Emma to wear something other than a nightgown and I walked the two of them to her car, just in case that douchebag was hanging around.

When they were gone I made a call to Kevin Reston. I didn't give him details, but asked him to put the word out to watch for a thick-necked prick with slicked back hair and an overpriced sports car. Kevin and I were still a little bit distant although we'd seen each other a bunch of times since the unfortunate night at Sheen's. Sometimes he accompanied Jane when she stopped by to see Colin or visited at the store. Even though things were rather cool between us he was always polite and he was polite now, didn't even ask a lot of questions, just said, "You got it, Nash," and let it go.

Colin was a pretty reliable nap taker and he started yawning around eleven. I brought him upstairs and read him a story about happy animals on a farm, hoping he'd nod off so I'd have the opportunity to go outside and do something about unloading the truck that was still sitting at the curb. It wouldn't take me long but it was an impossible task to complete while taking care of a baby.

As soon as he dozed off I deposited him in the crib, threw on a shirt and some shoes and went outside to deal with the truck. The baby monitor was stuffed in my back pocket and turned on full volume so I'd hear Colin if he woke up.

I grabbed the boxes first; clothes and books and some kitchen shit that might come in handy. I decided to stick everything in the living room for now because there was no better place. Houses that were a hundred and twenty years old didn't have garages. The bed frame and mattress were the biggest pieces and I planned to move them last.

I was on my way back to the truck to grab the remaining boxes when I noticed I had some company.

He'd just emerged from his car and he hesitated when he saw me coming. I stopped cold and assessed the situation. I could read men pretty well and he didn't appear to have the attitude of a guy spoiling for a fight. He even raised his hand in a tentative wave.

Still, just because he looked like less of an egotistical weasel than he had last night didn't mean much. I still hated him for creeping around after Kat, for scaring her, for wounding her so badly when she was young and trusting.

I pretended he wasn't there and returned to the truck. I wasn't going to move on him first but if he tried any bullshit he'd be sorry.

"Can I help?" Harrison stood a few feet behind the truck, looking up at me with some wariness, and maybe a touch of shame.

"Fuck off."

"I was really hoping to talk to you, Nash."

"How the hell do you know my name?"

"I heard Kat say it last night."

"Great. *Now* you can fuck off."

He nodded and stuffed his hands in his pockets. "You're pissed. I don't blame you at all."

"Nah, it's every guy's dream to come home and find his girl being assaulted on the front lawn by some cheesedick piece of shit with a receding hairline."

He was alarmed. "No, that's not how it happened at all. I swear to god I didn't mean to make her fall. I slipped and I guess I knocked into her. But it was an accident. I'd never intentionally hurt Kathleen."

This asshole was really pushing my buttons now. "Says every man who's ever hit a woman."

Harrison grimaced. "Cut me some slack, okay? I came here to apologize. The way shit went down last night was the last thing I wanted."

"So why the hell are you apologizing to me instead of her?"

"Because I think I've already scared Kathleen enough. And that was never my intention. I thought it would be better to approach you, maybe get you to see that despite my bad behavior I'm not the guy I seemed to be last night. I also thought maybe you could tell her that

I just want to talk."

"I have a better idea. You crawl back into your tiny cock compensation car and drive the fuck out of here."

He gave me a sad grin. "I can't do that."

"You can't, huh?" I hopped out of the truck so I could look him in the eye. "What do you want from her anyway?"

"Nothing. But the kid-"

"Is not yours."

"I know." He took a deep breath. "I know she's not mine. But she *is* my niece. I know Kathleen never wanted to see me again and even though I've been thinking lately I'd like to be there for the girl I would have left them in peace if it wasn't for my mother."

I crossed my arms, waiting for him to continue.

Harrison's face contorted and he looked incredibly sad. "My mother's dying. Colon cancer. It's everywhere now and we just found out she doesn't have long."

I wouldn't wish a dying mother on anyone, not even a total prick. "Sorry to hear that."

"The thing is, she never knew about Randall and Kathleen. She didn't know about the baby. And recently I finally told her she has a grandchild she's never met. After Randall died…" The man's voice trailed off and he looked away, unable to continue for a moment. Finally he swiped at his eyes and composed himself. "My mother was inconsolable. Frankly, so was I. Randall had been my best friend my whole life and then he was just gone in the most awful way. Worst of all, people had warned me that he had a big problem. Kat warned me. I just didn't listen. It was a bleak time and I thought we were all better off without any reminders of my brother around. The kid would have been a reminder."

"Emma," I said sharply. "Her name is Emma."

"Yes, I know her name is Emma," he said and I saw his face become wistful. "What's she like?"

"Smart and beautiful. Like her mother."

He smiled. "I'm glad to hear it." His smile faded. "My mother wants so badly to see Emma. That's why I contacted Kat. And like I said, she doesn't have long to live. That's why I've been so desperate."

I leaned against the truck, my mind trying to process everything. I'd been all set to despise this character but I found myself feeling vaguely sorry for him.

"I won't go to bat for you," I said. "But I can tell Kat what you said. It's her decision from there. And no matter what the outcome is I don't expect to find out you're doing anything to upset her."

He nodded eagerly. "Again, I really am so sorry. I got anxious because Kat didn't answer my calls or emails and every day my mother asks if she can see her granddaughter. I didn't want to go the route of lawyers and courts but I handled it badly."

"You sure as hell did," I said but there was no venom in my voice. I didn't hate him.

Harrison was contrite. "I didn't mean the things I said last night. Kathleen was amazing. And I was never good to her. She deserved better. But I don't think she got together with Randall out of spite. I think she cared about him and I'm glad. I'm glad he had someone. I'm glad that Emma is in the world."

"All right," I sighed. "You know, there was a time in the not so distant past where I would have pounded the shit out of you if I'd come home to last night's scene no matter what you said."

He raised an eyebrow. "What's changed?"

"I'm raising a little boy. I want to be a good example, to teach him that cooler heads should prevail and he should think before punching."

Harrison nodded. "That's a damn good lesson to learn at a young age."

I was going to say something else but I didn't get the chance because Kat's car drove up. I could see her through the windshield, slack-jawed with shock over finding me standing out here shooting the shit with her hated ex. I raised a hand to let her know all was well and she stared at us for another moment before exiting the car.

"What the hell do you want now?" she asked, her eyes darting from one of us to the other.

"It's okay," I assured her. "Harrison over here just wanted to apologize. There is something he wanted to talk to you about but he's told me everything and now he can leave. I agreed to tell you his story and he's agreed to live with whatever you decide."

Harrison shot me a look. I answered with a warning glare. Kat was visibly confused.

The door to Kat's sedan opened suddenly and Emma leapt out of the car.

"Emma!" Kat exclaimed. "What has Mommy told you about unbuckling your car seat?"

"Not to do it," Emma said cheerfully.

"That's right." Kat moved in front of her daughter, casting a wary eye on Harrison. Emma peeked around her mother's skirt and giggled.

Harrison was staring at Emma and looking as if he might cry. I couldn't blame him. Whatever his flaws, he'd evidently loved his brother and Emma was the last surviving piece of that brother. There were probably all kinds of emotions running through his head. I bet I'd be familiar with some of them.

Harrison cleared his throat. "Kathleen, I'm so very sorry. About everything, not just what happened last night. If I never hear from you I'll understand. You need to do what's right for Emma. But I really hope you'll consider getting in touch with me after you hear what Nash has to say."

He extended his hand to me for a handshake and I only hesitated for a second before accepting it. Harrison gave me a grateful smile, then took off in his car.

Kat was still stunned. "I don't even know what to say about all that."

I closed the back of the truck. It could wait.

I went to Kathleen and slid my arm around her shoulders. "Come inside," I said. "I'll explain it to you."

Chapter Twenty-Two

Kathleen

Nash was standing on the sidewalk along Garner Avenue, talking to a portly guy I recognized but couldn't recall his name. They shook hands and then parted. The man smiled at me as he passed so I smiled back.

"Did you make a new friend?" I asked Nash as he held the door open for me.

He snatched a kiss along the way and winked. "Maybe."

"Quite the social butterfly these days," I remarked.

Two elderly women were browsing in the aisles of the store. One of them nudged her companion and exclaimed over the wall of paintings depicting the Hawk Mountains.

"That was Ted Foster," Nash said.

I was still staring at the women as they admired the paintings. "What?"

"Ted Foster. The man who just left."

"Ah, that's right. I'd forgotten his name."

"He's one of the little league coaches. He wanted to know if he could count on our support to help sponsor the team in the fall league."

"What did you say?"

Nash grinned. "That the team could count on the Ryan family just as they had for years. I even promised to attend some of the games. Heck, maybe in a few years Colin will be out there playing."

"It might be more than a few years," I laughed. "Considering Colin isn't crawling quite yet."

Betty Carter, long time employee at Hawk Valley Gifts, waved to me with a smile and then approached the two customers to see if they needed assistance.

"What time are you leaving?" Nash asked.

"About five. I'll go pick up Emma as soon as I see my mother."

"You didn't talk to her yet?"

"No. Everything has happened so fast. But I need to tell her before I go."

Only three days ago I drove up to Nash's house to find him in the middle of a strangely friendly conversation with Harrison Corbett. Harrison left it to Nash to explain why he had been so desperate to contact me. Nothing about the situation was what I'd thought. I felt some sorrow that some of the ugliness could have been avoided if I'd chosen to answer one of Harrison's messages. I'd been afraid and I'd allowed that fear to rule me.

But now that I knew there was precious little time to waste. Down in Phoenix a dying woman was eagerly waiting to meet her little granddaughter. Harrison himself had been downright congenial when I called him after speaking to Nash. He thanked me profusely and offered to make himself scarce during the visit if his presence made me uncomfortable. I told him that wasn't necessary. I didn't expect he'd try anything funny in front of his dying mother. These people were Emma's family. If they were good people who would love her then I had no right to keep them out of her life.

So tonight my daughter and I were leaving Hawk Valley for a little while. Emma was excited when I told her this morning we were going away overnight. She'd never been to Phoenix and asked if we could get a pet rattlesnake. The plan was to drive down there tonight, stay in a hotel and then tomorrow spend the day with Randall's mother. We'd return home tomorrow night.

But before we left I owed my mother an explanation. I owed her the whole story that I should have told her four years ago.

"I wish you'd let me come with you to Phoenix," Nash said and I loved him for wanting to be there. I loved him for a lot of things. I'd tell him. Soon. Even if he didn't love me back I wouldn't be sorry for telling him.

"Emma and I will be just fine," I said. "You have your hands full with that sweet baby."

Nash checked his watch. "I told Nancy I'd be picking him up early today. We're planning a crazy night of eating pureed bananas and watching cartoons."

"I'm jealous."

I noticed one of the women was buying a painting. The other carried a basket full of carefully chosen souvenirs that I heard her say were 'for the grandkids'.

"I was going over the sales receipts from the last month," I said. "Looks like business is really picking up."

"Just like you said it would in the summer," Nash reminded me.

I reached for his hand. We hadn't yet discussed an official change in status but we weren't keeping things under wraps any longer. "So I'll call you when I get to the hotel tonight?"

"You'd better. I'll be waiting."

I kissed him. It was supposed to be a quick peck but Nash didn't let me go and turned it into the kind of kiss that left me breathless. When we came up for air Betty and the two customers were staring at us.

"Oh my," one of the women said and cooled her flushed face with a Hawk Valley folding fan.

That kiss left me feeling a bit woozy but I managed to stumble out the door with a smile that didn't want to leave my face.

An hour later I wasn't smiling anymore. I was sitting in my mother's kitchen, twisting my hands together as I awaited her reaction to the things I'd just told her.

"Why?" she asked.

I nervously tried to make a joke. "You sound like Emma."

My mother's brows knitted together. "Why did you ever try to hide something so important?"

I heaved a sigh and sorted through my memories to find the scared girl who'd come home four years ago with no prospects and carrying the child of a dead man in her belly.

"It was bad enough that I'd dropped out of school and was having a baby at nineteen. The fact that Randall was the father just made the situation harder to deal with. I was in pain and so horribly disappointed in myself. I couldn't handle the disappointment of others on top of that, especially yours." I swallowed. "I was a coward."

"Kathleen Margaret." My mother's voice rose. "One thing you have never been is a coward."

A tear fell down my cheek. It seemed I wasn't quite finished getting them all out yet.

My mother gazed at me and I wondered what she thought of this person crying in her kitchen, her only child. Other than our auburn hair and our affection for black coffee we had little in common. She'd worked her fingers to the bone for thirty years at the post office before retiring last spring. I'd never seen her read a book or even pick up a newspaper. She was very outgoing with a long list of friends, always active in a variety of charities. But, like me, she understood heartbreak. She'd suffered her own trials in the love arena with three failed marriages and a succession of inadequate boyfriends.

"I'm sorry, Mama," I said, calling her a name I hadn't called her since I was a little girl not much older than Emma. "I'm so sorry I didn't tell you the truth."

"Oh Kat." Now her green eyes were watery. "I'd forgive you for anything." She got out of her chair and collected me in her arms. "You're my baby, Kathleen. The love of my life. Don't you know that?"

Crying in my mother's arms while she stroked my hair felt childish and restorative at the same time. I was twenty-three with a child of my own but instantly I could recall being five and refusing to go back to sleep after a nightmare unless my mother stayed in my bed with me. And she did. She hummed a song that nowadays I sing to Emma and to Colin and that night she stayed with me long after I fell asleep.

Once my therapeutic sob fest was finished, my mother questioned my plans to drive down to Phoenix.

"Are you sure these people are trustworthy?" she asked. "I don't think you and Emma should go alone. I can go with you."

"Nash already offered to be our personal escort," I said. "But no thank you. I need to bring Emma down there by myself."

"If you're sure," she said and I could tell she was trying to weigh her words and avoid saying the wrong thing.

"I'm sure."

She watched me. "I saw Nash yesterday. I was passing by the store and hadn't been inside for a while so I took a look around. He was folding t-shirts. Folding them incorrectly I might add."

I grinned. "But I bet he looked great doing it."

She smirked. "I never said he wasn't easy on the eyes."

"He's a good guy, Mom. I swear."

She nodded. "All right. If you say so then I'm sure it's true. I trust you, Kathleen."

As I left my mother's house and went to go pick up my daughter I felt like a new chapter in my life was beginning. There was still one more big topic to sort out but it would have to wait. I was nervous because I didn't know what the outcome would be. In the beginning I'd promised Nash Ryan friendship and no hassles, no complications.

I couldn't keep that promise anymore.

I just didn't know if he wanted the same things I did.

Chapter Twenty-Three

Nash

I debated whether or not to bring Colin with me. I could have found someone to watch him for a few hours. But in the end I decided to pack up the diaper bag and bring him along. Today's journey belonged to him as much as it belonged to me. He had a right to be there.

Car rides usually lulled Colin to sleep and sure enough he was knocked out less than ten minutes into the drive. I turned the radio down to low volume and piloted the mini van up the winding roads that led deep into the mountains.

Years had passed since I'd been up here but I still knew the route by heart. Some of the hairpin turns were a little harrowing but there was no one else on the road. We were still a few miles away from the cabin when blackened vegetation began to appear on both sides of the road, a reminder of what had happened up here in the not too distant past.

There was something eerie and unnatural about the giant charred trees flanking the asphalt. This pocket of the world had always been lush and green and would be again someday. But it would take awhile.

I passed the turnoff to the small lake where my dad and I had spent our disastrous fishing excursions. I hoped it had been spared the devastation that rocketed through here on a night of high winds and brutal destiny.

Here and there were private unpaved lanes that meandered off the main road and led to rustic mountain homes. There were people who lived up here year round but not many and none of them were in the zone where the fire swept through with such ferocity. There was only one tragic story from that night and I was about to confront it.

My stomach clenched when I came to the turnoff. I pulled off to the side and idled at the mouth of the dirt road leading to the two bedroom cabin that had been in my family for fifty years. The tall pines that had once stood proudly along the half mile corridor leading to the cabin were now singed husks. I wondered if this had been a mistake. I wasn't sure what I hoped to gain by coming up here.

"In these parts you've always got to pay attention to the fire warnings, Nash. Take the No Burn days seriously and get the hell out of Dodge the minute you smell smoke."

Forest fires weren't that unusual in the mountains. On average there'd be a notable one about once every four or five years. Fatalities were uncommon. Typically there was a warning with enough time to escape the fire.

I turned up the road, unsure of what I'd find at the end of it. Kevin Reston had said the cabin was unsalvageable, just a burned out pile of logs. Steve Brown told me about some insurance on the place but I just told him to do what he needed to do and not bug me about it.

The damage was worse around here. This must have been where the fire had reached its peak before the combined efforts of fire crews and full rain clouds put an end to its ferocity. I hated to think of the two of them in the middle of it, their final moments of terror, their agonized thoughts of the baby boy they were leaving behind.

Someone had been here recently to pay their respects. A friend most likely. Chris and Heather Ryan had so many friends. There was a fresh floral arrangement in the middle of all the devastation, a spot of bright pink among the ruins. The cabin itself was unrecognizable.

It looked like someone had taken a pile of Lincoln Logs, scorched them in a barbecue and haphazardly rearranged them in the dirt. My father's truck had been towed out of here so there was no sign of where it had been parked but I would bet he'd parked in the same spot he always parked, a small clearing along the west side of the cabin. That's where they'd been found, beside the truck.

I opened the windows and cut the engine. There was absolute quiet but somehow it wasn't horrible. I'd imagined it to be horrible, a thick silence full of death. But this was more peaceful than I'd expected.

Now that we'd stopped moving, Colin stirred in his car seat. I hopped out and slid open the door to extract him, checking his diaper out of habit. My little brother blinked at the sunlight overhead as I settled him on my hip and grabbed the objects I'd brought along with me. I'd found them in the attic the other day when I was stowing some of the crap I'd brought from Oregon. At first I thought maybe I could used them sometime, when Colin was older. He might like to learn how to fish. But I decided the best idea would be to retire these poles and get new ones. These fishing poles had too much to do with my dad and me. Colin deserved one of his own.

I set the poles down in the middle of the clearing. One full-sized pole, one child-sized. They looked a little plain there so I plucked one of the pink roses from the flower arrangement and carefully set it on top. I assumed whoever had placed the flowers there wouldn't mind sharing.

Colin uttered a few babbling consonants, something he'd been doing lately. I was aware of how much responsibility I had. There was so much to tell him. Of course some pieces of the story he'd never have to know. There were a few parts I would have done over again if I could.

"Goodbye, Dad," I whispered, staring down at the fishing poles I'd placed side by side.

I still wondered about their reasons, why Chris and Heather had chosen me to take care of Colin if they couldn't.

"Because he knew you'd rise to the challenge, that you'd love and protect that baby boy. Chris and Heather never doubted you"

That's what Kat had said. I just didn't understand why it was true. What the hell had I ever done to earn this kind of trust from them? I wished there was someone I could ask.

If Kat were here she'd probably have some fitting words to say at an emotional moment like this. Kat was good at words. She was good at everything that mattered. But Kathleen Doyle's best talent proved to be awakening my heart in a way that no one else ever had.

I thought about her down there in Phoenix, bravely facing her own troubled past for the sake of her daughter. I was glad she'd decided to go. I'd be even more glad when she came back. There were things we needed to talk about.

"Let's get out of here," I said to Colin and kissed his cheek before carrying him back to the van.

The scars on the land would fade but I doubted I'd come back to this particular spot again. That didn't mean I wouldn't return to the mountains. Despite what happened I was sure my father would want Colin to know the woods, to have the satisfaction of pulling a fat rainbow trout out of the lake and appreciating how much brighter the stars are in the wilderness. I could show him those things. Maybe Kat and Emma would want to come with us.

Suddenly there was a plan in my head. Actually, it had been there for a while, right on the fringes. Now all the pieces were falling together and it was time to act. A new beginning could happen. All I needed was a little bit of help to get there.

I felt far more relaxed on the drive back down the mountain. Even though there was probably some kind of rule in the baby books against it, I took Colin to an ice cream parlor and shared a vanilla cone with him. He freaking loved it, practically gobbled my hand right off while I was holding the thing.

While we were sitting at the table closest to the window, I spotted my old nemesis Travis Hanson coming down the sidewalk. I'd heard how he'd been arrested last week. The story around town was that one of his employees had pressed assault charges against him. So it seemed that sometimes the wheels of justice turned just as they were supposed to.

Travis must have sensed someone watching him because he suddenly stopped and raised his head. Our eyes locked and I waved to him on the other side of the glass. He scowled and stalked away. I chuckled to myself and polished off the rest of the ice cream cone.

Unfortunately we couldn't hang out and eat ice cream all day because there was too much to do. In the parking lot of the ice cream place I drummed my fingers on the steering wheel and considered my options. Asking for help still wasn't a thing I got excited about.

I turned around and addressed Colin's head in his rear facing car seat. "Let's do this, little man."

He belched.

I grinned. Then I called my aunt.

"Jane," I said. "You free today? I was wondering if I could get your help with a few things at the house. And if Kevin's around it would be great if you could bring him along. Oh, and I don't have the number for Kathleen's mother but if you could call her and ask her to meet us there at the house I'd appreciate it. Yeah, I'm sure."

Before I drove home I stopped at the store and bought some moving boxes. I didn't know how many I'd need but I figured this stack was a good start.

It was time to move forward. Things would happen. I was determined that from now on they would be only good things.

Chapter Twenty-Four

Kathleen

"WHY DOES THAT TREE LOOK FUNNY?" EMMA ASKED.

I smiled when I realized she was pointing to a giant saguaro cactus. She'd never seen one before.

"It's a different kind of tree," I told her. "It's called a cactus. They only grow in the desert and instead of leaves they have needles."

"Is this the desert?"

We passed a residential neighborhood full of beige houses with tiled roofs. "Yes, honey. Phoenix is part of the desert."

"And my second grandma is here?" Emma sounded doubtful.

"Yes." The handful of butterflies in my stomach had swollen to a swarm now that we were getting close. I'd texted Harrison before we left the hotel and let him know we were on our way. He said they were eagerly waiting and gave me the gate code for the community.

I turned into the entrance and pulled up to the keypad to open the gates while feeling a brief stab of déjà vu. I'd been here a few times before, when I was with Harrison. The last time was a Thanksgiving holiday when I sat between Harrison and Randall, laughing at the way they playfully aggravated each other the way brothers did. Mrs. Corbett winked at me from across the table. Her husband had died the year before and I remembered feeling a little melancholy at the thought of her living alone in that big, elegant house.

And there it was.

The Corbett home was a sprawling Mediterranean-style building that blended into the upscale neighborhood. I spotted Harrison's silver Mustang parked out front and felt a surge of anxiety. I hoped I was doing the right thing for Emma. I thought I was.

They must have been watching through the window, waiting for us to drive up. I held onto Emma's hand as we walked up the front path and saw the door open. Harrison was there, his arm around the shoulders of a slender woman who looked to be in her late twenties. Her dark skinned beauty was complemented by the bright blue dress she wore. She looked right into my eyes with a warm smile that couldn't have been faked and I felt my misgivings disappear.

"Hello Kathleen," said Harrison. "We're so glad you both are here." His gaze rested on my daughter and I could see how emotional this moment was for him. I'd never given much thought to how shattered he must have been by the death of his only brother. They'd been very close.

"Hello Emma," he said, his voice catching.

Emma stared at him, then looked up at me as if unsure whether she should respond to this strange man.

The woman at Harrison's side took the initiative, stepping forward.

"Kathleen," she said. "I'm so happy to meet you. I'm Delia, Harrison's fiancé."

Her accent sounded vaguely Caribbean and instead of a polite handshake she enveloped me in a warm hug. I didn't mind.

Delia bent down to Emma's level. "Hello, Emma. We've been waiting to meet you."

My daughter looked her over. "Your dress is pretty."

Delia laughed and hugged her too. "Thank you sweetheart."

Delia was charming and Emma was all smiles as she took Delia's hand and followed her into the house. Harrison stayed back, by the door. He watched his fiancé pass by with his niece and then turned to me. An awkward moment of silence ensued.

"I don't know how to thank you for this, Kat."

"You already thanked me, Harrison. Anyway, I'm doing this for Emma. And for your mother." I paused. "I'm still not sure about you."

He nodded and looked embarrassed. "I'm sorry. And I'm sure you don't want to hear it after all this time, but you were never just some girl to me. I was devastated when I lost you even though I deserved to. And I know I said a lot of terrible things."

He had. Harrison found out about Randall and me just before his brother died and he didn't take the news well. I never got the chance to tell Randall I was pregnant. But in a moment of weakness I went and told Harrison. The last time we spoke he'd called me an evil slut, among other things. He said he and his family would have nothing to do with me, warned that he'd pay me off if he had to. I didn't give him the chance. In the months that followed there were many nights when I'd lie awake, feeling the baby kick inside my belly and remembering the hatred in the eyes of the man I'd once thought I loved.

"What happened between Randall and me," I said, "was not planned, and we weren't trying to hurt you. Don't get me wrong, I was furious with you for making a fool out of me. In fact I was crushed. Harrison, I swear I wasn't seeking revenge with your brother when I turned to him. But I know I shouldn't have and I'm sorry about that." I took a breath and looked at the house where Emma's father had grown up. "I really did care about Randall. I wanted to help him."

There was no hatred in Harrison's eyes right now. Only regret. "I can accept that," he said. "If you can accept my apology."

I thought about it. "I think we can both let the past go and move forward now."

He smiled. "How about we go inside and introduce Emma to her grandmother?"

I smiled back. "I'd like that."

Inside the house, Delia was listening to Emma talk up a storm.

"And she's so fun. And she makes me so happy. Roxie's the best dog in the world."

Delia listened with a polite smile. "Roxie is your dog's name?"

"Yeah. She's just Nash's dog now. But she will be my dog."

Delia nodded. "I see. She sounds wonderful."

"She is."

Delia looked over at us while Harrison closed the front door. The house was just as I remembered it, flawlessly and expensively decorated. Harrison nodded at his fiancé and she reached out to take his hand.

"Should we go in?" she asked.

"Yes," he said. "I'm sure she's listening."

Emma slipped her hand into mine as we followed Harrison and Delia down a long corridor. There was a room at the end and the door was open. Delia looked over her shoulder and offered a smile of encouragement.

Harrison poked his head in the door. "Mom?" he said softly. "Are you awake?"

"Yes," answered a high, quavering voice. "Are they here? Is Emma here?"

Emma suddenly pulled back and looked up at me worriedly.

"It's okay," I assured her and led her into the room.

The woman in the bed only faintly resembled the fashionable middle-aged woman who'd smiled indulgently at her two rowdy sons across a table one Thanksgiving evening. Her head was covered by a scarf and the king sized bed only emphasized how her once stout frame had been ravaged by the cancer. Harrison immediately went to her side when she struggled to sit up. There were pill bottles and other medical paraphernalia collected on a small table and the room was very warm, probably for Mrs. Corbett's benefit.

Harrison carefully propped his mother up on the plush bed pillows and her gaunt face surveyed us. The only unchanged feature was the color of her warm brown eyes that widened when they landed on Emma.

"Hello darling," she said and held out her hand, beckoning Emma to come forward. "I'm your grandma and I'm so happy to meet you."

I'd tried my best to make Emma understand the reality of the situation. Her grandmother was very sick. She would look sick and probably wouldn't be able to get out of bed. Emma was a sensitive child but she was also three and a half and unpredictable at times. I wasn't sure how she'd react to all the emotion in the room.

"Hi," Emma said and willingly approached the bed. Emma and her grandmother examined each other up close for a few seconds.

"How come you're wearing a hat in bed?" Emma asked with curiosity and Mrs. Corbett chuckled.

I breathed a sigh of relief. This would be all right. Everything would be all right.

Mrs. Corbett told Emma she had something very special for her and motioned to Harrison to bring forward a large pink gift bag. Emma wasted no time getting the tissue paper out of the way and pulled out an adorable stuffed animal that kind of looked like a plush puppy version of Roxie.

Emma's eyes widened and she clutched the toy to her chest. "She's bee-yoo-tiful," my daughter said in an awed voice and I thought poor Mr. Ford might have just been demoted.

There were tears in Mrs. Corbett's eyes. "*You're* beautiful."

Emma looked at the woman. "Are you sad?"

"No, honey. I'm not sad. This is a happy day. I was just remembering how your father used to have a stuffed dog just like that."

"Is he here?" Emma asked.

I flinched. Harrison glanced at me with a worried expression. I'd also attempted to explain Emma's father to her but there were only so many complicated topics you could burden a preschooler with.

"Emma," I said gently, bending down to her side. "Remember when we talked about your father? About how he's gone?"

She nodded slowly. "Like Aunt Heather and Uncle Chris," she whispered and I thought how unfair it was that she'd already been exposed to so much death when she scarcely understood the concept. She'd lost her father. She'd lost the people who were practically surrogate parents to her. And soon she would lose this grandmother she'd only just met. No, it wasn't fair. But I had hope too. I hoped she wouldn't forget that life is a fragile thing, to be cherished unreservedly.

"That's right," I said and hugged her close, stuffed dog and all.

Emma was quick to rebound and began bouncing her new toy on the bed. Suddenly she noticed Harrison standing on the far side of the room.

"Do you live here too?"

He seemed startled that she was speaking directly to him. "I used to. Now Delia and I live about fifteen miles away."

"Why?"

"Because when you grow up you move away and find your own home."

"Why?"

He smiled. "It's just something people do."

Emma didn't like that answer. "I don't want to move away from my mommy."

I laughed. "Don't worry about that anytime soon, Ems."

"Kathleen." Mrs. Corbett was addressing me in a gentle voice. She held out her hand and I reached out to take it, noting how thin and frail hers was.

"I'm sorry I never brought her to see you sooner," I said but she shook her head vehemently.

"No. You've given me an incredible gift. There have been so many misunderstandings." She cast a sharp look over at her remaining son. "Let's not have any more. I'm so grateful to you for bringing Emma here. And I'm very thankful that Randall's child has such a wonderful mother." She turned to Emma and beamed. "Emma, will you come sit close to me? There's a book I'd like to read to you."

Delia took that as a sign. She reached for a faded children's book on the dresser and handed it to Mrs. Corbett. I caught a glimpse of the title. It was *Love You Forever* and I figured it must have belonged to her sons when they were little.

Emma settled herself and her new stuffed toy on the bed and prepared to listen to the story. Emma loved books. Even more than she loved strawberries.

Perhaps not quite as much as she loved dogs.

"Kathleen," Delia whispered and I saw she and Harrison had left the room and were standing just outside the door.

Mrs. Corbett began reading to Emma in a voice that was now surprisingly strong and clear. I stood up and backed out of the room. They were already so engrossed in the story they didn't see me go.

Delia was holding onto Harrison's arm and I got the impression he was nervous. She looked at her fiancé as if urging him to speak but when he didn't she forged ahead.

"Kathleen, we don't want you to feel pressured in any way. There aren't enough words of thanks to express our gratitude."

She looked at Harrison again and this time he cleared his throat. "We'd love to see Emma again," he said. "If that's okay with you. She's my niece and when I look at her I remember how much I loved my brother. And how much I miss him."

I looked behind me, into the room where Emma was hanging on every word her grandmother read to her. I'd been so used to having Emma to myself it almost felt strange to share her with another family. But I shouldn't feel that way. This would be her family too.

"I think Emma would enjoy that," I said.

Harrison looked relieved. "And if you need any financial help we'd be happy to-"

"I don't," I interrupted, bristling. "I don't need any financial help."

He backed off. "I didn't mean that the way it came out. We have no intention of intruding on your life or dictating terms. But Emma is Randall's little girl and I just wanted to let you know that we're here for her."

"And for you," Delia added. "We're here for you too, Kathleen. I'm really hoping we can be friends."

They looked so earnest, so hopeful. In the other room Emma

and her grandmother broke into laughter.

"I'd like to be your friend," I told Delia and I meant it.

The three of us stayed just outside the room for a little while longer, giving Emma and her grandmother their privacy to get to know each other. I learned Harrison had become a financial advisor and I had some trouble imagining the brash football guy I'd known in college sitting across a conference table and advising couples on 401K plans. But things change. People change. Delia was pursuing a PhD in biochemistry and planned to eventually become a professor.

"That used to be my plan," I said. "To become a professor."

She was thoughtful. "You still can. It's not too late."

I considered the idea. "You're right," I said. "It's not too late."

A hospice nurse arrived just before lunch to check on Mrs. Corbett. Her presence was a sobering reminder that the woman in the next room did not have long to live.

Harrison thought his mother was getting too tired but she protested and begged if Emma could stay a little while longer. A compromise was reached where she agreed to rest for an hour while Delia made lunch. The adults enjoyed lemon chicken with quinoa while Emma munched on a grilled cheese sandwich with a side of strawberries. Emma delighted the table with tales from preschool and after I finished eating I excused myself for a moment to text Nash. He'd been a little apprehensive about this trip and I just wanted to let him know he didn't need to worry about anything.

Everything is fine. Emma met her grandmother and was gifted with a synthetic Roxie replacement. Thinking of you guys.

I was about to stick my phone back in my bag but then decided on one more line.

I miss you so much.

When our roles had been reversed recently Nash had said that to me. I hadn't said it back at the time even though he was constantly on my mind. I waited for a few minutes but there was no reply. Maybe he hadn't seen it right away. Nash didn't always keep his phone right by his side.

Delia's rich laughter came from the dining room, followed by Emma's high giggle. I stayed where I was for another few seconds and just listened. We'd spend a few more hours here and then hit the road so we'd be back in Hawk Valley before dinner. I was already thinking I'd offer to drive Emma down here again real soon. The memories Emma was building today would be precious to her. She should have the chance to make more.

I'd decided something else too. Before we went home tonight I'd stop to see Nash. I needed to tell him how I felt about him. If he didn't feel the same it was better to know that now, while I might still be able to salvage pieces of my heart. If I fell for him any harder I wasn't sure if I'd recover.

"Mommy!" sang Emma. "Where are you?"

"I'm here," I said, smiling as I returned to the dining room.

Chapter Twenty-Five

Nash

We were still deciding on categories when Kathleen's mother showed up.

"What's all this?" Eleanor Doyle demanded to know after she barged through the front door. I guess that served me right for not locking it.

She frowned when she saw all the boxes on the living room floor. Kevin was hunched down, scrawling on one with a black marker while Jane wrapped a crystal vase in bubble wrap.

"Hello Eleanor," Jane said.

"Are you moving?" Kathleen's mother asked me. I thought she sounded a little too hopeful.

"No," I answered. "We're working on boxing up some of Chris and Heather's personal effects. I figured it was about time and since Heather was your niece I thought we could use your help to decide what's best."

All of that was true but I also had another reason for calling Kathleen's mother. I was shamelessly trying to insert myself into her good graces because I wanted to impress her daughter.

"Hey there, Eleanor," Kevin chimed in.

She looked in his direction and nodded before turning back to me.

"The important things, the sentimental things, will be boxed up and stored in the attic," I said. "But I'm guessing most of the clothes can go to charity." I paused. "What do you think?"

Eleanor continued to stare at me, then slowly nodded. "I think Heather would approve. And my church is having a rummage sale on Saturday. So anything you're looking to donate I can certainly take off your hands."

I smiled. "Thanks, that would be great. I knew we could count on you." I was piling it on a little thick and Kevin raised an eyebrow at me as if to say he detected a significant rise in my bullshit meter but Eleanor blushed and seemed satisfied.

She offered to start in the master bedroom and sort through Heather's things, which was a relief because I still felt a little weird being in there. I'd have to get over that. I couldn't just close off the room forever and keep it as some kind of gothic shrine. It wouldn't be healthy for Colin, for any of us.

Jane followed Eleanor up the stairs with some boxes, leaving Kevin and me alone in the living room.

I picked up a glass plate that was on a display stand on the end table. It looked old, probably an antique.

"You want to box up *all* the breakables?" Kevin asked.

I nodded. "Most of them. Colin's almost ready to crawl. Then he'll be walking. So a lot of baby proofing is in order." I picked up some bubble wrap. "This stuff will go in the attic for now."

"Nash."

I looked up and found my father's old friend with a pained expression. "I've been meaning to talk to you for awhile, about that night at Sheen's."

"No need for that."

"Yes there is. You were right about Travis, no mystery there. But I need to apologize for what I said to you. I told you I thought you'd fucking grown up a little, implying that you were still the same reckless kid you always had been."

I tore off a length of bubble wrap. "I remember."

"I was wrong," Kevin said flatly. "You've stepped up around here in a way that I didn't expect. I see the way you are with Colin, how hard you're trying. And I admire you, Nash. Your dad knew what he was doing when he put you in charge."

I saw him glance at a photo of my father and Heather on their wedding day. Their arms were wrapped around each other and their faces were ecstatic. I wished I'd been there that day. I wished I'd let go of whatever anger I'd been holding onto. I'd wasted so much time. At least there was no more anger left now. I realized suddenly that I'd forgiven both of them a long time ago. They'd found each other and fell in love and it had nothing to do with me. I should have said that. Now it was too late.

Except it wasn't. Because there was Colin. Perhaps that's why they'd chosen me as his guardian. Maybe it was my father's way of saying that he knew I wouldn't hold a grudge, and that he had more faith in me than I'd ever guessed. They had to have known somehow, Chris and Heather. They'd been confident I'd step into this role if it was ever necessary. I'd never squander that faith.

"Maybe we can go catch a drink sometime," I said to Kevin. "Someplace other than Sheen's."

He grinned. "You got it."

I finished wrapping up the antique plate. It would be put away. But the pictures would all stay. Colin would be able to see his parents and maybe feel as if they were watching over him somehow.

"You think we have enough bubble wrap?" I asked.

Kevin looked around. "I can run out and get more if necessary."

The baby monitor had been left on the couch and it crackled to life as Colin woke up in his crib and started babbling. I knew he'd probably entertain himself for a few minutes before demanding some attention so I wrapped up a few more valuables in the meantime.

When five minutes had passed and he wasn't howling to be picked up I wondered if he'd dropped back to sleep so I went upstairs to check. I could see into the master bedroom where Eleanor Doyle was folding clothes with marvelous efficiency and placing them in organized piles on the bed. She didn't notice me as I passed by and went straight to Colin's room. I was a little surprised by what I found there.

Jane had picked up Colin and was rocking him in the chair beside the window. Jane rarely picked up the baby and whenever she did she seemed eager to put him down again as quickly as possible. She was showing him something on her phone, a cartoon maybe. I didn't know how much Colin was getting out of it but he appeared to be interested.

"Everything okay?" I asked and Colin's face immediately turned to the sound of my voice. He bounced with excitement in Jane's lap.

"He woke up," Jane said, lowering the phone. "I just came in to see him. I hope it's okay."

I leaned against the changing table. "Of course it's okay. You're his aunt."

She cupped Colin's head in her palm and regarded him thoughtfully. "I remember you when you were this age, Nash." She looked over at me. "It's hard to believe now. You're taller than your father was."

I gestured to the phone. "What were you guys looking at?"

"Oh! I found a video I'd taken at the hospital the day Colin was born so I was showing him. Here." She held the phone out to me. "You really should watch it too."

The video was only a few minutes long and I started it from the beginning. They were in the hospital, probably mere hours after Colin's birth. Heather looked tired but radiant as she cuddled her new bundle of joy. She was staring down at the baby when my father appeared. He knelt by the bed, peered into the blue blanket that swaddled his newborn son and gave his wife a soft kiss. She smiled at him, then returned her loving gaze to the baby.

"Hey Jane, what do you think of your new nephew?" my father asked.

"He's beautiful," Jane's voice said from behind the camera.

"Just like his brother," my dad said. He leaned against the wall and crossed his arms with a happy grin plastered across the face. "Can't believe I'm a new dad again at forty-five."

"Old timer," Heather teased with a laugh.

"But you want to know something?" he said. "I've learned to treasure every moment, something I didn't know how to do when Nash was born."

"Did you call him?" Heather asked. "Did you call Nash?"

"I called him, told him he's finally got a brother. He sounded happy." My dad looked thoughtful, hopeful. "I'm thinking he might come for a visit."

Colin made a noise and Heather soothed him while my father stared at them.

"Two sons," he said, sounding a little awed. "Two perfect boys who are my pride and joy." He then looked straight at the camera. "I still can't believe my luck."

"Colin." Heather sang the name as she rocked the baby back and forth. "Colin, did you know you have a big brother? And he's going to love you." She kissed the sleeping face in her arms. "I promise he's going to love you."

My father sat on the edge of the bed and placed an arm around his wife and son. The camera continued to watch the family for another thirty seconds but they didn't seem to be aware of it.

Chris Ryan hadn't been perfect. Nobody was. But as I watched the last few seconds of the video I realized I could learn from his triumphs. And his mistakes. That's the best any of us can do.

"I promise he's going to love you."

And I did. I loved that baby so damn much it hurt. He'd grow up with the pain of losing his parents before he knew them. I'd do anything I could to help him navigate the strange and sometimes excruciating realities that challenged us in this life. Because it could also be wonderful. And loving other people was what made it worthwhile.

"Oh, Nash," Jane said when the video finished playing and I was wiping at my eyes. "I'm sorry. I didn't mean to upset you."

My aunt looked distressed, on the verge of tears now herself.

"No, it's okay," I said, swiping at the last of the sudden tears. I handed her the phone back. "Thank you for showing me that. Actually if you could send it to me that would be great. Colin will want to see it someday."

"Of course."

Colin shifted in her arms and she started to look a little flustered so I reached out to take him.

"It's a really good thing you're doing," Jane said and stood up. "Staying here, raising him in this house. You're giving him the life Chris and Heather wanted for him. I knew you would. You're the only one who could have."

"Thanks, Jane," I said as Colin tried to grab my left ear.

My aunt's smile now turned a little devilish. "I knew you'd love her too. I knew it when I saw you together."

"Who?" I asked even though I knew damn well who.

"Kathleen."

I didn't answer. I bounced Colin and he squealed with delight.

"You do, don't you?" Jane pressed. "You do love her."

Eleanor Doyle suddenly appeared in the doorway.

"Are there more boxes?" she asked. "I'm going to need at least three more for the clothes alone."

"There are some more downstairs," I said, glad for the chance to escape Jane's scrutiny. "Follow me."

Before I left the room I looked over my shoulder and Jane gave me a knowing smirk. There was an easy answer to her question but I wasn't ready to disclose my feelings for Kat until I actually talked to Kat first. I owed her that and anyway I might be barking up the wrong tree. Kat might be happy keeping things just the way they were and I wasn't excited for everyone to witness a savage blow to my pride. And to my heart.

Kevin was already taping up some of the boxes downstairs and offered to start moving them into the attic. Eleanor and Jane grabbed more boxes for the clothes and headed back upstairs.

"You must be hungry," I said to Colin after I'd changed his diaper.

"Babababa," Colin answered. I didn't know if the sound had any meaning for him but it was awesome to hear him try.

After I mixed up a bottle I found my phone on the kitchen table. There were a few messages from Kathleen. I was glad to hear everything had gone well. She and Emma had been on my mind a lot. Her second text made me smile.

As soon as she got back to town I'd corner her for a very important conversation. I just hoped she liked hearing what I had to say.

Chapter Twenty-Six

Kathleen

Hawk Valley probably didn't look like much to people who were used to more exotic places. You have to drive north on the Interstate out of Phoenix for a hundred miles, then merge onto the smaller state highway for another thirty miles before you catch your first glimpse of the valley at the base of the stately Hawk Mountains.

I drove past one landmark after another, feeling the sweet familiarity of coming home. There was the small campus of Hawk Valley College, then the restored old courthouse, just before the main drag, Garner Avenue. I squinted as I passed Nash's store, wondering if he was there today. Even if he was, chances were he'd left by now to go pick up Colin.

It was nearly 7 p.m., later than I'd expected to return. Emma napped in the backseat with her arms around Roxie Jr., as she'd christened the stuffed animal from her grandmother. I couldn't have asked for a better day for my girl but I was relieved that it was over.

On the seat beside me in a paper shopping bag were some things that Mrs. Corbett had wanted me to keep for Emma. One was the book they'd read, a favorite of Randall's when he was her age. There was also a photo box filled with Corbett family pictures and a framed eight by ten photo of Randall taken during his senior year of high school, just a few years before I met him and his brother at Arizona State.

I found myself wondering what Randall would have said about today, how he would have felt about being a father. Yesterday I applied for a change to Emma's birth certificate to show the rightful name of her father. The two of us would not have ended up together no matter what. It just wasn't meant to be. But maybe the knowledge of impending parenthood would have convinced him to get the help he so desperately needed. Or maybe not. In any case Randall had a gentle heart so I liked to think that he would have adored his daughter if he'd known her.

It was mid summer and the remnants of sunlight lingered well into the evening. I liked this time of day, suspended between daylight and darkness, when the light became soft and generated friendly shadows.

At the stoplight on Garner Avenue I peeked back at Emma. We'd stopped for dinner along the way and she might be ready for bed after such an exciting day.

But her eyes were open now and she was looking out the window.

"This is home," she said, sounding surprised and delighted.

"Yup, we're back in Hawk Valley."

She yawned. "What do we do now?"

I knew exactly what I wanted to do now.

"Would you like to introduce Roxie to Roxie Jr.?" I asked.

Her face lit up. "Yes!"

"Good. That's what we're doing."

I made a right turn at the light, into the neighborhood dotted with old Victorian homes. There was a brief twinge of doubt as I approached Nash's street. He'd never texted me back today and I hadn't called to let him know I was stopping by. Maybe this would come across as needy, intrusive.

I brushed aside the thought. I'd closed my heart to the possibility of love for too long. Even if I humiliated myself today and was forced to face the fact that Nash didn't feel the same way, I still wouldn't be sorry. It was time to put myself out there and find out what could come of it.

But when I pulled up to the curb in front of Nash's house I did a double take.

"Is that Grandma?" Emma asked.

"Uh, sure looks like her," I said, cutting the engine.

My mother was standing on Nash's front lawn and and holding Colin while Nash loaded some boxes into the trunk of her Toyota. She was laughing. Then she waved at me. It was odd.

Emma didn't think so. She unbuckled herself from her car seat, which I have ordered her at least seven hundred and twenty six times *not* to do, and tried to bolt from the car.

"Mommy," she complained. "I can't get out!"

I sighed and released the child lock. Emma bounded across Nash's front lawn with Roxie Jr. hanging from one hand.

"Look what I got! My other grandma gave him to me!" Emma held up the toy as proof. Colin hiccupped and stared at her with fascination. My mother caught my eye as I made my way over.

"So it went well?" she asked me.

"Yes. We had a lovely day, didn't we, Ems?"

Emma was trying to place Roxie Jr. in Colin's arms. "I had fun."

Nash closed the trunk of the car and headed toward us. He was wearing faded jeans and a white t-shirt that had definitely seen better days and he looked so good my knees nearly gave out. Then he smiled at me and I had to remind myself to breathe.

"You're home," he said.

I wanted to run to him, jump into his arms, bury my face in his neck and inhale the warmth of skin.

"I'm home," I said and we stared at each other. There was more heat in that mutual stare than there was contained on planet Mercury.

"Well," my mother said. "Who wants to take this little gentleman? I've got to go."

That reminded me that I still didn't understand why she was here in the first place. Nash held his arms out to receive his baby brother.

"Thanks for all your help today, Eleanor," he said.

"Of course," she said and pecked me on the cheek. "Call me tomorrow, Kat. I want to hear all about your visit." She bent down to kiss Emma, then folded herself into her car and was gone.

I turned to Nash. "What on earth just happened?"

Nash was amused. "Your mom and I were hanging out today. She's actually a pretty cool lady."

"I know she's a cool lady."

"And I see where you get your organizational skills from."

"That's not really a complete answer to my question."

"I see where you get your bossy instincts from too."

"Nash!"

He grinned and without warning locked a hand around my neck, pulling me in for a kiss. We couldn't get all exotic about it with two kids looking on but the touch of his lips was enough to get my head spinning. It was also enough to shut me up. Which was probably what he'd intended.

"We did some work on the house," he said.

"You and my mother?""

"And Kevin and Jane."

I was confused. "What kind of work?"

"Baby proofing. This little guy is getting ready to be mobile." He held Colin up high above his head and the baby laughed with delight. Nash was smiling when he brought him back down. Then his smile faded. "We also cleaned out the master bedroom. It was time. Kept the sentimental items, boxed them up and put them in the attic. Your mother took the boxes filled with clothes because she knew a good cause that could use a few more donations."

"I see," I said, a little stunned that Nash had taken this step. The last time I'd addressed the topic of Chris and Heather's belongings he'd cut me off and changed the subject.

"Where's Roxie?" Emma demanded. "I want to show her Roxie Jr."

Nash pointed to the stuffed dog in her arms. "Is that Roxie Jr.?"

Emma nodded. "I love her less than Roxie but I love her too."

He laughed. "Roxie's been in the backyard most of the day. I know she's been waiting for you to come back though." He held out his hand. "Come on. Let's go see her."

Emma slipped her little hand into Nash's large one and they walked toward the wooden gate that led to the backyard. For a second I couldn't move. I just stood back and admired them; Nash carrying Colin in one arm while Emma trustingly allowed him to lead her with his other hand. I wanted to imprint the vision in my mind forever.

Nash unlocked the gate and looked over his shoulder. "You coming?"

I nodded. "Where else would I go?"

Roxie was so happy she cried and darted from person to person in search of affection. Emma allowed her face to be licked and then ran everywhere in the grass while Roxie zoomed all around in circles. A near tragedy occurred when Roxie grabbed Roxie Jr. around the neck but Nash intervened in a flash, returning the toy to Emma, who was very forgiving.

"You don't know how much she loves that dog," I laughed when he returned.

He sat down on a cushioned patio sofa. "I have an idea." He looked me up and down, setting off another involuntary chain reaction in my body. "Sit down, Kat."

I plopped down right beside him. The light was fading fast now. Emma was a short, pale tornado in the grass, Roxie a hairy whirlwind.

"Long day," I commented and rubbed at the back of my neck.

Nash balanced Colin on one knee and reached over to massage the spot for me. I let him. He was so much better at it.

"Tell me," he said.

"Later." I wanted to talk about something else first. "How come you decided to do this today? To clean out the house?"

"I told you. It was time. They would have wanted it this way. They would have wanted life to keep moving."

"Chris and Heather?"

He nodded. He was staring out at the backyard shadows, watching my daughter and his dog.

"Besides, I needed to make room."

"For what?"

"The new residents."

"Are you renting out rooms or something?"

"Or something."

"I don't get it."

He stopped massaging my neck and turned to me with a penetrating stare. "We have to talk."

I swallowed. "About what?"

"I'm no longer satisfied with our arrangement."

I looked down, not sure if I wanted to hear this or not. "Is that right?"

"Yes." He pulled me close and softly brushed his lips over mine, sending chills through every inch of my body. No one else had ever done that to me. No one else ever could.

"I want more from you, Kat," he said and curled his strong arm all the way around me. "I want more from you and I have more to give you."

"You told me you don't like hassles," I whispered. "Or complications."

"You are neither."

I touched his face. "What am I?"

He didn't hesitate. "Mine. You're mine."

He'd just uttered the words of my dreams. Maybe that's why I found myself unable to talk.

Nash was watching me. "Kat?"

I blinked.

"I love you," he said.

This moment is everything. He is everything.

But now he was looking a shade worried because I'd become catatonic.

"I love you," he repeated. "Live with me. You and Emma. You said you'd have to find a new apartment soon. So live here with us. Kat, this old house could use some happiness. We all could."

Colin waved his arms in the air. Maybe he was imitating Emma as she pranced around in the grass. Maybe he was trying to weigh into the conversation.

"Nash," I said and closed my eyes. There were so many thoughts racing through my head and yet I had no words. I'd always been great with words and now they'd deserted me when I needed them the most.

Suddenly I found the words I'd been searching for. They weren't hard to say at all.

"I love you too."

Chapter Twenty-Seven

Nash

SHE WAS RIGHT ON TIME. OF COURSE.

Kat strolled through the door of Hawk Valley Gifts with her laptop bag on her arm and those rowdy curls contained in a loose bun. Her long navy blue skirt would have looked modest on another woman but on Kat it highlighted the shape of her incredible ass and beckoned to me like an invitation to that luscious back door.

"Are you ready for our meeting, Mr. Ryan?" she asked and from the way she smirked I could tell she guessed the trajectory of my thoughts.

I cupped my hand over my dick and rubbed just enough to make sure she understood what I had in mind. "I'm ready."

Kat set her bag down, unfastened the first two buttons of her white blouse, then released the front clasp of her bra. God bless her. And those tits.

She watched me while I walked around her and locked the door after ensuring the CLOSED sign was still out. We wouldn't open for another half hour and the college student who would be running the cash register this morning wouldn't be here until then.

"Not so careless anymore," she remarked, referencing the fact that I hadn't always bothered to lock the door. Kat set her hand on her hip and I got a tantalizing peek of a nipple.

"I just don't want any interruptions," I said, closing in. I was ready to get my hands on her. I ran my palms over her hips and around to her ass so I could press against her hard. I wanted her to feel how hard I was. That breathy little sigh escaping her lips told me she was getting all kinds of hot and bothered. If I slid my hand down into the waistband of her skirt and went exploring I knew I'd find some damp panties and eager flesh.

And, lo and behold, that's exactly what I did find.

"Fuck," she moaned, straining against my hand, trying to get my fingers to go deeper. I liked her like this; needy and dirty. Ready to let me finger her or fuck her in the middle of an aisle full of coffee mugs and cheesy Hawk Valley t-shirts.

But I was in the mood to take my time so I didn't do either one. I withdrew my hand from between her legs and wordlessly led her to the back office. I barely had time to shut the door before Kat dropped her skirt.

"Shirt too," I demanded because I always demanded that.

She finished escaping her clothes and sat down on the plush sofa I'd recently bought for this room just for this reason. Kat smiled at me then reached up to set her glorious hair loose. It spilled in riotous red waves past her shoulders and she looked so sexy it was sick. Then she took it a step further, leaning back and opening her legs while touching her tits.

Meanwhile, my dick was conducting a major tantrum over all this torture so I did us both a favor and yanked my pants down to my knees. I'd been brooding about today's planned meeting ever since we kissed goodbye just after breakfast.

Our mornings at home were blissfully chaotic these days, a hectic hurricane of diapers and preschool plans and barking dogs. There was no time for fun and games while all that was going on. But moments like this more than compensated.

Kat was ready for me, lying back on the sofa and widening her legs so I could fit between them. I hooked one of her knees for leverage and two seconds later I was buried in heaven.

It didn't take too many thrusts to get her to come. She must have been thinking about this since breakfast too. I looked down at her, this gorgeous creature full of humor and intelligence and kindness and marveled over the fact that she belonged to me.

"I love you, Nash," she moaned as she was still shuddering in the wake of her orgasm.

"I love you too," I said and pulled out to come all over her tits. Just because I could. Because she was mine and because she liked it when I did moderately kinky shit.

Afterwards I grabbed a box of tissues and helped her deal with the aftermath. Then I collected her in my arms and held her close for a few peaceful moments.

"You'll be opening the store soon," she sighed as she ran a finger up and down my bare thigh.

I checked out the time. "Yeah, I guess so."

"And I've got to get to another meeting. A *real* meeting," she emphasized, giving me a playful slap.

I tipped her chin up and kissed her lips. "There's nothing more real than this."

Her eyes softened. "No, there's not."

She let me kiss her soft and slow, both of us getting all excited again in the process.

"But I do need to get out of here," she said, wriggling out of my embrace and seeking out the clothes that were strewn all over the floor. I just stayed where I was and watched her get dressed. I never got tired of looking at her.

"You'd better put on some clothes," she said while buttoning up her blouse. "You can't sell souvenirs to tourists while naked."

I laced my hands behind my head. "Actually I think that's a fucking great idea. A naked gift shop. I bet no one's tried that gimmick before."

She threw me a look and tossed my boxers at my head. "And no one's going to try it now." She looked around. "Where'd I leave my laptop?"

I pulled my boxers up and grabbed my jeans. "In the store I think."

"Oh, right." Kat tied her hair up into a prissy bun once more and bent down to give me a kiss. "See you at home."

I pinched her ass. "See you at home."

Kat blew me one last kiss before she was out the door and I finished returning to a state of decency while reflecting on the sad fact that nothing nearly as exciting would happen for the rest of the workday.

The store opened. An overly perky employee named Hayden arrived and industriously dusted every surface of the store. People stopped in to buy postcards and key chains, mugs and Christmas ornaments even though it was months until the holidays. The busy summer season was officially over but the Hawk Valley Chamber of Commerce had invested in an expensive ad campaign hoping to lure people to the area in autumn. After all, the mountains were even more stunning in the fall. Most of the trees were evergreen but some did change colors and with the cool bite in the weather it was a popular daytrip for the folks still sweltering down in Phoenix. Yet another new tagline was invented: Hawk Valley, The Best Place You've Never Been. Surprisingly, it was starting to catch on. There was a new steakhouse opening at the end of Garner Avenue and an old mansion on the edge of town was being renovated into a bed and breakfast. There was more optimism in town than there ever had been.

And I was damn glad to be here.

After lunch Jane arrived with a new painting she'd just finished and wanted to sell. She also had some news. Kevin had been asking her to marry him for two years and she'd finally said yes. I was happy for her, for both of them. Kevin adored my aunt and he was a good guy. They both deserved some permanent happiness. Seeing Jane was nice but I was still counting down the hours until I could head home.

Right after Jane left Betty showed up. I'd just given her another raise because she'd proven how indispensable she was. Betty liked having her mornings free and then working until closing, which worked out great for me because I could be home for dinner every night. We chatted about inventory orders and last month's fantastic sales receipts in between customers.

Kat texted me that she was finished running around on all of her errands earlier than expected. She wanted to get Colin from Nancy Reston's right after she picked up Emma. Kat was as devoted to Colin as she was to her own child. It was just one of the many reasons I worshiped her.

At five o'clock I told Betty I was taking off. She was studying the art gallery wall in search of a place for Jane's new painting. She waved and cheerfully told me to have a nice night.

"Thanks," I said, thinking about everything that was waiting for me at home. "I will."

As soon as I turned down my street, the distinctive yellow Victorian house loomed into view and I could feel myself grinning already. I couldn't help it. I'd become one hell of a cheerful motherfucker lately.

One month ago Kat and her daughter had moved into the house and every day was a new adventure in the best way. Life could be amazing if you embraced it.

The sound of a bark coming from the backyard meant Roxie had been alerted to my presence. I could hear Emma's laughter coming from there too so I followed the sound through the back gate.

Emma was currently in the midst of a Wonder Woman phase, inspired by the early purchase of a Halloween costume. Then Kat had to buy three more because Emma was temporarily refusing to leave the house in anything else. At present she was running around the backyard with her arms out and a red cape streaming behind her.

Roxie was waiting by the gate with her tail wagging so hard you'd think she hadn't seen me in a year. I paused to give her a few seconds of attention so she would let me pass.

Kat relaxed on a large blue picnic blanket in the grass while Colin sat up beside her and avidly watched Emma's every move as she conquered the backyard.

"I'm all powerful!" Emma cried, still flapping her arms.

Kat made room for me on the blanket and I knelt down at her side. Colin babbled with delight and immediately tried to crawl into my lap.

"Badabadabadabada," he said and I wasn't sure what the sounds meant to him but they must mean something. I picked him up and gave him a sloppy kiss on the cheek and he clung to me for a moment before demanding to be released.

My eyes swept over Kat, who had changed to jeans and a plain gray sweater. Her hair was loose again, her face free of makeup. She was a vision, a rare beauty with the power to be gorgeous even in old jeans and a baggy cardigan.

"You're beautiful," I told her.

She tipped her face up for a kiss. "I'm so glad you're home."

"Mommy!" Emma shouted with impatience. "You're not watching me!"

"I'm watching you, Ems," Kathleen called.

"Hi, Emma." I waved to the little girl who stared at me for a second and then broke into an impish smile. She picked something up out of the grass and came bounding over with Roxie eagerly following.

"Nash," Emma said breathlessly and handed me a heavily chewed tennis ball that had been slimed with dog slobber. "You're a good thrower so throw this."

"Say please," her mother prompted.

Emma offered up a winning grin. "Please."

Roxie was excited now, jumping around and waiting for the chance to catch the ball. I got to my feet with the rather disgusting ball in my palm and threw it high in the air to the opposite corner of the yard.

Emma bounced on her toes and clapped when Roxie caught it in her mouth like a pro and came running back over to deposit it on the picnic blanket.

"Again!" Emma insisted. Then she glanced at Kat and added, "Please."

How could I refuse? I threw that ball about a dozen more times while Kat dashed into the house to check on the food in the oven.

"Fifteen minutes until dinner," she announced, returning to the blanket.

Emma had become distracted by a hole Roxie had dug and was in the process of filling it with leaves. I saw an opportunity to abandon the game of fetch, dropping the slimy ball in the grass and wiping my hands on my jeans.

"What's for dinner?" I asked, settling down between Kat and Colin.

"Roasted chicken," she answered. "With peas and biscuits. Is that okay?"

"Hell yes." I surveyed the happy scene in the backyard. "That's perfect." And it was. I only wished Chris and Heather Ryan were somehow able to see this, the legacy they'd left behind.

Kathleen snuggled against me. Colin ripped out a handful of grass, became disgusted at the sight of the detached green blades and hurriedly dropped them.

"Oh, there's some good news," I said and told her about Jane and Kevin while the shadows of oncoming dusk approached.

Kat was delighted. "That's amazing. I'll have to call her tomorrow."

I pushed a red curl out of her face. "Maybe there's more than one wedding in the future for this family."

"A bold assumption," she said but she blushed and I could tell how the words had thrilled her.

"A bold prediction," I corrected and possessively slid my arm around her body.

"Badabada!" Colin exclaimed.

"See? Even Colin agrees."

Kat smiled. "Then maybe you're onto something."

I smiled back. "You're damn right I am."

Epilogue

Kathleen

One Year Later

"COLIN, LOOK AT ME. WHAT A GOOD BOY! EMMA, PLEASE smile. I promise we're almost done."

The kids looked adorable today and I had my heart set on catching some memorable shots of them on the gorgeous grounds of the brand new Hawk Valley Inn .

Emma kept making a face and Colin was determined to avoid standing still for an instant but I finally got them to smile at the same time while sitting on a stone bench beneath a sprawling cottonwood tree. I snapped a series of photos with my phone in a hurry.

"Can we eat now?" Emma asked.

"You just ate, sweetie. You had a bowl of strawberries."

"I want more."

"Me!" Colin shouted. "Me eat!" Then something else caught his interest and he scrambled down off the bench. "Doggie woof woof!" he said, determinedly toddling after a golden retriever that was obviously a service dog belonging to a woman in a wheelchair.

"No no." I scooped him up and kissed his chubby cheek. "You come with Kat now."

"Kat!" he said. "Katkat."

"That's right."

I escorted the children back to the lobby where the inn was

celebrating its grand opening. Since Nash was on the Hawk Valley Chamber of Commerce as well as a minor investor in the new place, we'd all been invited to attend the ribbon cutting ceremony.

The event was crowded. The free food and the fabulous early autumn weather had drawn everyone who had any interest in the inn. There were local politicians, business owners, educators, and just about anyone who was well known in the community.

Emma made a beeline for the food buffet and pouted when I limited her strawberry consumption but cheered up when she found some finger sandwiches.

"Baby sandwiches," she marveled as I put several on a plate.

"Just don't eat the toothpick in the middle," I said.

For Colin I found a soft buttery biscuit that I planned to break up into small pieces, if I could manage to get the job done before he snatched the thing out of my hand.

Once we had some snacks I considered our seating options but there weren't many. I spotted my mother cozied up beside Steve Brown, who happened to be her new boyfriend. She would have welcomed us but I opted to give her some privacy.

Jane and Kevin were by the inn reception desk chatting with the high school principal but there were no seats nearby. I watched as Jane laughed at something her husband said and he wrapped an arm around her, planting a kiss on top of her head. They were married this past spring. And Nash had been right about something. A year ago when he'd predicted theirs wouldn't be the only wedding in the family.

"Where's Nash?" Emma asked, echoing my thoughts. She was always looking for Nash. He was devoted to her. He treated Emma like a daughter. Before he'd presented me with an engagement ring he'd gone about the very solemn task of asking for Emma's permission to marry her mother. Of course she said yes. And so did I.

"I don't know," I said. "Let's go back outside."

The three of us wound up sitting on the same stone bench where

I'd posed the kids for pictures earlier. Emma primly ate the contents of her plate while I offered Colin-sized pieces of the biscuit to his hungry mouth.

"More," he said every time he swallowed a bite. It seemed he would keep his light hair, at least through childhood. He looked a little like photos of his mother at this age. But his mischievous blue eyes were just like his big brother's.

"Nash!" Emma abandoned her plate and took off to fling herself into the arms of her soon-to-be stepfather.

Nash had arrived outside in the middle of a conversation with several other Garner Avenue business owners but he stopped talking and crouched down to receive Emma's hug. Damn, he was a gorgeous man in every way.

"I'll catch you later," he told his companions and swung Emma up, carrying her over to Colin and me.

"I was looking for you guys," he said as he sat down next to me.

"Mommy was making us take pictures," Emma said, scrambling out of his lap with some indignation in her face.

"Oh." Nash nodded. "Well I'm glad because you look so pretty in your new dress, Emma."

She looked down at her pink dress that was really more suited to the Easter season, but it had been her undoubted favorite so it was the one I bought.

"I do look pretty," she agreed.

"You sure do," I said, glad that my girl did not suffer any shortage of self-confidence.

"Hi-oh," said Colin.

Nash grinned down at his brother and smoothed his hair. "Hey there, handsome."

"Hi-oh," Colin repeated.

Emma spotted a flowerbed about twenty feet away that she wanted to get a closer look at. Colin cried to go with her so Nash asked her to please hold his hand.

"And don't pick any of the flowers," I called.

"Okay, Mommy," Emma said as she slowed her steps to accommodate Colin's toddling.

Nash slipped his arm around me. "Hi-oh."

I grinned. "Hi-oh."

He kissed me. A familiar thrill rolled through my body, as it always did when he got close.

Emma and Colin were in front of the flowers now. Emma held tight to his hand like she was supposed to and pointed out the different colors. Colin seemed enthralled.

I touched Nash's knee. "Did I tell you I got a letter from the college?"

"No. What kind of letter?"

"One congratulating me on my scholarship and saying my financial aid package was approved, which means I can register for next semester's classes."

Nash's smile lit up his face. "That's fantastic, Kat."

I bit my lip. "You don't think I'm a fool for abandoning my accounting career?"

"No. I think you're following your dreams."

Nash had been supportive ever since I brought up the idea of enrolling in Hawk Valley College to finally finish my philosophy degree. When I was a kid I would have balked in horror at the concept of attending the tiny liberal arts college right here in my hometown. Frankly, I would have balked at the idea that I'd end up in Hawk Valley at all. It was funny how things turned out. Life was full of surprises.

Just like how once upon a time Nash Ryan had been an object of my fantasies. Unattainable. A dream.

I held out my left hand so that the sunlight caught the diamond on my fourth finger. "I think I *have* followed my dreams, Nash Ryan."

He picked up my hand and kissed it. "We still need to set a date."

"Any date will do. I'd marry you tomorrow."

"Tomorrow it is."

"Actually," I said, "I was thinking about Valentine's Day. It'll be too cold for an outdoor ceremony but I was thinking maybe we could have it here at the inn. We were planning on a small wedding anyway and I noticed they have a good sized party room."

Nash liked the idea. "I'll make it happen. Before you change your mind."

I rolled my eyes. "As if that's a possibility." I nudged him. "You're stuck with me now. We're a family."

Nash stared into my eyes and I felt the electricity crackle between us.

Then Colin face planted into the flowers and Emma shrieked. Nash was up like a shot.

"I got him," he said and ran over to rescue Colin from the flowers.

Nash picked him up and Colin's face was red and crumpled, as if he was still deciding whether or not this event was worth a few tears. Nash brushed some flower petals out of his hair and spun him around. Colin forgot his tears and let out a scream of laughter.

"Me too!" Emma begged, holding her arms up. "Spin me too!"

Nash picked her up in his other arm and spun them both around and around while the children howled with delight.

"Mommy," my daughter called to me, laughing. "Take a picture. Don't you see us?"

"We're a family."

Families are beautiful. They are always intricate and unique. They are created in different ways by different events for different reasons. Yet all are cemented together with one precious and irreplaceable thing.

Love.

And there's nothing more valuable.

Not in this life.

"I see you," I called back and lifted my phone to capture the priceless image.

The End . . .

THANK YOU for choosing to read IN THIS LIFE!

This story has meant so much to me and I was almost sorry to end it.

Authors depend on reviews so I really hope you will consider leaving one.

Email me: corabrentwrites@yahoo.com

Sign up for my spam-free newsletter: bit.ly/1QFyYJE

Join my Facebook group: www.facebook.com/CoraBrentsBookCorner

Get your hands on the latest hot new releases

www.ingramcontent.com/pod-product-compliance
Lightning Source LLC
Chambersburg PA
CBHW021009120726
47905CB00009B/2933

9780999002100